HART OF REDEMPTION

THE HART SERIES

S.B. ALEXANDER

Cover Design by: Hang Le
Photography by: Kruse Images & Photography
Model: Drew Leighty

Hart of Redemption
The Hart Series Book 3

First Edition: March 2024

E-book ISBN — 13: 978-1-954888-50-0
Paperback Print ISBN — 13: 978-1-954888-51-7

1

FALLYN

The fishy odor from Boston Harbor wafted on the cold November wind as I lay on top of a shipping container, my focus resolute as I looked through the scope of my rifle. My heart was punching my ribs left and right. I swore that anyone within a five-mile radius could hear it.

As many times as I'd been part of a raid with the ATF, my adrenaline was always off the charts. I never had any expectations that I would like this type of job, but it was in my blood.

My dad was a retired FBI director, and my brother, Jason, had been an FBI agent—a good one until he'd gone undercover to bring down Brian McCauley, a front man running drugs for the Colombian cartel, and been killed. At least I believed he was. There wasn't enough evidence to convict McCauley or any of his associates. According to Jason's autopsy, he died from a drug overdose, and though he might've succumbed to drugs while inside, he would have never taken his own life.

I'd made it my mission to uncover the truth behind his death, but I took a different route and joined the ATF instead of the FBI. I believed it would be the quicker path to finding answers. Unfortunately, by the time I was out in the field, McCauley had already shifted his focus solely to the drug trade and left the work of illegal arms dealing to his longtime friend and associate, Duke Hart.

Sadly, the truth about my brother's death may never come to light. But I refused to give up. Over the last four years, I'd spent countless hours examining the evidence we had, but there was nothing to indicate he was murdered. The only way I would ever have closure would be if the person responsible for Jason's death confessed or was caught, and that felt like an impossible task. McCauley's world was not one where people sought redemption or admitted their guilt easily.

"Fallyn, report," Special Agent Howard said through my comm.

"All quiet for about twelve hundred meters."

Special Agent in Charge Kyle Howard was leading the raid based on information from his informant, who worked around a few of the Colombian cartel soldiers in Boston.

I wished Brian McCauley were the target for tonight's operation, but the tip we received pointed at Duke Hart, front man for Rosario Mendoza, head of the Colombian cartel.

Apparently, Duke was meeting with Rosario's lieutenant, Gustavo Gutierrez, to transfer the weapons—the first step in the chain of custody—before Duke sold them to multiple buyers.

"Stay alert," Howard said through his comm to the rest of our team, scattered throughout the container yard.

In the dead of night, with only the crescent moon providing a smidge of light, we were essentially ghosts, hidden by shipping containers.

I inhaled and exhaled, regulating my breathing and trying to steady my hand around the rifle. I was the newbie on the team but not new to long-range rifles. I'd recently transferred from LA to Boston's ATF field office. So I had something to prove.

Agent Bruce Griffin, one of my colleagues, had issues with me. I believed he felt threatened because I was the daughter of a retired FBI director, and he thought I got special compensation and privileges because of my dad. Bruce was off his rocker if he thought my dad's status would open doors for me. I had to bust my freaking ass through ATF training and do everything by the book.

Lights bounced in the distance, catching my eye.

I swiveled the rifle in that direction. "We got company."

"We don't move unless we see the guns. Fallyn will give us the signal," Special Agent Howard said.

We were assuming the parties would meet inside the warehouse, where I had a bird's-eye view from my scope into a large window carved into the building.

A moving-style truck rolled to a stop sign about a thousand yards away. Behind it, a cargo van pulled up. In seconds, two masked men jumped out of the passenger side of the cargo van, guns in hand, ran up to the moving truck, and pumped bullets into both of the men inside.

No loud boom, indicating the perps were using suppressors to silence the sound.

"We have a problem," I said into my comm as the masked perps yanked out the limp bodies and threw them to the ground. "I think it's an ambush."

Both masked perps hopped in the moving truck and sped off, with the cargo van on the tail.

I turned the dial one click to my right. "Two bodies are on the ground, not moving. Truck with possible gun shipment is gone."

"Son of a bitch," Agent Howard growled out. "Any other activity, as in Duke Hart, his men? The cartel?"

"Negative," I said as headlights bounced on the cross street. "Wait. Another vehicle is approaching."

The SUV pulled up to the four-way stop.

The passenger—a beefy guy with a gut—jumped out, jogged over to the bodies, felt for a pulse on both of them, then shook his head at the driver.

I swung my scope to the man behind the wheel.

"Fallyn, what's going on?" Agent Howard asked, sounding perturbed and antsy.

I dialed in the focus even more. My long-range scope had the means to see close to a mile.

The driver climbed out and lingered close to the SUV, searching the industrial neighborhood.

"I got eyes on Duke Hart and Vince Russo," I said in a low voice.

I'd read through both of their files until I had just about everything memorized. Vince Russo, second-in-command for Duke, had been joined at Duke's hip since they were teenagers. No family to speak of, except a brother in prison. The same age as Duke—thirty-three. And, like Duke, had yet to do any jail time.

"Everyone, hold your positions," Agent Howard ordered. "They might come into the warehouse."

If they did, we had no evidence to arrest them unless Duke had guns in his SUV. Even then, he wouldn't have the mother lode we'd been hoping for.

Duke focused in my direction, lifting his cell to his ear.

My freaking heart was pumping blood at warp speed as I held steady. Surely, he couldn't see me. I was far enough away, and it was dark.

I steadied my breathing, sizing up the imposing criminal I'd seen in a slew of pictures in his file. He was hot as fuck—angular jaw, patrician nose, cold reddish-brown eyes that were more mahogany-colored, close-shaven beard, and thick sandy-brown hair, shorn over the ears.

Duke straightened the beanie on his head as he continued to scan the area, like an expert soldier looking for the enemy in a war-torn city in Iraq. The only thing he didn't have was a weapon.

"Are you sure it's Duke Hart?" Agent Howard asked.

The streetlight at the corner provided ample light, and I had no doubt I was looking at Duke Hart.

"Affirmative," I responded.

Duke lowered his cell, shaking his head furiously as he banged on the hood of his SUV.

"They're getting in their vehicle. Hold tight," I said.

From my vantage point, Vince and Duke appeared to be arguing. A beat passed, then Duke made a U-turn and drove back in the direction he'd come.

I blew out the breath I'd been holding. "They're gone."

"Everyone, hold your positions in case the cartel shows up," Agent Howard ordered harshly.

After five minutes, I gave the all clear, muttering several expletives. I thought this was our shot. My teammate and friend, Agent Gwen Holiday, had been attached to the Boston field office for five years, and in that time, she'd said that anything involving Duke Hart was like playing a cat and mouse game. But the cat never won.

A dirty agent came to mind. How could Duke or even McCauley skirt the Feds on every turn? But no one within the federal government—DEA, FBI, or ATF had been investigated. According to my dad, if anyone within the government agencies was corrupt, they were covering their tracks really well.

I doubted a dirty agent was involved tonight. I speculated someone who wanted to fuck Duke or the cartel was responsible for this ambush.

By the time I packed up my gear, most of my team had been deployed to scour the area for anyone suspicious, as in Duke Hart or members of the cartel, who might be idling nearby.

I threw my gear in the van not far from the dead bodies and joined Gwen, Agent Howard, and Bruce by a stop sign.

Gwen, a striking blue-eyed brunette and a badass agent, said to our boss, "Sir, an ambulance is on its way."

Agent Howard lifted his ATF hat, swiped a hand over his flat brown hair, and shoved his blue ball cap back on. "My informant got it right, but something went wrong."

Bruce, who was in his late thirties with blond hair and a muscled body, handed our boss the driver's licenses of the dead. "I believe they're cartel."

"Fallyn, did you get a good look at the ones who killed them?" Howard asked.

I shook my head. "They had masks on, but both were lean. I didn't see the driver of the cargo van either."

"It seems either Duke or the cartel have an enemy in play here." Bruce latched on to the collar of his bulletproof vest.

"We don't know that Hart is innocent here," Gwen said. "He could've staged this to screw with the cartel."

"Hart seemed pissed when he drove up and found the bodies," I said.

Agent Howard read both licenses. "Hart is Rosario's front man. He works for her, and he would never fuck with her. Whoever did, I pity them. Rosario is one mean bitch and takes no prisoners, especially when she loses good soldiers."

"And guns," Bruce mumbled. "A lot of money is gone."

"The Mexican cartel has been trying to get a foothold in the gun market," Gwen said. "You think they're involved?"

Agent Howard rubbed his jaw. "If Arturo Rodriguez is involved, we might be seeing a cartel war play out on the streets of Boston. Motherfucker. When are we going to catch a break? Bruce, I need you to start pulling all the files on Arturo. So far he's stuck to drugs, which is the DEA's department." Agent Howard addressed Gwen. "I need you to poll your contacts on the streets. See if there's any scuttle on Arturo. Also, we need to take the temperature of the gangs. Gwen, take Fallyn with you."

I hadn't been with the team long enough to have any contacts or informants, but I had an idea. "Maybe it's time to send someone undercover. Either in the cartel or Duke's organization."

Everyone stared at me like I'd said I was a dirty agent.

Gwen gnawed on her lip. "Not a bad idea, although if I had to choose one, I would say Duke's camp. But I'm not volunteering. I've had friends who went inside and never came out the same."

My brother's plight certainly spoke volumes to her last statement. While a dangerous assignment had more cons than pros, it was a chance for me to maybe learn if Jason's death had been murder or suicide. After all, I could kill two birds with one stone, so to speak. Duke was friends with Brian McCauley. Maybe Duke knew of Jason or the details behind his death. Plus, if a cartel war was on the horizon, maybe I could help prevent that from happening.

"It can't be you, Fallyn," Bruce scoffed. "You're a newbie."

I clenched my teeth. "The fuck I'm not. I've been with the ATF for two years. Granted, the majority of that time was in LA. So what if I've only been on this team for six months? I still have the experience."

My boss studied me, his dark gaze in thinking mode. "No one has real-world experience in undercover work. Not even you, Bruce. However, I do think it's time to take things to the next step. But not in the cartel. Rosario has a team in Boston, but it would be easier to focus on Duke Hart, since he also has legal businesses that we could blend in well. But, Fallyn, your father would never agree. Not after what happened to Jason."

"My father isn't ATF, and he's retired," I argued, even though Agent Howard was right.

Agent Howard chuckled. "Your father still carries weight within the agencies."

"Fallyn." Gwen's voice was soft and sorrowful. "Your brother, Jason, lost his life inside. Are you willing to risk yours?"

A sharp pain stabbed my chest, as if she'd rammed a dagger into me. "I appreciate your concern. but we risk our lives every day on this job."

As if a light bulb brightened for Agent Howard, he said, "If you're volunteering because you think you'll find answers about Jason, then you might not be the right person, Fallyn. Our attention needs to be solely on the issue we are facing and the potential war that could happen."

"Which is why I should go in," Bruce said, his shoulders tense.

I pressed my lips into a thin line. "I'm not going to lie. I want answers on Jason, but I understand what we're facing. I will do my job, and if the stars align and I find what I'm looking for, then it's icing on the cake. Besides, I am the perfect candidate because no one on the streets knows me since I am a *newbie*." I darted my gaze to Bruce.

Gwen hooked her thumbs in the sleeves of her bulletproof vest. "I'll check with my sources, but the recent scuttlebutt among the gangs is Mateo Alvarez is looking to make a name for himself since he was forced out of the Southside Creepers. Let's not forget his brother, Tito, who was pinched four years ago because Hart's brother, Denim, was trying to break into the gun trade then."

Sirens wailed in the distance.

Agent Howard chewed on his bottom lip. "I'll run the undercover op by my superiors."

Bruce snarled. "Fallyn is wet around the gills."

I rolled my eyes, wanting to strangle the man. "Is it my newbie status, the fact that I'm a woman, or you dislike that I'm the daughter of the former FBI director?"

"Careful how you answer that, dude," Gwen said to Bruce.

Bruce shook his head. "All I know is Hart is cunning and lethal and can sniff out a cop before you even realize it. He'll chew you up and spit you out, and you won't even know what happened."

"That applies to you too," I said between clenched teeth.

"Enough. Sending anyone undercover is not my decision or yours." Agent Howard flicked his head at the dead bodies. "Gwen and Bruce, help the paramedics. Fallyn, over here." He stabbed a thumb at a spot by a fence that surrounded another shipping company.

I pushed out a long breath when we were alone. "I can do this."

He tightened his mouth. "You'll lose your soul. No one comes out as the same person they were before they went undercover. Are you prepared for that?"

"I'm prepared to do my job." That was the only answer I had. "And before you say anything, I'm not my brother. Drugs are not my thing." Jason had experimented with drugs in high school but nothing serious—or so I thought.

A beat of silence bounced between us.

"About two weeks ago, there was an opening for a bartending position at the Monarch nightclub that Hart owns," Agent Howard said. "I don't know if it's still open, but you were a bartender in college, right?"

I nodded. "I also did some moonlighting as a bartender for a friend in LA."

He sighed. "You should talk to your father. I'll work my end."

My stomach churned with excitement and apprehension. "Thank you. If this happens, I'll do my best."

"I know you will. I think you're a great agent. Your superiors and colleagues in LA speak highly of you. I also agree that you're not Jason. You have fire in you to seek the answers you're looking for. That alone should help you to stay focused. It's Hart I'm worried about. Bruce was right. Hart has a nose for cops. So if this op happens, then you need to become a chameleon and adapt to the profile we put together for you."

I'd taken acting in high school—not that the starring role in *Romeo and Juliet* deemed me worthy of playing someone I wasn't on the world stage of criminals and illegal firearms.

But I would do whatever it took to stop a war, and maybe in the end, I would finally get closure on Jason's death.

2

———

DUKE

An hour after the clusterfuck at the container yard, I was pacing in a run-down empty building in Dorchester that I was considering purchasing.

I was trying to shed my criminal businesses little by little to build a life in which I could settle down, maybe have kids, open a boxing gym, and spend more time with my siblings. I had to do something soon. Or I was afraid I would end up in a body bag or prison. I'd skirted the Feds for years. But my good friend and associate, Brian McCauley, believed it wasn't if but when we faced our fate.

I had to get out on my own terms—hand the business over to Vince, my second-in-command, who was eager to run the empire.

"We're fucked." Vince sat on a crate, elbows on his knees. "Those were Rosario's men. They were driving the truck full of guns. What happened? It wasn't the Feds."

I'd been racking my brain on who the fuck would have done this. The Mexican cartel came to mind, but I couldn't find a reason why Arturo Rodriguez would steal Rosario's guns. He was a dick and had the army, but surely he knew that it was suicide. Then again, Arturo Rodriguez was right up there with Rosario as a lethal motherfucker.

"Maybe Rosario pissed off Arturo." I walked up and down the dirt-covered floor, smelling the disgusting odor of piss that was permeating the air.

Vince flashed his blue eyes my way. "He has been trying to move into the gun business, but why take her guns?"

"To get her attention. Actually, anyone could've stolen the guns, but who knew of our meeting? On our side, only you and I knew. Unless one of our men overheard the details and is stupid enough to cross me."

We'd been fucked over the years by a few who'd worked for us. Either they'd leaked info outside our circle or had been caught stealing from us.

"You can cut off my fingers if we have a leak," Vince said. "I assure you we don't."

I ripped off my beanie and shoved a hand through my sweaty hair. "Are you sure you want to run this business?"

"I go back and forth." He straightened, his big gut sticking out. "That topic is for another day. What if the Alvarezes are behind this? If anyone has the balls to pull this off, it's Mateo Alvarez. He's been kicked out of his gang. And don't forget that his brother, Tito, tried to move in on the gun trade. Plus, they do have a vendetta against your family."

The Southside Creepers, a large gang that had been around Dorchester for eons, had been led by Tito Alvarez until he was sent to prison for murder. Mateo had taken the helm but was recently forced out of the gang. Like Tito, Mateo was a loose cannon, murdering anyone who pissed him off, which attracted the wrong kind of attention to the Creepers.

I hadn't been bothered by the Alvarezes since my brother Denim set up Tito to take the fall for a gun shipment four years ago. But during that meeting, Denim had worn a wire for the Feds, and instead of Tito bragging about a gun shipment, he'd been coerced into confessing to two murders. But that was a story for another day.

"If you're right about Mateo, then he's working with someone in Rosario's camp." I punched the chipped cement wall as fury flooded my veins. Rosario was going to rain hell down, and I would be right in the middle of it, doing her bidding.

"Why isn't Gustavo calling me back?" I asked myself more than Vince as I wiped blood off my knuckles. I'd left Rosario's lieutenant a voicemail after Vince and I found the bodies.

"You think Gustavo is aware of what happened?"

He better not be the one behind this. I could never be sure who was stabbing who in the back in Rosario's organization. In the past, she'd had a few leaks, not only filtering information to her enemies but to the Feds as well.

I blew out a painful breath as I rubbed a spot below my chest. "No idea. But I wasn't waiting around for his ass, not with dead bodies." My ulcer was giving me problems as of late. At least I thought I had an ulcer. I'd never been medically diagnosed.

The ringing of my cell echoed through the run-down building as Vince whipped his gaze at me.

No Caller ID flashed on screen. Gustavo and Rosario's calls always came through with no name or number.

"Yeah," I answered after hitting the speaker button.

"What the fuck is going on?" Gustavo shouted, his gruff voice echoing in the empty space.

"Are you at the container yard?" I asked.

"No, I'm pulling a bullet out of my shoulder. We got ambushed at a light. I just found my phone. I tried to contact Manuel and Joe, who were in the truck, but no answer."

"That's because they're dead."

"Fuuuuuck!"

Vince and I glanced at one another, feeling the same way.

"By the time Vince and I got there, your men were dead. No truck in sight."

"Motherfucker." The sound of glass breaking came through the line. "What the fuck is going on?"

"Million-dollar question. But Rosario is going to rain hell down."

"I don't want to make that call," Gustavo said. "She is going to yank my balls off."

Rosario Mendoza, head of the Colombian Cartel and a bitch of a lady, ruthless and deadly, was one person not to fuck with.

I rubbed a knot on the back of my neck. "Who has Rosario pissed off lately? Because I can promise you no one in my organization is responsible."

He growled. "The fucking world. I'll do some digging on my end. You do the same. We'll be in touch." The line went dead.

Vince cleared his throat. "I have another thought. We were using Jeremy Pitt's warehouse. Do you think he could be behind this?"

The Russian mob boss wouldn't steal from the cartel or me. "Pitt would never kill for guns. That's not his style, and he has access to them through me. Besides, he has enough of an arsenal for his security firm, but I will talk to him. Let's get out of here."

I needed a drink, a good fuck, and an hour in the gym, in that particular order.

By the time Vince and I reached my nightclub, Rosario's harsh and screeching voice was blaring over Bluetooth in my SUV.

"Find those guns, Duke. I want you and Gustavo picking apart the city."

"I will do my best," I said as calmly as I could. "But which one of your enemies has a mole inside your organization? Arturo Rodriguez? He's been trying to gain market share."

"Who says your people aren't behind this?" she asked.

She had the drug and gun trades sewn up to about ninety percent in the New England area. McCauley handled her drug business while I managed the illegal firearms side. But Arturo was making more inroads in Boston, using low-level gangs to filter his drugs through the pipeline. He might be trying to do the same with guns.

"Rosario, I respect you, but I would never fuck you. And the only people privy to the meeting tonight were Vince and me. I would stake my life on that. So I suggest you find your mole."

"If Arturo is involved," she said, "this is war."

Vince and I shared a grim look. That was all we needed, bloodshed on the streets of Boston. The thought of ending up in a body bag or rotting in a cell seemed more like a very real possibility than ever before.

3

———

DUKE

I kicked off the sheet, peeled the woman's arm from my chest, and climbed out of bed. The blonde rolled over, pulling the cover with her. I'd forgotten her name. Cara or Maura. I tried not to remember their names. If I did, then I would care, and I couldn't. Emotions other than those in keeping with my stoic nature would only create more problems for me and also for her. The last and only woman I'd let in was six feet under because of the life I led.

I crossed the wood floor into the bathroom, wincing at the pain in my jaw. I'd been grinding my teeth since I found Rosario's men dead and the guns were stolen.

I had to call Pitt and McCauley today to ask if they could put feelers out. I needed all hands on deck for this one. More importantly, I had to alert my siblings, especially my sister. My enemies— or even Rosario's—wouldn't think twice about using our loved ones to fuck with us, and my sister, Grace, was a prime target. Many around me knew I would die to protect her.

I'd failed her once as a teenager, and she ended up in a sex-trafficking ring at sixteen. I blamed myself for that. I'd left her with our alcoholic father while I built a new life away from the abuse and torture of our old man.

She'd taken off for the same reasons I had and was sold to some fucker who'd beaten her into submission. After four years of torture, she'd found a way out by killing her captor. Ten years later, while she was tougher, more aware, and surrounded by my two brothers, the men we had watching her, and me, I still worried.

I flipped on the shower and slid under the cold spray, not waiting for the water to heat. My stomach felt queasy. It didn't help that I'd polished off a bottle of bourbon or that my ulcer was becoming more of a problem.

Stop drinking, asshole.

The way I was going, I would be an alcoholic before long. *Like father, like son.*

I closed my eyes, feeling the water pressure beat down on me as my problems bombarded me. I needed a quiet space to think, and I knew the perfect place. Besides, I was planning to visit Savannah's grave next week.

The only woman I'd ever loved had been murdered in prison on the orders of Tito Alvarez. I slapped a hand on the tile. Fucking Tito. If my brother hadn't been wearing a wire, I would've ripped out his throat.

As it stood, guilt rode me hard for Savannah's death. I couldn't have stopped the choices she made, but I should've returned her repeated calls from prison. I was afraid if I had, my enemies might've gotten to her. A lot of good that had done. I failed her. I failed everyone that I loved.

I had to find a way out of the hell I was living in. It seemed for every step forward I took to redemption, I had to take five steps back. Freedom was like climbing a hill but never reaching the top.

Freedom. I'd never really felt free in the thirty-three years of my existence. I wouldn't know what it felt like.

After my mother had abandoned us when I, the oldest of her four children, was seven, we grew up with a monster of a father. He thought his kids and wife were his personal punching bag to work out on after a long day at the factory.

I'd forgotten my mother over the years. Didn't even know if she was alive. But one memory that seemed to bombard me over the years was the day she'd walked out the door.

I rubbed my sleepy eyes as I lifted my head off the pillow. "Mom, what's wrong? Did Dad beat you again?"

A light in the hall spilled into my bedroom, giving me a glimpse of my mom's tears.

She sniffled. "I'm leaving, Duke. I'll be back when I'm settled." She kissed me on the forehead. "You're a good boy, Duke. I know you'll take care of Grace, Dillon, and Denim. You'll protect them from your father."

I shook my head. "You can't go," I pleaded, throwing my arms around her, basking in her lavender scent. She loved that floral fragrance.

I'd stolen bottles of perfume from the local store and had wrapped them for her Christmas present.

She squeezed me to her. "I'll return as soon as I can." Then she ran out.

I bolted after her, watching her grab her suitcase and purse.

She was halfway out the door when she glanced over her shoulder. "I love you."

I wiped the water from my face as I jolted back to the present. If she'd loved her kids, she never would've left.

I learned a valuable lesson after she walked out—don't let anyone in. She'd pulled out my heart that day, and since then, I pushed away Dillon, Denim, and Grace. Love had yet to drop from my lips for anyone.

I rushed through my shower, trying to wash away the memories that haunted me. My mind was still reeling from thoughts of my family and Savannah. God, Savannah.

I had never had a steady girl in high school. Never had the desire to stay with one for too long. Over the years, I became a hardened individual. Women wanted more from me than I was willing to give—money, a safe home, my heart, hell, my fucking soul.

But I would've given Savannah all that and more. She got me. I got her. We both had flaws. However, she had one I couldn't deal with—drugs. I experimented in high school. I even sold them for a while like Denim had. But I hated what drugs did to people, and seeing Savannah strung out broke my black heart.

Since her death, I slept with women at most twice. I hardly remembered their names, and if they whined or begged, I walked away. The only begging I wanted was when I was balls deep, and she pleaded for me to fuck her harder.

I rubbed my bruised knuckles as I stared at myself in the mirror. My reddish-brown eyes looked tired, although my mother would say I had chestnut-colored eyes like her. I was starting to see wrinkles on my forehead and—dare I say—gray hair amid the sandy-brown color.

Whatever. With the world I lived in, I was surprised I didn't have a full head of white hair.

After shaving and the normal morning bathroom routine, I was dressed in a pair of black pants, a blue button-down shirt, and a pair of loafers. I grabbed my watch off the dresser and secured it around my right wrist.

The blonde stirred before raising her head and opening her sleepy blue eyes. "Duke, why are you up at"—she looked at the clock on the nightstand—"five a.m.? Come back to bed."

"Vince will see you out in a couple of hours."

I could be an asshole and kick her out now, but I wasn't that much of a dick, although others around me would argue that point.

She pouted as she flashed her tits at me. "Duke, you don't want these babies?" She pinched her nipples as she threw the sheet off her lower body. "Or this?" She opened her legs wide and stuck a finger inside her pussy.

My dick stirred for the briefest of seconds, but I shut that shit down. "This will be the last time I see you." I grabbed my suit jacket off the chair by the closet.

"But Duke—" she protested.

I ignored her as I walked out. I had nothing in my room for her to take or use against me. All my important information and valuables were kept in a safe behind a wall in my old penthouse where Denim and his wife, Jade, lived. Denim knew about it. He even knew what to do if I was ever arrested or found dead.

"You're a cold bastard," she shouted at my back.

"I am," I admitted.

I ran a multimillion-dollar criminal empire, and the only way to succeed was to put up my steel armor. No one could get a glimpse of what lay beneath my hardened exterior. No one.

I navigated the hall on the top floor of the Monarch, which was where I lived.

I read the text that Denim had left about twenty minutes ago.

Denim: *Call me when you're up.*

I tapped on his name in my favorites as I unlocked my office and went straight for the Advil in my desk drawer.

"Bro," Denim said, sounding like he had been dozing.

"Are you just getting home?" I asked.

He yawned. "Yeah, I was guarding a musician all night. It seems young pop singers ask for me when they're doing gigs in Boston."

I swallowed the Advil without water. "At least it's legal work and pays well. I'm happy for you, bro."

"The Guardian isn't exactly legal."

"Jeremy Pitt keeps you legal, though, right, Denim?" My big-brother tone kicked in. "I don't want you in jail again."

"Dude, I'll worry about my life. Enough about me. I got your text about dinner tonight. What's going on? You never do dinner with the family."

I went into the small kitchen behind my office in search of coffee. "Not over the phone. But you still know what to do in the event anything happens to me?"

"Duke, please tell me you're not about to go to war with your enemies."

I pressed on my ulcer. "Not sure of anything yet. I need to be prepared. I'll explain things tonight. Also, we need another man on Grace."

"Motherfucker. Seriously, bro. Find a way out, please."

"I'm working on it. I'll see you at Yvonne's at five. Oh, and please don't bring Jade. I don't want wives there. Maggie neither. Can you pass that along to Dillon?"

After he agreed and we ended the call, I blew out a painful breath. I hated to discuss my business with them, but if I wanted them alive, I had no choice.

4

——————

FALLYN

"**D**ad," I called out as I entered my childhood home in Weston, Massachusetts, the following day after the raid.

The smell of coffee drew me toward the kitchen in the back of the two-story, country-style home that my mom had decorated and adored.

"I'm in the sunroom," my dad called out.

I breezed by the dining room we never used, where dust was collecting on the table and chandelier. The last time we had dinner in that room was six years ago, if my memory served me correctly. Dad, Jason, and me. Dad had cooked a turkey for Thanksgiving—or attempted to. The meat had been dry, and the stuffing tasted like stale bread, but it was the thought and effort that had made that day special.

I veered left off the breakfast nook, the sun's rays spraying into the kitchen through the French doors, then stepped through an arched doorway and into the best place in the house.

My mom loved lounging in here, watching the birds through the wall of windows or admiring the colorful fall trees that were currently shedding their leaves.

My father flashed his hazel eyes over the rim of his gold-frame reading glasses, closing the novel in his hand. "You're early." A warm smile melted my heart as he picked up his coffee cup from the table beside him.

I leaned in and gave him a kiss on the cheek then skirted the coffee table, dropped my purse by the cushioned recliner, and shed my wool coat. "I love this room. I still feel Mom's presence every time I come in." I sank into the chair, inhaling the floral aroma of the bouquet of flowers on the stand in the corner.

He followed my line of sight, beaming as if he, too, was thinking about Mom. "How was traffic for a Sunday morning from Boston?"

The weight of sorrow crushed me as I recalled the day my father came to pick me up from high school, the same day my mother had died from a pulmonary embolism. I had never seen my father cry before, but that day he wept like a newborn baby.

I regarded the man I resembled right down to his thick golden-brown hair, freckles splattered around his nose, and hazel eyes. "Minimal."

He swung his melancholy gaze to me. "I'm going to pass on the cemetery visit today. I'm feeling a little under the weather."

Since his retirement two years ago, he seemed out of sorts. I knew Jason's death had hit him hard. Neither of us was dealing with loss very well. At least I kept busy with my job, though Dad fished and played golf. Both sports were something Jason had liked to do. I knew Dad felt closer to Jason on the golf course or fishing on the lake.

"You do sound nasally," I said. "A cold? Nothing serious?"

He sipped his coffee. "Change of weather always messes up my sinuses."

"It won't be the same without you at the cemetery, but I won't be long. I'll be back in time to watch the football game with you." Cozying up by the fire in front of the TV sounded wonderful after last night. "I'll pick up Chinese for us too."

"There's a bouquet in the kitchen to take with you." He went to the cemetery every Sunday with my mom's favorite flowers—black-eyed Susans and carnations.

I swallowed down the emotions, which always seemed to bubble to the surface whenever I came home.

He moved the book to the coffee table. "Tell me what went wrong last night."

I titled my head. "News travels fast. Did Agent Howard call you?"

"No. The deputy director of the ATF."

Deputy Director Malone was a nice enough man but not keen on women in the field. Gwen and I had a few choice words for Malone whenever he made a comment about allowing the men to take the lead on field ops.

"What did he tell you?" I toed off my boots and curled up in the chair for the long conversation.

If I knew my dad, he would grill me as if I was a perp. He often had whenever Jason or I had gotten into trouble as kids.

"That we might be seeing a cartel war. Do we have any idea who stole those guns?"

"Well, it wasn't Hart. I saw how mad he was. Plus, he wouldn't screw the hand that feeds him."

Dad regarded me with his sharp, fatherly expression as if he was about to scold me. "So you want to go undercover? I told you many times, Fallyn, that we might never know if Jason was murdered. You know he got hooked on drugs inside."

"And you know Jason would never take his own life and overdose on drugs." I tried to keep my voice from cracking or sounding caustic, but I failed on both counts.

Dad removed his glasses and rubbed his eyes. "I don't know what to think anymore."

"Dad." My voice was soft. "I've been thinking of going undercover long before last night, but this opportunity presented itself. The cartel and those who work for them, like Duke Hart, are always five steps ahead of the law. If we don't do something other than relying on informants, we could be chasing these guys for years to come." I chewed on a hangnail.

"Fallyn, I don't know."

"It's not your decision, Dad. It's the ATF's."

He gave me one of those "are you serious" expressions. "No one in the FBI, ATF, or even DEA would send you undercover knowing what happened to Jason without running it by me. I don't want to lose another child."

I didn't want to die or have him mourn my death. I had plans for the future. I had my master's in math and had always planned to teach college but had yet to start working on my doctorate, although I was enjoying the ATF more than I'd counted on. I also wanted a husband, kids, and a nice house with two dogs and a cat.

"You can't always protect me, Dad."

"A father can try."

I flopped my head back on the chair. I knew he would react like this. I couldn't blame him. He was scared. In a way, I was too.

I straightened. "I became an ATF agent because of Jason. Of course you know that. But, Dad, this could be our opportunity to finally put away the bad guys, take guns off the streets, and prevent a war. Through all that, what if I could find out what happened to Jason? Wouldn't you sleep better? Don't you want closure?"

"Not if it means your life," he said.

I closed my eyes briefly, rubbing the tightness in my chest. That was a definite possibility. "But I risk my life every day as an agent. You did as well in the FBI. Mom worried about you constantly. I did too." I stifled a yawn. The loss of adrenaline and several drinks last night were catching up to me.

I knew this would be a hard sell. "Give me your blessing to go undercover, and when I come out, I'll leave the ATF and teach like I intended to do before Jason died."

He frowned. "You're enjoying the ATF, I thought."

"I like the action, but I love you."

"Come here." He patted the cushion beside him.

I skirted the coffee table and curled up against him.

He draped his arm around me. "I love you dearly. I want to see you happy." He kissed me on the head. "I also want closure on Jason. It's been eating at me, and I've gone through Jason's files, the autopsy, and every piece of information available multiple times. You're right. He would never commit suicide."

Tears escaped as I listened to the pain in his voice. "I miss him, Dad. I'm gutted that I didn't have a chance to see him or spend more time with him."

Dad squeezed me. "It's a cruel world out there, sweetheart. I would sleep better knowing you weren't risking your life. I also know that feisty and determined side of you. You're going to find answers with or without my approval."

"It would be easier with your blessing," I said honestly.

He rubbed my arm. "The ATF deputy director has given the thumbs-up for the op. He's suggesting Agent Griffin."

I shrugged out of his hold. "Are you serious? Why Bruce? And please don't tell me the deputy director thinks a woman can't do the job because I know he believes women should be barefoot and pregnant."

Dad chuckled. "Agent Howard and I believe you're the better choice."

I leaned away, eyeing him with confusion. "*You* think I am? Why?" I was bursting at the seams with pride that he thought I would be good for the job.

He'd been holding his coffee cup in his free hand, and he set it on the end table beside his half-eaten scone. "Because you're stalwart and persistent, and you have a purpose. I'm not saying Agent Griffin couldn't do the job, but you're more perceptive, and your gut always leads you in the right direction."

My dad always told me he believed in me, but it meant more at this juncture in my life. He wasn't treating me like his baby girl either.

I held his hand. "Thank you for saying all that. Does that mean I'm in?"

"Not yet. We need to discuss a few things."

I leaned my elbow on the back of the couch, facing him, prepared to argue if I had to.

"As a woman going undercover, there are certain ways you can befriend Hart that someone like Agent Griffin can't."

"You mean my sex appeal."

He cringed. "I'm not naive, Fallyn. Agents have done what was necessary while undercover to get close to the source and find evidence. Jason comes to mind. Not to mention, men like Duke Hart don't get to the top without knowing how to manipulate people. On top of that, you're beautiful, and—"

"Dad, I'm not a teenager anymore, and Duke isn't that drummer I dated, if that's where you're going with this." My dad had wanted to hunt down Axel after he'd broken my heart during my first year of college. Dad also knew the type of men I was drawn to—bad boys with that air of confidence, ready to conquer the world. In a way, Duke was that type. "Besides, Duke is the enemy."

"He's also a human, and I've heard he's charming," Dad said, raising an eyebrow.

I sighed. "The job comes first, no matter what, and I'll do my best."

He swiped a hand over his unshaven face. "I know you will. Agent Howard has already begun the process of setting up a profile. I'll be involved in helping him. It will take about a week. In the meantime, I want you to really think about this."

Nodding, I rubbed my hands down my legs. It was something I did when I was nervous. I would hope that in this situation I wouldn't succumb to falling for the bad boy. After all, Axel was a drummer not a front man for the cartel.

"Dad, I will try my very best to make you proud. But I'm not making any promises."

He moved hair off my cheek. "I don't expect you to, and if you did, I wouldn't approve. There's one thing, though. Duke, the cartel, and the guns are your first priority. This assignment isn't about finding out what happened to Jason. Frankly, I prefer you stay away from McCauley."

"We're forgetting one important thing. I have to get a job at Duke's club first. We don't even know if that bartending position is still open."

If the stars did align for this op, finding answers to my brother's death would be tricky.

5

———

DUKE

Cumulus clouds skated across the sky, blocking the sun every now and then as I trudged around headstones at Linwood Cemetery in Weston, Massachusetts, several miles outside of Boston.

Not long after Savannah's death, I had a gravestone set up in her honor away from the seedy underworld of the city. A peaceful place where I could visit her without any distractions. She didn't have a resting spot because her sister, Jade, had her cremated.

Linwood was the perfect spot for the woman to whom I'd never told the depth of my love. The forty-five-acre property was well landscaped, with variations of trees, shrubs, flowers, and roads that wound through the vast expanse of the burial grounds.

For late morning on a Sunday, the cemetery was practically empty. I didn't expect the place to be crawling with mourners, but I glanced around with a mechanical precision just the same. After last night, my radar was on high alert. Then again, I was always looking in the rearview mirror or behind me.

I placed the lily on the step of her headstone and read the

epitaph I'd written. *A vibrant woman who knew how to steal a heart with her brilliant smile.* That was exactly what she'd done with me.

I clawed my fingers through my hair, pulling at the roots as I inhaled the sweet aroma of flowers carried on the wind. "Savannah," I gasped through gritted teeth, my chest aching with longing and pain. "I wish you were here, but part of me is relieved you're not. The world has become more of a treacherous place since your death." I paused to catch my breath, clenching my fists as I continued, "The good news, though—Tito is behind bars, where he belongs." My voice dripped with bitter satisfaction. Yet prison was too lax of a punishment for Tito for taking Savannah's life.

"He will die in the joint," I mumbled, feeling the need to hit something, to take away the numbness I've had inside for so long. "I'm so sorry, babe. I'm sorry I didn't answer your calls from prison. If I could change things, I would."

You keep beating yourself up, man. You need to make peace with Savannah's death.

That was my problem. I didn't know how.

"But I've been planning on walking away from the cartel and my empire. I feel like I've aged fifty years. I haven't relaxed since we took that vacation to the Maldives. Remember sitting by the pool, laughing, good sex, just you and me and no outside world?"

I rubbed the back of my neck as fallen leaves whirled around me as if she were answering my question.

I placed my hand over my heart, remembering her words that still echoed in my mind from that day on the beach when she was straddling me. "Duke, being far from home suits you. You need to break free. We both do."

I clenched my jaw, feeling the weight of guilt more heavily than ever. It was like a knife twisting in my gut. Seeing my brothers with their wives made me more envious of what I didn't have and would never have but still longed for deeply.

With a trembling hand, I pulled out the flask from my jacket pocket and slammed back a swig of bourbon. The fiery liquid burned its way down my throat, but it wasn't enough to numb the pain. Last night's rage had left me with a throbbing hand and aching knuckles, but that wasn't enough either. I needed more. I needed to feel raw bone against raw bone in the ring, sparring with a partner until blood leaked from my wounds. Only then would I find release for the emotions boiling inside me.

After another swig from my flask, I returned it to its original place when my phone vibrated in my suit jacket.

I fished it out and answered Jeremy Pitt's call. "Hey, man."

"Duke." His voice was calm as always.

The Russian mob boss, who hardly showed any sign of emotions, was intelligent, well respected in Boston, and a wealthy individual, running a multitude of illegal and legal enterprises. Yet through it all, he seemed invincible, as if the law couldn't touch him.

What are you complaining about? You haven't been arrested or spent any time in jail.

"How's my brother Denim doing for you at the Guardian?"

He chuckled. "Don't worry. I won't bring him into illegal shit. He's happy with his role as a bodyguard. Now, I know you didn't call me to talk about Denim. I heard the news about the dead cartel members outside my container yard. Cops are roaming the place, asking questions."

"I'm not sure what's going on, but I wanted to check with you on your cameras around the property. Did you turn them off for me?" He normally did if I was brokering deals there.

"Always," he said.

Thank fuck. "I owe you." I relaxed my muscles, silently thanking my lucky stars I had Jeremy Pitt in my court.

A hard wind whipped up, carrying the scent of flowers that served to ease my panic even more.

"I'll check with my contacts at Boston PD and take the temperature of the water. If you need my help, I have an army."

He came from several generations of mafia families and knew the pitfalls, ways to stay below the law's radar, and how to build relationships with key city officials to ensure he kept his freedom. That army he had included a few men in blue.

"I appreciate that, man. I hope I don't need you."

"We need to stick together," he said. "I'll let you know if I hear anything."

After we ended the call, I scanned the property for nothing more than to clear my head. The man I'd seen early was gone, and there wasn't anyone around as far as I could see.

For just a moment, I reveled in the quietness and emptiness of the area, listening to the tree branches rustle, leaves blowing on the ground, and my pulse beating in my ears. I stared at Savannah's headstone, my brain a whirlwind of thoughts—past, present, and future.

I couldn't keep going at a thousand miles an hour, looking over my shoulder, worrying about my siblings, wondering if or when I would finally end up in prison or a body bag. Denim, Dillon, and Grace had been pleading with me to find an out, to leave everything behind. Maybe even leave the country.

But that wasn't me. I didn't run. I attacked my shit head-on, and I needed to clean up the mess from last night. If I left Rosario hanging, she would cut off my limbs but not before she did the same to Grace and my brothers. Besides, I owed Rosario. She'd gotten me out of a tough situation with Arturo Rodriguez a few years back. If she hadn't, I would be six feet under alongside Savannah.

After a few deep breaths, I touched Savannah's headstone. "I need to go, babe." I picked up the lily that had fallen off the ledge of her headstone. "I hope wherever you are, Savannah, that you're having the time of your life. That you're walking in the sunshine, laughing in the rain, and free from the darkness. You will always have a place in my heart."

I buttoned my jacket, took one last long look at her headstone, and walked away, releasing my emotions, wiping them away, because feelings would only make me weak, and weakness was a flashing neon sign for a death warrant.

I slid into the driver's seat when my phone vibrated in my hand, with Vince's name on the screen. And just like that, my scowl was in place, the door to my heart locked tight. My ulcer pricked my stomach.

Answering, I started the engine. "What?"

Vince didn't reply. I looked at the phone, and the call had disconnected.

"Call Vince," I said into my SUV speaker.

Nothing. My cell should've automatically connected to the SUV. The damn system had been giving me problems as of late.

I fiddled with the SUV's screen as I slowly navigated the winding road in the cemetery, every now and then checking the road. I tapped on the Bluetooth option, glanced up, and found myself slamming on the brakes.

But it was too late.

I clipped the back of a beat-up Ford truck that probably belonged to the groundskeeper. Or rather, tapped the bumper of the vehicle, although I heard glass break. My right headlight was probably busted.

My damn cell rang again.

"Vince, I have to call you back," I barked after tapping the accept button.

"Duke." Vince had that edge to his voice that told me something was wrong, so I stayed on the line.

I couldn't even begin to speculate what had him rattled, unless he'd found a narc among our ranks.

"What happened?" I asked.

"Duke Hart," a baritone voice I didn't recognize said. "I'm Detective Branski. I need you to come in for questioning."

I rubbed my temples, laughing. The Advil I'd taken earlier was wearing off. "For what?"

"We found two dead bodies last night near a shipping container yard," Branski said. "Where were you around midnight?"

"Screwing a beautiful woman." Not at that time. More like three a.m.

"She can vouch for you, then?" he asked.

"Why would you think I was there?" I asked. Pitt had just told me he'd turned off the security cameras.

"I understand from Detective Hughes that you might know the deceased. They've been identified as belonging to the Colombian cartel. Rosario Mendoza's men, in fact."

I belted out a hefty laugh. "You can tell Ted—or, rather, Detective Hughes—that he shouldn't stick his nose where it doesn't belong and run his gang unit for the BPD and not anything else."

Ted Hughes was my sister-in-law Maggie's foster dad. He'd been nosing around me for years but could never touch me. In fact, he'd been Denim's arresting officer. It sure was a small fucking world, though.

"Don't leave town, Mr. Hart," Detective Branski said. "I might return with more questions."

Like I gave a fuck. He had nothing on me.

Climbing out, I said, "You do that. But the next time you show up, you better have a warrant." I growled as I hung up. That peaceful moment I'd been enjoying vanished in the blink of an eye.

Even more so when I spotted a woman running toward me, tits bouncing, nice ones, too, and fury stamped on her face.

She breezed past me and examined both vehicles, fists clenched, then whirled on me and froze as if she'd seen a ghost.

All I saw was an extremely beautiful creature with big hazel eyes, high cheekbones, warm caramel-colored hair that was blowing in the wind, big tits, and a curvy waist.

I lifted my hands. "I promise I don't bite, and I'm sorry about this."

As if my apology was the key to snapping her out of her zombie mode, she said, "What are you, drunk? I can smell whiskey on you." Her voice was silky and smooth, causing my groin to react.

What the fuck? No. No. No. I'm here for Savannah. My mind was on board, but my dick was having a good old time. I brought up mental images of blood and guts, which was helping.

"Not drunk. I might've had a few swigs of liquor." I was sure several glasses of bourbon the night before were filtering through my pores as well. "I didn't see your truck until it was too late. Why are you parked haphazardly on the bend of a curve? That's idiotic."

She pursed her lips. "Are you calling me an idiot?"

I cocked an eyebrow. "Lady, I don't have time for this. I'll pay you for the damage." Upon closer inspection, I had a busted headlight, and she barely had a scratch on her Ford.

"We need to file an accident report for my insurance. I'm calling the cops."

Chills careened down my spine at her threat. The last thing I needed was more lawmen on my ass.

"I'm a businessman. We can work this out."

She puffed out her chest. Her low-cut green sweater was showing very nice cleavage.

Stop lusting over her. You're at Savannah's grave.

She stuck her hands on her hips. "Okay. The price is fifteen hundred because that's how much it's going to cost me to repair that dent."

I studied her as she locked gazes with me.

She had a small nose, a smattering of freckles, full lips, and a scar on the corner of her forehead the size of a thumbtack.

I was curious about where she'd gotten that scar, but my heart decided to skip a few beats as we continued to stare at one another. What the fuck was happening? No one had that effect on me since Savannah, but I couldn't break away. Her hazel eyes had warm tones of browns and greens but mostly golds, and against that caramel hair, she was stunning.

Maybe I'd had too much to drink. I'd been nursing my flask of bourbon on the way here. Liquor made me want to do nothing but fuck sometimes, but this quivering feeling in my black heart wasn't from the alcohol.

Shit! Today is not the day to be ogling a curvy, beautiful creature.

I shrugged off the instant connection, her long-ass legs, and every other dick-squeezing thing about her.

I silently apologized to my girl when my cell went off again—that time with Vince's name unless Branski was using his phone to screw with me.

"I need to take this. We'll settle things in a second," I said as I strode off.

The only thing I needed to settle was my damn libido that was opening up like a Venus flytrap.

6

———

FALLYN

I stared at the backside of the criminal, my jaw slack, my stomach knotted tightly. What were the odds I would run into Duke Hart at a cemetery in Weston, Massachusetts? He lived in Boston, and to my knowledge, I hadn't seen anything in his files to indicate he had loved ones buried here.

I texted Agent Howard, breathing in and out slowly in the hopes my nerves wouldn't give me away. I might not wear my emotions on my sleeve, but like at the raid, my hands tended to shake when my heart was pumping adrenaline through me at warp speed.

Me: *You're not going to believe this, but I'm standing with Duke Hart at the Linwood Cemetery. Call me.*

I inhaled the newly cut grass, examining my bumper. Not much damage.

I rested against the cold metal of the classic Ford that my dad had surprised me with for my sixteenth birthday.

As I watched Duke, I recalled the files I'd read on him. His two brothers and sister lived in Boston, as did his alcoholic father, who'd been in and out of jail for drunk and disorderly conduct. But there was little info about his mother. Maybe she was buried here.

Duke was shaking his head as he talked with his back to me about thirty yards away. He was at least six feet two with powerful thighs that showed through his suit pants. Fuck. A suit sans the tie was sexy as hell. The pictures of him didn't do him justice.

Sandy-brown hair—thick with a slight curl on the edges. Reddish-brown eyes—sad yet cold. On top of that, there was no doubt Duke had a dangerous aura about him. The kind of guy you didn't want to be caught with on a dark street late at night.

I would bet that small bulge in his lower back beneath his suit jacket was a gun.

Duke glanced in my direction.

I raised my hands in a "I don't have all day" gesture, even though I did. This was my chance to seize the opportunity with Duke. This wasn't just a random encounter. Destiny was giving me a sign, opening the door for me, and now all I had to do was walk through it.

Ask him to settle the accident over coffee. A laugh broke out in my head. He didn't seem like the type to sit in a coffee shop and chat. However, he was emitting liquor like he'd doused himself in it. Maybe I could ask him to join me for an alcoholic beverage.

My phone vibrated with Howard's name on it.

"Hey," I said quietly.

"I got your text. Are you serious? Duke is with you?" Shock colored his tone.

I rubbed my lips together. "He hit my truck at Linwood Cemetery. He's on the phone right now."

"You're visiting Jason?" His voice held a hint of sorrow.

"And my mom. It's a ritual my dad and I have, but he didn't come with me today. I think this encounter with Duke could play in our favor, but I can't go into it right now. Duke is coming toward me. I'll call you later." Smiling at the criminal overlord, I lowered my phone.

"Are you calling the cops about this?" He stabbed a finger at our vehicles.

"Why are you so intense? It's not like the cops will arrest you."

"You said that I smell like alcohol. So they could bring me in for driving under the influence."

He had a point, and him being detained by the cops would throw a wrench in my plan.

He lost his ire. "I'm sorry. I'm having a bad day."

"Me too. A cemetery isn't exactly a place to be happy."

His fingers danced through his hair. "Can we settle this like adults? I have more damage than you do anyway."

"I didn't call the police, but if you must know…" *You need that bartending job.* An idea bloomed like a spring flower. "I was talking to a potential employer who called to tell me that I didn't get the job I'd recently applied for."

The wind kicked up errant yellow-and-orange leaves around us as the tree branches swayed.

He slipped his hand into the front pocket of his pants and removed a wallet as he turned his attention to the damage I had on my bumper. "That scratch won't cost fifteen hundred. I'll give you five hundred, and we'll call it even." He held the hundred-dollar bills in his hand. "Do we have a deal?"

I snagged the bills from him. When I did, my fingers brushed his, and a zap of electricity made me flinch.

He tilted his head, his gaze lowering to my mouth.

I squeezed my Kegel muscles together. My damn body was about to betray me as I found myself pushing out my chest.

As if the liquor on his breath were an aphrodisiac, I found myself leaning closer to him, but that only served to make me sway. Luckily, my truck was there to catch me.

He didn't waver, keeping my lips in his sights.

If he kissed me, I wasn't sure what I would do. Kick him in the balls or climb his strong body like a monkey.

Wake up, girl. He's the enemy, remember?

Still, my heart banged against my rib cage as silence strung us together, the sexual tension heightening.

Clenching his jaw, he pinched my chin as if he was a second away from throwing me into the bed of my truck and feasting on me.

I wouldn't protest, either, given the way my body was so freaking heated in all the right places. Maybe my dad was right. Or Agent Howard. I'd even forgotten who'd said I would lose my soul.

A bird chirped loudly nearby, zapping our connection—or at least mine. "Thank you." I wadded up the bills in my hand. "Since I don't have a job, I could use the cash." Liar, but keep going.

A slight grin emerged on his gorgeous face. "What do you do?"

Hallelujah! "I bartend. Though around here, it seems no one is hiring."

"I'm sure there are plenty of opportunities in Boston," he said. "If you're interested in driving into the city, stop by the Monarch nightclub." He started for his car door. "I know for a fact the owner is hiring."

This was my lucky day.

"Are you the owner?" I asked.

His gaze lingered for a beat before he slid sleekly and smoothly into the driver's seat and started the engine. Then he pulled out, stopped, and rolled down the passenger window. "I didn't get your name."

I smiled at him. "I didn't get yours."

Think, Fallyn. If you're going undercover, you'll need an alias. I hated to come up with a name, since Agent Howard was working on a fictitious bio for me.

"Duke Hart," he said proudly. "I own the Monarch."

Ah, shit. Now I had to respond in kind. If I didn't, he might get suspicious.

"Joy Whitlock."

I'd read that last name when I was walking by a headstone earlier. The first name was how I felt. Joyful. Stupid way to come up with a name, but I didn't care.

He leaned toward the passenger side and extended his business card. "Call me this week, and we can set up a time for you to come into the club."

I took the card, smiling like I'd won the lottery.

7

———

DUKE

After tossing my keys to the valet at Yvonne's in downtown Boston later that evening, I entered the restaurant, trying to clear my mind in preparation for the biggest challenge I had yet to face—dealing with my siblings. This was a conversation I didn't want to have. Nor did I want to hear Dillon chastise me over how I should've gotten out when Grace finally escaped from that sex-trafficking ring. Denim understood my plight. Even Grace did, too, to a certain extent. But Dillon was the good brother, although he'd sold guns for a short time after he returned home from the Merchant Marine. I'd forgotten about that until now. Still, he shaped up and made his mission in life to help battered women get off the streets.

I applauded and admired my brother. In fact, he made me want to be a better person, which was one reason I was trying to jump on the straight and narrow path.

The aroma of garlic overwhelmed my senses as I strode up to the hostess station, where Brittany was helping a customer.

She smiled at me like she always did when I came in with Grace. Yvonne's was my sister's favorite restaurant in the city. I had to agree. Yvonne's had better garlic bread and spicy food than any of

41

her competitors. My mouth watered and my ulcer protested at the thought of diving into a basket of bread.

Brittany finished with her customer. "Duke, it's so good to see you." The cute brunette rose on her toes and gave me a hug. "Your family is all here and in the private room we have reserved for you."

I wound around the carved path of the main dining room, the place buzzing with voices competing with silverware clanging and the faint sound of music overhead.

I dug deep for the strength I always had, recalling the advice McCauley had given me on the phone only minutes ago as I was driving back to the city. "The best way to keep them safe is to tell them the truth. They need to know who to watch out for and the players involved."

I had yet to share that kind of info with Dillon and Grace. As much as I wanted to keep Denim at arm's length as well, I needed one sibling to confide in. Besides, he understood my world to a tee. He'd lived it for years. On top of that, I wasn't worried any of them would narc on me. I just didn't want to make them complicit in the event I ended up in a legal situation in which they would have to testify against me. I wouldn't fault them if they had to, but I knew it would gut them if they were responsible for sending me to prison.

Making my way toward the back of the restaurant, I spotted a woman seated with a clean-cut guy, and I did a double take. For a second, the tawny blond looked like Joy Whitlock. It wasn't until she smiled at me that I realized it wasn't Joy.

A laugh zipped around in my thick skull. I hardly remembered the names of women I slept with. Yet I couldn't forget Joy's, though she didn't strike me as a Joy. I pictured someone with that name as bubbly and giddy. Joy was anything but. I saw her as a tomboy who drove a truck and wore army boots. Most women who caught my eye were nothing like Joy.

But the reason she was affecting me vanished as I entered the private room with the built-in bookcases and the eclectic artwork that Grace loved about the place.

"I always feel like I'm among knowledge when we eat here," Grace had said a time or two.

Dillon and Denim, with beers in hand, were sitting at the only table in the room while Grace was browsing the bookshelves.

My sister lit up when she saw me, and my heart swelled. "You look tired." She gave me a hug.

"I always look this way." I kissed her on the forehead. "But you…" I eased away. "I haven't seen you in a month, and it seems like you're prettier."

Her cheeks flushed as she moved waves of her brown hair over her shoulder, exposing her colorful hummingbird tattoo. My sister had a love for tats. "The only thing I've done recently was a trip to the hairdresser."

Denim cleared his throat as he rose from his chair. "What? No love for your youngest brother?" His blue eyes flashed as he feigned a pout.

"I have to say, it's odd to have all of us in one room." Dillon stood behind his chair. "But I know this isn't a social call for you."

Acid swished in my stomach at his dig and the roughness in his voice.

I didn't want to argue with him, so I put on the best grin I could muster. "Thank you for coming."

Dillon dragged a hand through his dark hair. "You sound like you're about to deliver bad news."

Denim and I exchanged a knowing look, and Dillon caught on.

"You are," Dillon said. "Denim knows? I'm trying to decide if I'm more pissed that you confided in Denim more than any of us or the fact you only call us when you need to tell us to watch our backs. That's what this is about. You're into some shit that is life or death."

"Sit." Denim nodded at Dillon. "I don't know the specifics."

Our waiter breezed in to take my drink order, his goofy attention on Grace.

"Bourbon," I said to him. "And close the door on your way out."

He scurried away like a rat being chased by a mouse.

Silence bounced around the table once all of us were seated.

Denim, the only blond and blue-eyed sibling who resembled our old man, took a swig of his beer. "Well, where do we start?"

I was trying to soften the blow, but there was no way to do that in my line of work.

"We're in danger," Dillon said. "Start there."

I dealt with lethal individuals. I brokered illegal weapons deals. Yet I was having a difficult time talking to my brothers and sister. I'd practically raised them. I loved them and put food on the table by any means I knew how. I fought off assholes who fucked with them, stayed up with Grace when she had nightmares, and acted as my old man's punching bag so he wouldn't beat Denim and Dillon to a pulp.

"You're going to jail, aren't you?" Grace's voice pitched.

I reached over and grabbed her hand. "While that could happen, it's not why I called you here."

As if the light bulb came on for Dillon, he flinched. "This is about the dead cartel guys they found last night by Pitt's warehouse."

The media had been reporting it. In fact, Dillon's wife, Maggie, was a popular TV reporter for a Boston news station.

"I've always been reluctant to share my business with you. One, it's dangerous. Two, the more you know, the more you're in it. But it's time."

Our waiter returned with my drink then flew out as if he knew I would bite off his head if he said the weather was cold.

I tossed a look over my shoulder to be sure the door was closed. "What went down last night at the container yard could have bloody repercussions that might blow back on all of us."

"You mean me," Grace said. "Your enemies always use me as a way to force you into deals. I'm not stupid. Anytime you warn us, it's always the same thing. But, Duke, I can handle myself. No one will ever touch me in a vulgar or dangerous way again."

I gave her a sad smile. "I would like to believe that, but there are men five times your size that you don't stand a chance against, no matter how skilled you are in kickboxing, boxing, or self-defense."

"Or one shot from a drug to knock you out," Denim said. "That's all it would take."

"Let's not forget what happened when Maggie was kidnapped," Dillon added. "They shot her up good."

Grace crossed her arms over her chest and leaned back in her chair, as if she knew they were right.

I rested my forearms on the table. "Rosario Mendoza, the woman I work for, had her gun shipment stolen last night, and two of her men were killed. We don't know who's behind the ambush. Vince and I suspect it might be the Mexican cartel. My point is things could get bloody, and I need you to be on high alert."

"What about the gangs? Could any of them be involved in the ambush?" Denim asked.

Dillon harrumphed. "You mean like Mateo Alvarez?"

I shrugged. "Possible. The Alvarezes want us dead. That was the last thing Tito said to Denim and me before the cops carted him off in handcuffs, but this isn't about us. Someone is fucking with the Colombian cartel. I'm just a soldier in the game."

"I'll swing by and see the Southside Creepers and talk to Chris," Denim said, referring to Chris Vargas, the leader of the organization. "If any of the gangs are involved, he would know."

"I prefer you not to." I narrowed my gaze at Denim. "But you're going to anyway."

He nodded with a cheeky grin. "I still have street cred, even more so now that the gangs know I didn't kill Hector Alvarez."

"I'll see if Mags has any insight," Dillon said. "She comes across all kinds of information and has several informants she works with for the inside scoop."

I hung my head, feeling a sense of déjà vu that the three of us brothers were teenagers again in a gang in which we had one another's backs. But the work I was in wasn't child's play like our gang days.

I gulped down a mouthful of bourbon. "I can't tell you what to do anymore. Hell, I'm tired of trying to keep all of you at a distance. Please, please be careful. I might not have said this before, but I can't lose any of you."

Quiet dropped over us like a thick coat of paint. Each of them looked at me as if they didn't know who I was, but what had my heart about to stop were the tears in Grace's eyes.

She grasped my hand. "We can't lose you either. Please, Duke, start a new life. We want you to be part of our Sunday dinners. We want to see you fall in love. We want you to really find something that will make you happy."

"She's right," Dillon chimed in. "I want us to be the family we never had. It's time to hang up your hat, bro. Come to the legal side. It's sunny and bright over here."

Dillon had been gushing about a cohesive family unit for the last few years since he befriended the tight-knit Maxwell brothers, who Dillon admired to a point that was sickening. He wanted us to be close like them and to do things on Sundays and holidays together. He'd even mentioned that all of us should live in the same neighborhood, like the Maxwells did. Each of them had built a house next to one another on a lake in the small town of Ashford, Massachusetts.

I couldn't see that far into the future. Nor was I in any position or even mindset to consider Dillon's dream.

"I've been on your side, Duke," Denim said. "So I know the addiction. I also know it's not that easy to break free. However, it is doable. Clean up this mess, and then call it quits."

My laugh was anything but nice and happy. It wasn't like I could snap my fingers and the cartel would be gone and I would be living in euphoria. "I didn't ask you here for an intervention."

Dillon grunted. "But you knew it would lead to this."

"Okay." Grace let go of me and patted the tears from her cheeks. "Let's talk about something happier. Dillon wants to ask you something."

Dillon picked at the label on his beer bottle. "Duke doesn't do fancy dinners, but why not ask?" He leaned back in his chair. "I'm hosting a charity gala to raise funds for the Hart of Hope House. My business is growing, and I'm planning on finding a larger space."

Grace beamed with pride. I had to admit I was proud of Dillon too.

"When I had the vision for a women's shelter," Dillon continued, "I never expected it to grow as fast as we did. All of us here support the cause of battered and abused women."

"Of course," Denim chimed in.

I gave Dillon a nod. "How much do you need?"

He grinned. "As much as you would like to donate. Tickets for the gala are two hundred dollars a plate. I want all of you there."

Grace batted her long lashes at me. "You can be my date. Or we can find you one."

I couldn't say no to my sister. "I'll think about it. At the very least, I'll write a check."

"Good," Dillon said. "I'll send you the details, but it's set up for next month. The second Sunday in December, in fact. I'm making the theme Holiday of Hope. It will be a black-tie affair."

I did at least own a tux.

"While Duke is in the giving mood," Denim said, "Jade and I are hosting Thanksgiving."

I held my breath. I hated the holidays. Every year, my siblings tried to coax me into all that gooey crap about being thankful and shit. The only thing I was thankful for was the fact that they were alive and happy.

Once again, Grace was blinking those pretty lashes at me. "Please come. Please. You've never spent a holiday with us."

I knocked back the rest of the liquor. "Maybe."

She squealed. "I'll take that answer. I have over two weeks to turn that into a yes."

Her happiness was everything to me.

"You know what would be awesome?" she said. "A nice woman to settle Duke down."

I almost choked. "Grace, please don't start with that." Give her an inch, and my sister took a mile.

"She's right." Dillon jumped on Grace's bandwagon.

"It's time to move on from Savannah, bro," Denim added.

"All of us know you had a headstone erected in Weston in her honor," Dillon said. "We know you go out there every year around this time. Is that where you came from today?"

"Are you following me?" I asked, rearing back in my chair until I remembered Grace had seen the receipt from the cemetery on my office desk when I'd first purchased the headstone.

Grace frowned. "I'm sorry that I told them."

I waved her off. "I would rather not talk about Savannah."

Denim flicked strands of hair off his forehead. "Fair enough, but we want you to be happy. If it weren't for you when we were kids, our father might've crippled us or, worse, killed us from all his beatings. It's time, big brother, to let us help you. It's time to stop worrying about us."

"I will never stop worrying about you. Frankly, if it came down to it, I would die to protect each of you. So please heed my warning."

I didn't plead for much. Hell, I wouldn't even beg for my life if I had a gun to my head, but I would die for my brothers and sister.

8

FALLYN

F lurries floated to the ground as I pulled into the Monarch. It was early afternoon on a Sunday—exactly one week since Duke had hit my truck.

Only a handful of cars were parked in front of the warehouse-style building. If it weren't for the sign on the brick facade, I would've assumed I was about to walk into an Amazon product facility or even one of those data centers with private servers that usually didn't have any signs for security reasons.

My stomach had been pitching and rolling the entire drive from Weston to Boston. The powers that were within the ATF had approved my undercover assignment, and between them and my dad, they'd built a fictitious profile under the name of Joy Whitlock.

Today was do or die. When I'd spoken to Duke to set up this interview, he'd given me a link to the job application on his website and instructed me to fill it out before I came in for the interview.

I knew he wanted to check out my background, as any employer should before he hired me. Luckily, I waited until the ATF had my profile in place before filling out the application so I didn't risk the opportunity for the undercover assignment.

If for some reason Duke didn't hire me, my backup plan was to use that spark Duke and I had in the cemetery to start up a dating relationship, but that was a tall order. According to what we knew about him, he went through women like water.

The swish of the windshield wipers resounded, removing snowflakes that almost melted instantly in the heat blowing out the defroster vents.

I checked myself in the visor mirror and fluffed up my hair then made sure my makeup was perfect, although I hardly wore much on a daily basis. My hazel eyes appeared more gold than green today. Probably because I was wearing a patterned scarf that had streaks of yellow and gold in it.

I dragged a finger lightly over my glossy lips then rubbed them together before sighing. "Hi, my name is Joy Whitlock. I can do this. I will succeed."

I closed the visor when an SUV with a busted headlight rolled down the deserted street in front of the Monarch.

Nerves had my heart banging against my ribs like the little drummer boy, even more so when Duke climbed out of his vehicle and immediately glanced in my direction.

Yeah, handsome, it's me. I've come to make your life a living hell. Although I'd been silently repeating several mantras all week. *He's forbidden. He's the enemy. He's going to prison for a long time.*

I had six months at most to pull off this op, regardless of whether I succeeded. My dad felt that the reason we'd lost Jason was because my brother had been inside too long.

Putting on my metaphorical acting hat from high school, I cut the engine, jumped out, and gave myself a silent pep talk, taking the first step toward the handsome gangster.

Gwen had counseled me on what to do—or rather, what she would do. "Let him make the first move. Draw him in. Don't engage until he does." Her theory was if I came on too strong, Duke might get suspicious or throw me to the curb like he had with other women in his life.

Duke watched me intently, waiting by his SUV.

The man was sex on a stick. Sharp black suit, white shirt—sans the tie. His thick sandy-brown hair seemed wavier today and, of course, damp from the snowflakes landing on his head.

I will not give in to my desires.

I inhaled deeply and expelled the jitters as best as I could and waved at him as I approached.

He kept his expression blank, sizing me up.

I suddenly felt as though I was having an out-of-body experience in which I was about to step into an alternate reality—lightheaded, nauseated, and shaky.

I tucked my quaking hands into the pockets of my wool coat, my hair blowing in the snowy wind.

"You're early," Duke said in a raspy voice that tickled my lady parts. "It's probably best with the storm coming in." He sounded like he was worried about me driving in snow.

Odd coming from a cold, calculating man.

"I'm a big girl, and I have four-wheel drive on my truck. If the weather is bad by the time I leave, I can always stay at a hotel." If he hired me, then my new home would be a short-term rental in Boston. I couldn't stay at my current place, which was in my name and not far from the ATF field office.

Duke studied me, his reddish-brown—or rather, mahogany-colored—eyes appraising as if he'd made me.

"Is something wrong?" I flicked melted snow off my nose.

Lines dented his smooth forehead. "One thing has been bothering me about you since we met."

I swallowed an elephant. "You've been thinking about me?" Shock wove through my words.

I was made. I was screwed. I was dead.

I held steady, hoping beyond hope that he hadn't done a background check on me before my alias had been set up.

"You don't look like a Joy. Is that your real name?"

I flipped my hair over my shoulder then rubbed the back of my neck. "Why would you ask me that?" Fear swished in my stomach.

"When we met, you could've given me an alias, since I was a stranger," he said. "My sister does that as one way to protect herself."

Grace Hart, twenty-six, youngest of the four siblings and a victim of sex trafficking. I could see how she would pull out all the stops to protect herself.

I relaxed under his scrutiny. "Do you want to see my driver's license?" Yep, I was officially Joy Whitlock in the DMV system, and any background check would confirm my profile.

"I've already done a background check. I don't need to see anything."

One tick mark in the right column. Now he just needed to hire me.

The rumbling of an engine tore Duke's gaze away as he tensed, his hand going to the small of his back, which was where his gun was, no doubt.

Without looking at me, he said in a lethal tone, "Joy, go inside the club. The door should be unlocked."

I didn't move as I followed his line of sight.

A black Hummer with tinted windows came toward us.

"Move now!" he practically shouted in a deep voice, removing his gun and angling it down at his side.

My curiosity kept my feet planted and my legs locked. I almost went for my piece that was in my boot but thought twice. Duke would surely become even more suspicious than he already was about my name if I drew a weapon.

He reached out and grabbed my wrist. "When I tell you to do something, you obey. Get your ass inside the club." He tugged me behind him. "Go."

Do as you're told, Fallyn, or you'll give yourself away.

I walked at a fast pace, my attention glued over my shoulder. I had to see who was in the Hummer that was now stopped behind Duke's SUV, blocking my view.

"Oh, it's you. Is this your new car?" Duke asked the driver.

I lingered by the entrance as I listened.

"New one that came in today at my dealership," the man said. "You got a minute?"

I suspected it was Brian McCauley since he owned several car dealerships in the city.

"Any word from your camp about the stolen guns?" Duke asked.

"Nothing."

"We'll talk in my office," Duke said.

I grabbed the door handle when Duke strode up quickly—shoulders tight, gaze hard, and nostrils moving in and out. "I thought I told you to go inside."

"You don't have the right to tell me what to do." The words fired at him machine-gun fast, my anger melting the snow in my hair.

"I do if you're working for me. If you can't follow orders, then you're not the right person for the job."

"You're hiring me?"

He opened the door. "Do you want the job or not? I don't have time to dick around. It's a yes or no. If not, I'll escort you to your beat-up truck."

Bite your tongue, Fallyn. "Before I commit, I need to know the pay, as in hazard pay." My gaze went to his gun.

He slipped the weapon into the back of his pants. "We'll work that out later, but I can assure you that I pay well and you're safe here."

I snorted. What the heck? I never snorted. "It seems your definition of 'safe' and mine differ," I mumbled as I crossed the threshold in my new alternate reality.

The pungent odor hit me first—a mixture of cleaning supplies, booze, and sweat.

The right side of the club had cages suspended from the ceiling, while the back wall displayed a long wooden bar with a polished mirror and neatly stacked liquor bottles on shelves. And on the left side, stairs led up to a second floor filled with scattered tables and chairs.

My college days came roaring back—drunken students, late nights, loud music, raves, and frat parties. But this wasn't a time to reminisce, and I certainly wasn't in college anymore. Losing my senses to alcohol and hot guys wasn't on the agenda either.

I pointed at the cages. "What do you keep in those things?" I asked for nothing more than to temper my nerves.

I knew men and women were hired to dance in them. As someone who hated small spaces, I would pass out if I had to stay in a cage for more than five seconds.

He came up alongside me. "Not important. I'll have Carlo, my club manager, help you with the paperwork, and he'll show you around. You'll work on a trial basis for thirty days. If you're still here after that, then the hazard pay will kick in. For now, you'll be paid the going wage and split the tips with your bar partner."

"When do I start?"

The floor was rather sticky as he ushered me in the direction of the bar.

"Tonight, if you're ready. We're short a bartender."

I skirted around a support beam. When I did, I bumped into him.

He placed a hand on my lower back to steady me. "Are you nervous?"

My legs felt like saltwater taffy. "Not in the least," I lied.

"Joy, we'll get along just fine if you don't lie. I despise anyone who does. My employees will tell you that I only give a person one chance."

"Or what?" I couldn't stop the question from flying out.

Note to self: Have my bulletproof vest close by because when Duke learns I'm a fraud, he'll pump a round of bullets in me.

He ignored me as he waved to an older, well-groomed man behind the bar. "Carlo."

"Yes, sir." He set the wineglass down and flipped the towel over his shoulder.

"This is Joy Whitlock," Duke said. "She's our new bartender. She already filled out the application online. Can you show her around? Prepare her for tonight. I want her shadowing Matt."

Carlo gave me a polite smile. "Sure thing, boss."

Heavy footsteps echoed behind us.

As I suspected, Brian McCauley strutted up to the bar. The man was a beast. Large, intimidating, and like Duke, a shrewd, sharp, man who took no prisoners. What I knew of him came only from what I'd seen on paper and in photos.

Jason had never been able to gather any concrete evidence that would stick. He had, however, been successful in sending Brian's lieutenant to prison on a weak drug charge.

McCauley swept his green eyes over me. "Duke, you didn't tell me you were dating."

The word "dating" scraped along my skin like rough sandpaper. The last guy I dated was in LA, but we were more friends with benefits. Neither of us wanted to tie the other down, and with my ATF job, it was hard to think about a long-term relationship.

"Bartender," Duke said. "Nothing more."

McCauley's big blond head bobbed. "Right. You'll have her in your bed by tomorrow night. I know you, Hart."

Maybe that was the reason Duke had hired me on the spot. Whatever the reason, I wasn't complaining. I was in, and that was all that mattered at the moment. Except I wouldn't mind interrogating McCauley about my brother. He had to know how Jason died. But in due time.

I snarled at McCauley. "You don't know me."

He gave me a cheeky grin. "And you don't know Duke Hart."

I had several comebacks for McCauley, but causing trouble wasn't how I wanted to start my new job. Plus, I had to act like someone I wasn't. Joy Whitlock—bartender and regular civilian. Regardless, I wouldn't be treated like I was about to become Duke's play toy.

Duke straightened. "My office, McCauley. Carlo, show Joy the ropes."

"Isn't that how you met Savannah?" McCauley laughed as he and Duke headed for the stairs. "She was a bartender at one of your clubs. Déjà vu, man."

I dipped into my memory, recalling the names listed in Duke's file of the people around him, but the name Savannah didn't ring a bell. I got the feeling she was someone special to Duke.

"Shut the fuck up." Annoyance dripped in Duke's caustic tone.

McCauley's laugh was loud and obnoxious. "I love rattling your cage, Hart."

After watching the two walk into Duke's office, which overlooked the club, I closed my eyes briefly, erased Fallyn Williams from my psyche as best as I could, turned to Carlo, and extended my hand.

"I'm Joy Whitlock. I'm excited to be working here."

Nervous was more like it.

9

———————

DUKE

I slammed the door to my office after McCauley and I were inside, the geometric art on the wall rattling with the force. Even the lamps on the end tables on either side of the couch shook.

"What's eating at you?" McCauley dropped his big body onto the couch and kicked up his booted feet onto the coffee table.

I cocked an eyebrow. "Seriously? It's been a week, and I don't have any leads on the stolen guns. I won't even talk about how I can't sleep for more than an hour."

"Nah, my friend. That pain on your face doesn't compute with the tension about the guns. That shit is second nature to you. You deal with problems all fucking day." He wagged a finger at me. "You want that spitfire and stunning beauty downstairs. I can see it in your eyes." He laughed. "You like her as more than a nightly conquest. I bet your dick is hard, thinking about her. I know mine would be."

I sat in a chair across from him. "I hate that you can read me. You're like Vince. You two see right through me."

I was sexually frustrated more than anything. I jerked off in the shower to mental images of Joy. I hadn't had a woman in my bed

57

since I'd met her either. Maybe that was my problem. Still, when she'd called to take me up on my offer, I knew I would hire her. I didn't care if she couldn't make a drink.

Though I'd done my due diligence yesterday and had Pitt's tech team do a background check on her, like he did for all my employees.

"Why not act on your urges?" he asked. "No harm in tangoing with a beautiful lady."

"Are you forgetting Savannah?"

He folded his arms behind his head. "Duke, you need to move on. You need to live a little."

I needed a drink. Sighing, I glanced at the blank wall above the couch. "She just started. I don't want to scare her."

"Then find a way to break the ice."

"What are you? My shrink?" I went over to the bar and fixed two drinks.

"Nah. Just a good friend."

"More like a brother," I added.

Brian didn't have any family except his daughter, Fran. He'd never been married. Fran was the result of a surprise pregnancy from a woman he'd dated for only a month. Sadly, Fran's mom died in a car accident three years ago. Brian was devastated more for Fran than anything. After her death, he'd sent Fran to a boarding school in upstate New York.

"We've been joined at the hip since we were nineteen," he said, sounding as though he was remembering our younger days—lots of girls, fast cars, and our initiation into the world of the mob. "Speaking of those days, where's Vince?"

I handed him a drink then sank into my seat. "Shacked up with Amber for the day." My lieutenant was in love with my most popular waitress.

"You mean that strawberry blonde?" he asked.

"Yeah, the two are sickening."

"If I recall, Amber is hell on wheels. She might see Joy as competition."

I rolled my eyes. "Don't care. So, do you have any news for me? Any scuttlebutt on the streets about missing guns?"

He swirled the ice around in his glass. "Seems no one is talking, but they will. Something as big as stolen guns doesn't stay hidden for long."

"Gustavo is striking out as well. Rosario is fuming. She can't get hold of Arturo, and none of her other enemies want to speak to her."

"You know I would rather wrestle an alligator than work for her, but she keeps my bank account filled to the brim."

"She's loyal to the people who are under her command. Hell, remember she saved my life from a crazy buyer who thought she fucked him on the amount of guns he bought. The man strung me up by my ankles, naked, and stuck me in a meat locker until she came to my rescue."

"I remember that." He snapped his fingers. "It was your first job with her, but wasn't that buyer operating on orders from Arturo Rodriguez?"

I gave him a nod. "Which is why I believe Arturo is behind the stolen guns. He's been trying to take Rosario out since she mowed her way into the Boston market four years ago."

"And she hasn't been in the States since," Brian added. "She stays protected in Colombia. Maybe stealing her stash is a way to force her to come to Boston."

"Whatever the reason, the end result won't be pretty," I said, needing to change the subject because my ulcer was acting up the more we talked about Rosario, Arturo, and the impending doom we were about to face. "What brings you by?"

He dropped his booted feet to the floor, straightening. "Can't I come see my friend?"

I chuckled. "Sure, but it's Sunday, and you're usually in front of the TV, watching the Pats."

"I guess you know me well too." His sarcasm rang through. "I need a favor. I could've called, but I wanted to test out my new Hummer. Anyway, Fran has a father-daughter dance in December at her boarding school. You think you can give me Grace's number? I thought Grace could take her dress shopping. Fran will be home for Thanksgiving. I'm sure my daughter doesn't want my big ass watching her try on dresses. Hell, I don't even know anything about dresses."

"I'm sure Grace will oblige, but back up. You're going to a school dance?"

He stuck out his middle finger. "You wait. If you have a daughter, you'll want to do anything for her."

"If I ever have kids, I hope they're all boys. A daughter would make me insane, trying to protect her from assholes like us. Look at how crazy I am in safeguarding my sister."

He chuckled. "Believe me, I'm not all there when Fran is with me. I want to tear out throats when boys look at her."

I leaned my elbows on my knees, cupping my glass. "By the way, do you need dancing lessons? Dillon is hosting a charity gala in December. Not sure of the date yet, but if it works out, you and Fran can practice."

He lifted a shoulder. "Maybe. Depends on the date."

Another idea came to mind. "If Fran is going to be home for Thanksgiving, why don't you and Fran join us at Denim's place?"

His green eyes widened. "You're going to a holiday shindig with the Harts? That dinner last week with them must've gone well or your brain has misfired."

I shuddered, recalling the initial tension, hating myself for putting my family in danger. "My brothers are ready to fight alongside me. Even Grace."

"It was never your family that didn't want you, Duke. It was your sorry ass that pushed them away. I don't ignore my daughter. She needs to know I love her and protect her, and for fuck's sake, I will do that all day long."

I opened my mouth to speak, and he held up his hand. "Hear me out. I'm not comparing myself to you. What I'm trying to say, as your friend, is I understand why you don't include them. It's not only for their safety, but you've been estranged from them pretty much since you left home. It's guilt that drives a wedge between you and them."

"Yes, Dr. McCauley," I said sarcastically.

"I should charge you. Kidding aside, you only get one chance at this life, and you and I both need to break free from this industry."

I chewed on the inside of my cheek. "I can't do squat right now. But come to Thanksgiving dinner, and you and I can discuss our futures." I needed support and someone who got me.

He considered me for a moment. "Fran is missing her mom terribly. It's been three years since that car accident, and Fran could use some adult female companions instead of our sorry asses."

"Good, then it's settled," I said.

"Look at us, bonding more than ever," he said jokingly.

I refilled our glasses.

"I'm curious about how you met Joy," he said after several seconds of silence. "When I was driving up, you two looked chummy. Do you know her from somewhere?"

I returned with his drink. "I met her at the cemetery."

He choked. "The fuck."

"I hit her truck. Long story. Anyway, she needed a job. Before I realized what I was doing, I was handing her my card."

"Oh, yeah. You're screwed. I can see the love affair starting already." He smirked. "But in all seriousness, it is time for you to move on from Savannah and stop blaming yourself for her death."

"The guilt will always be there," I said.

"Maybe so, but moving on will help you resolve some of your issues." He stabbed a finger at the window. "If you have no interest in that pretty lady, I'll take her for a spin."

"Like fuck you will."

He laughed hard. "I thought so. Twenty bucks says you'll have her in your bed by the end of the week."

I wasn't about to take that bet. Because every fiber in me was itching to touch her, taste her, and feel her against me.

With Joy, I would break my rule about not sleeping with a woman more than twice. And that scared the fuck out of me.

10

FALLYN

ALIAS: JOY

The club was rocking for a Saturday. Lust was in the air as the night scene was at its peak, with music blaring and alcohol-infused people dancing, some dry humping while others had their tongues down someone's mouth.

At the age of twenty-eight, I would like to say I missed this type of atmosphere, but I didn't. I hardly drank, and if I did, it was a beer or maybe a vodka drink but nothing that would get me to the point of stupid drunk.

"Is it like this every weekend?" I asked Matt, my bartending partner.

He waggled his thick light-blond eyebrows at me. "Can you feel the vibration? It's fucking awesome. I love this job."

A very busty brunette leaned over the bar, her cleavage on display for the young handsome bartender with a man bun. He met her halfway, turning his ear so he could hear her.

I was appointed the bartender for the waitresses tonight. They came first, and if I had a lull, I helped Matt. The man could work a bar like I'd never seen before. He reminded me of that movie *Cock-*

63

tail with Tom Cruise. Matt even twirled a liquor bottle or two with expert ability.

I continued to make Long Island iced teas for a party of five in the VIP section on the second floor. Every now and then, I would steal a look at the window of Duke's office.

The only time I saw Duke was through his window. At times, I thought it was creepy how he stood above the crowd, watching down like he was the king of the castle. Actually, he was. He commanded attention, oozed sex appeal, and made women crazy if he dared to come down from his perch.

I was feeling antsy that I hadn't attempted to snoop. How could I? I wouldn't know where to begin. My guess was he locked his office if he wasn't in the building. I hadn't even been able to use my womanly charm to cause Duke to make the first move, like Gwen had advised me.

It's only been a week. Give yourself a break. You're still trying to get to know the lay of the land.

Though it was hard to do much with Duke's second-in-command, Vince Russo. He had an eagle eye like his boss, always scanning the club. But Vince had the manners to check in with me every now and then.

I could at least say Vince was nice and a gentleman, opening doors if I was around or trying to get to know me. Unless Amber, one of the waitresses, was near. She seemed to bare her teeth at me whenever Vince and I chatted.

Matt relayed to me that Amber saw me as competition. She and Vince were fuck buddies or maybe more. If I wanted to know gossip, Matt was my guy. He didn't initiate it, but he had his ears wide open.

Matt nudged me out of my stupor. "Did you hear Amber calling you?"

I followed his line of sight to the petite strawberry blonde waiting for her order at the end of the bar, fuming red.

I could hardly hear over the *thump, thump, thump* of the bass. At least the noise was my excuse. There had been a few times before we opened, when the club was quiet, that I hadn't answered to my alias.

She threw her hands up, clearly wanting to tear off my head. "Hurry up, Joy. Time is money around here."

I couldn't argue that point. Matt and I had been racking up the tips. I usually left the club with about five hundred per night in my pocket from my portion of the tip jar. The crowd might lean more toward the younger generation, but the weekends brought out the rich business folks who wanted to let their hair down, particularly the women.

I placed the drinks on Amber's tray. "Sorry."

"You need to step it up," she said rudely. "You're slow. You're always looking up at Duke's office, and you're deaf. Matt heard me, and he's on the other side of the bar."

I bit my tongue and smiled. An argument with Amber would only draw attention to me that I didn't want, but maybe a brawl would light enough of a fire under Duke's ass to bring him out of his castle.

"Thanks for the advice." I pivoted on my heels and helped a bald guy sandwiched between two groups of rowdy ladies at the bar. "What can I get you?"

He watched Amber breeze off as if he knew her.

I snapped my fingers at him. "Dude, I don't have all night."

I was tired, my feet hurt, I was starving, and I needed to use the bathroom. I'd forgotten how exhausting working on my feet for hours on end could be.

"Heineken." His strident tone carried over the music.

Vince ponied up to the bar. "Joy, Duke wants to see you in his office when the show starts." He gave me a warm grin as his blue eyes sparkled beneath the strobe lights overhead.

"'Kay," I said.

The dancers in the cages put on a show on the hour. I had a few minutes before it started and maybe a chance to use the bathroom.

I popped the top of the Heineken and took the bald guy's money. Then he melted into the crowd.

I cleared empty glasses and beer bottles from the bar, feeling like someone was watching me. Sure enough, Duke was in his office window, dressed in black pants and a light-blue dress shirt rolled up on his forearms. He was always *GQ* ready, except for the night I'd been watching him through my scope. Then, he'd been wearing black jeans and a T-shirt with a skullcap on his head—a far cry from a business suit, for sure.

"Does Duke always stand like an eagle up there?" I asked Matt.

The corners of Matt's lips curled upward. "Always. He's kind of scary. But I caution you—don't dip your pen in the company ink, if you know what I mean. Many waitresses past and present have tried, and those who've succeeded have walked away with broken hearts. He's not the settle-down kind of dude."

Matt had no idea what I knew about Duke. I wondered if he had knowledge of Duke's illegal enterprises. I would guess not. And if he did, I doubted he would share.

"Good to know. I don't do steady anyway." I just needed intel about guns, the cartel, and a possible war with those who'd stolen the guns.

Besides, an ATF agent and a criminal weren't exactly a recipe for success.

Matt closed the distance between us, his gaze tracking mine. "I'll give you one last piece of advice. Keep your nose behind this bar, and don't give Amber any reason to screw with you."

I laughed, thinking he would have warned me about how dangerous Duke was. "What's so scary about Amber?"

"As I told you, her and Vince have a thing. If she has Vince's ear, then she has Duke's. Vince and Duke are tight."

I nodded at him. "Duke wants to see me, and the show is about to start. Are you cool for a few minutes?"

"Girl, I can work this bar in my sleep without any help." He gave me a lopsided grin. "Go. I would hate to see you get fired."

I hoped I hadn't done anything wrong. Or worse, maybe Duke knew who I really was. But I threw the towel I had over my shoulder on the counter below the bar then headed to the restroom.

I dodged sweaty patrons, thinking about what Duke wanted when someone grabbed my arm.

I whirled around to find my attacker was the bald guy I'd served the Heineken to. "What?" I asked rather than kicking him in the balls. He was a customer, and I didn't want to cause a scene.

Instead of verbally answering me, he shoved me into an empty hallway where the restrooms were located.

Fuck causing a scene. Actually, maybe this was a perfect opportunity to bring Duke out of his castle like I wanted to, if he'd seen the dude strong-armed me.

Baldy pinned my arm around my back, grabbed my neck like the jaws of life, and pushed me into a glass case that housed a fire extinguisher. My temple caught the edge of the wooden frame, and instant pain ricocheted through me.

"What is going on?" I shouted, only for my voice to die amid the blaring music from the show, which the club goers were riveted to, hooting and hollering.

"Listen carefully, Fallyn," he said into my ear.

My stomach dropped to the floor. How the fuck did he know my real name? Duke had made me. My cover was blown. That was the reason Duke had called me into his office.

"That's not my name. Now, let me go, or I'll scream." That was the only recourse I had. Even my free arm was caught between the wall and my stomach. I couldn't even use my legs because all two hundred fifty pounds of him was pressed against me.

A lot of good my weeks and weeks of physical training and self-defense classes did. I couldn't even bend low enough to grab the gun out of my boot.

"No one will hear you," he said. "And I know who you are."

My heart stopped.

"Listen closely. I'm only doing this to make this look real. I could kiss you, but you would probably knee me in the balls. Gwen needs you to meet her at noon tomorrow. She said you would know where. Oh, and to check your messages."

Gwen and I weren't due to meet until next weekend. So for her to send someone in, she must have urgent news. Still, I'd looked at my burner phone yesterday but not today. I'd been running late for my shift because my alarm hadn't gone off. I normally took a three-hour nap before work.

My pulse was soaring. I should be relieved at the mention of Gwen's name, but I wasn't just yet. Duke could have an inside man within the ATF or FBI or even Boston PD. I had to be cautious.

"I don't know a Gwen," I countered, just to play along for a moment.

"I promise, I'm legit. Now, someone is probably going to show up soon, as in Hart. I noticed him watching you most of the night. So work with me."

Maybe I had nothing to worry about, and if he was right that Duke would show up, then this might give me a great opening with Duke.

Baldy dragged his lips over my ear, eliciting a string of tingles along my arms. "I'm sorry I hurt you. Now, you could kiss me." He released his hold on my neck.

But when I turned to face him, Duke was pulling Baldy off me.

"Do you like hurting women?" Duke's face was red.

I shook off the soreness in my arm and attempted to slide between the two until Baldy got in Duke's face. "My business with her is none of yours."

Standing eye to eye with Baldy, Duke wrapped his hands around the other man's throat. "It is my business. I own this club, and I despise assholes like you who shove ladies around. If I see you in this club again, I'll break your knees. Are we clear?"

Baldy snarled and bit out, "Then tell your employee to pay up by the end of the week, or it's her knees I'll be breaking."

What the heck was Baldy doing? Saying? He was digging me a hole, not him.

Duke whipped out his gun and pressed it under Baldy's chin. "Touch her, and I'll make it so you never walk again."

Baldy shot a cheeky grin my way, appearing not the least bit fazed or frightened by Duke's threat.

I touched Duke's arm—the one not holding the weapon. "I can handle my own shit. Let him go."

Duke hesitated as a crowd formed to use the bathroom now that the cage dancers' show had ended.

"Duke, please," I begged, swallowing the dryness in my throat. "You're not a monster." I didn't exactly know if he was or wasn't. The government had yet to pin murder, drugs, guns, or money laundering on Duke. Hell, anything, for that matter.

Duke finally lowered his weapon. "Don't show yourself in this club again," he all but growled out.

My pulse began to slow as Baldy was sucked up into the crowd.

Duke examined me. "You're bleeding. Follow me."

I touched my temple, feeling the wetness of blood. "It's nothing." I flicked my finger behind me. "I can clean it. I need to use the restroom anyway."

"You can use the one in my place." His offer wasn't a suggestion but rather a demand.

I mashed my lips into a thin line, acquiescing not because he was ordering me but because my bladder was protesting to the point that if I didn't go soon, I would definitely have an accident.

11

FALLYN

ALIAS: JOY

A few minutes later, I found myself standing in the en suite attached to Duke's bedroom. It was hard to believe he was allowing me into his personal space.

After taking care of my immediate needs, I washed my hands then leaned over the pristine marble sink and examined my temple. The cut wasn't that bad. Head and facial wounds bled more, making it seem much worse than it actually was.

"I haven't talked to Grace yet," Duke said on the other side of the closed door.

I eavesdropped as best as I could.

A second of silence, then Duke said, "I'll see you and Fran at Denim's on Thanksgiving."

If I wasn't mistaken, Fran was the daughter of Brian McCauley.

A knock on the door startled me, and I slapped a hand over my mouth to swallow my screech.

"Joy, are you okay?" Duke's husky voice slid over me like warm butter on freshly baked bread.

The damn guy was attacking my feminine side like a soldier at war, only in a good way. Between his beautiful face, the way he dressed like a model out of *GQ*, and his raspy tone, I would be a goner if I didn't erect my shields.

"I think I need a Band-Aid." My voice cracked.

Fallyn, get your shit together and drop the nerves.

I shook my head like a wet dog then wiped blood off my wound.

"Can you let me in? I have a first aid kit in my hand. I don't keep one in the bathroom."

I'd been so consumed by my thoughts that I hadn't even bothered to snoop in his closet or cabinet. If I didn't start paying more attention, I could end up like my brother.

Duke raked his gaze over me when I let him in. "Sit on the counter."

On his command, I ambled over to the sink, feeling his heated gaze on my back. My legs felt unsteady, as if his eyes were causing tremors in my body, tingles on my skin.

Once I was where he wanted me, he rolled up his shirtsleeves, opened the small first aid kit, and set it beside a bottle of Sauvage cologne by Dior. The name seemed to fit him, as did the spicy fragrance that filled the room.

I suddenly felt lightheaded, vulnerable, and more jittery than ever.

"Who was that guy?" He began to clean my wound, his touch gentle yet firm, concentrating like he was performing a unique surgical procedure. "How much do you owe him? And for what?"

Swallowing, I shifted in my seat, thinking of a believable lie. I had never been good at telling fibs when I was a little girl. Dad always knew I was lying. He'd even warned me to be cognizant of my tells when I was nervous, like rubbing my hands on my thighs.

Duke positioned himself between my legs. "You haven't answered me."

"You've played doctor before?" My brain was fogging with the proximity and closeness of his body to mine. It didn't help that he smelled so freaking good.

He's forbidden. He's the enemy. He's going to prison for a long time.

No matter how many times I repeated those lines, my body was telling me to fuck off.

With the tips of his warm fingers, he curled my hair behind my ear. "I'm the one asking the questions."

I'd never been one to fluster easily, but he was making it difficult for me to think.

He placed a small round bandage on my temple. "Are you going to answer me?"

"Maybe when you're not touching me," I said honestly.

He studied me as if I was a nutjob. "You're nervous because of me?"

I rolled my eyes. "You're quite scary."

Handsome. Deadly. He's everything I don't need yet suddenly want. And that want has nothing to do with the job.

I licked my dry lips, waiting for him to respond to my comment, but he seemed mesmerized as he fixated on me.

I sighed quietly. "If we're done here, I would like to go back to work."

He blinked as if the sound of my voice broke whatever was going through his head. "Not until you tell me about the bald beast."

I snorted, more to calm my nerves than anything else. "Beast, huh?"

He lightly touched the scar on my forehead, and I could see intrigue washing over him. "What happened?"

I circled my fingers around his wrist. "Childhood accident."

"Tell you what. I'll answer one question from you if you promise to answer mine."

"I only get one?" I fake pouted.

He narrowed his gaze.

I let go of him. "Fine. Who's Savannah?"

Brian had made a big deal about throwing Savannah in Duke's face the other day.

"None of your business," he snapped.

I'd hit a nerve—a strong one.

"Exactly," I had the courage to say. "The bald guy is none of yours."

Fire burned in the depths of his eyes, and the devil came to mind.

Ever so gently, he tangled his fingers through the ends of my hair, as if he, too, was trying to do something to keep his nerves at bay. "I'm going to make you a deal, Joy." His actions didn't match his stern tone.

At that moment, Duke Hart reminded me of my father. Dad always had a way of being gentle with me before he scolded me.

"You tell me who that bald beast is, or I'll give you your final paycheck tonight. We'll part ways now."

Fuck me. He sounded serious.

I didn't know what to say or do. Cry, laugh, walk out, beg, kiss him? Whoa!

It didn't seem as though crying would work on him. He was a hardened individual. I pictured him with a strong partner. Begging wouldn't work. It would make me seem too weak, though men like Duke tortured their subjects into submission. Kissing him wouldn't be appropriate, but it sure might be fun.

I was going to be true to who I really was. I thought about what Fallyn would do. I didn't need to put on an act now that I'd decided on a course of action. I also couldn't let him think he had me cornered.

"Then I guess I'll take my paycheck and part ways." I leaned forward, motioning for him to move so I could leave.

He didn't budge, searching my face, those mahogany eyes sucking me in.

"Can I go?" My pulse shot through the roof. I was beating myself up inside, not only because I wanted to feel his lips on mine but because I was about to blow my assignment with nothing to show for it after one freaking week on the job.

He shook his head. "How much do you owe him?"

"Why do you care?" I touched the scruff on his jaw. "You gave me an ultimatum. That means you just fired me over something that is none of your business. I'm a good bartender. I do my job, and as much as I need the money, I won't sell out my personal life for you or anyone."

I barely had time to register his next movement when he cupped the sides of my face with a possessive grip and crashed his lips onto mine. The kiss was sudden and consuming, igniting a fierce desire within me.

His tongue explored my mouth, gentle yet demanding. I was lost in the moment, my body responding to his every movement. For a second, I forgot where we were, who we were supposed to be. Criminal and federal agent. Boss and employee.

His hands fell away from my cheeks, and he took a step back, his expression unreadable.

My heart raced, my breath coming in short gasps.

"I shouldn't have done that," he said, his voice brittle. "I'm sorry."

"Am I fired or not?" I asked, hoping I wasn't showing any sign that I was dying inside to have him kiss me again—or take me to his bed.

"No." His fingers flew through his hair. "Tell me how much you owe him at least. You can borrow the money from me."

You earned his respect. Or maybe he's testing you. A man like him needs to see that. He needs to see how you tick. Let him do this. If you push too hard, he might send you packing.

"Two grand, but I'm paying you back." I was cheering inside, relieved that I didn't have to tuck my tail and tell my team I blew the ops gig.

"One more thing." He closed the distance between us. "I want you to take self-defense classes. A guy like that is no match for you. I can protect you in the club, but once you leave here, you're on your own."

"Duke, I'm a big girl. I can handle myself."

His lopsided grin tickled places that were soaking in lust. "My sister says that all the time." He slid his hands along the sides of my thighs. "If you know how to fight, then you won't mind showing me. That way I would feel better."

"You won't take no for an answer, will you?" The more time I spent with him, the better chance I had of gaining intel or—call me crazy—falling for him.

He touched my scar again as if he were fascinated with it. "No."

I pushed out much-needed air from my lungs. "Fine. Tell me where and when. I'll be glad to kick your ass."

He laughed, the sound loose and dark, as he dragged his knuckles along my cheek. "We'll see about that. Also, one thing you'll learn about me, Joy, is I despise men who beat women."

"Sounds to me like an asshole hurt a lady close to you. I don't want to know," I rushed out. "But I do want you to understand who I am. I don't like ultimatums."

"Clearly," he volleyed back.

"Duke," a female voice called from his bedroom. "Are you in here?"

My stomach dropped. The last thing I wanted to do was to have a woman he might be dating get the wrong idea about us.

Duke eased away. "Grace?"

His sister breezed in, assessing the situation as her gaze bounced from Duke to me. "Oh. Vince said you were helping the bartender. I thought he meant—"

"Don't finish that sentence," Duke said. "What are you doing here this late?"

Grace Hart was stunning, with long, wavy locks that tumbled to the middle of her back. Her makeup brought out the sparkle in her copper eyes, and she was dressed in a shimmery low-cut top over black leggings, with ankle-high boots to complete her outfit.

Ignoring her brother, she turned to me. "I'm Grace, Duke's sister. Bartender? Are you sure you're not a model?"

I was flattered. "Bartender."

A tall blond man waltzed in and sidled up to Grace.

Duke stiffened. "Denim? What's going on? Everything okay? Dillon with you?"

Denim Hart, tall, blond, blue-eyed, and the youngest Hart brother, had spent time in the slammer for a murder he hadn't committed. He'd also been instrumental in putting away Tito Alvarez for the exact murder Denim had been accused of.

Denim glued his attention to me. "Are we interrupting?" He was smiling as if he was proud of his brother. "Who's the pretty lady?"

"Bartender," Grace answered for me.

"No shit," Denim said.

I slid off the sink, smoothing my hands down my denim-clad legs. "I'm Joy. Duke was playing nurse." I pointed at my temple. "Rowdy customer."

"Really? My brother hasn't done that since we were kids." Shock wove through Denim's words.

Grace sashayed over to Duke then felt his forehead. "Are you feeling okay?"

Duke rolled down his shirtsleeves as if he didn't have a care in the world, or maybe he was avoiding his inquisitive siblings. "Grace, please don't read anything into this. You know I take care of my employees."

Denim guffawed. "Not personally, you don't. You have men to do your dirty work, including bandaging."

If looks could kill, Denim would be dead. "Denim," Duke warned.

As if Grace were the peacekeeper, she said, "Denim needs to chat with you, and I tagged along. I wanted to see Matt."

Duke raised his eyebrow.

She huffed. "I'm not dating him or anything. He wants to help me with my college application to Boston University. Of course, not at this time of night, but I need to ask him a few things. He's hard to track down during the day. Plus, I got your message about giving Brian my phone number. I'll let him know I can take Fran dress shopping when she's home for Thanksgiving. I need a dress for the gala anyway."

"Our sister is going to be a college girl," Denim said. "Can you believe that?"

The smile on Duke's face was blinding. "I'm proud of you. Also, thank you for helping Fran. Brian will be happy." He kissed her on the head. "Do you need my credit card to buy your dress?"

She batted her pretty eyes at Duke. "That would be nice."

The man melted on the spot again. "Of course. I want you to be the most beautiful woman in the room."

As I watched the bonds among the Hart siblings, I was crying inside. Jason and I had shared that kind of love, but I would never again have that sibling connection—the laughter, the holidays, the big brother watching over me like Jason had done when we were growing up.

On the flip side, anger rifled through me, my muscles tightening. Duke, Brian, and criminals like them were happy and building family ties. Yet they were simultaneously profiting from violence and fueling other thugs with weapons and illegal drugs, resulting in bloodshed, death, and destruction.

"Joy, did you hear me?" Grace asked, yanking me out of my thoughts.

I feigned a smile. "I'm sorry. I didn't."

"My brothers need to talk. I'll walk with you to the bar," she said.

"We'll talk before you leave for the night," Duke said at my back. "About self-defense classes."

I was in a daze as Grace hooked her arm through mine. "Duke is a great trainer."

I was sure he was good at everything.

The brothers began talking as Grace guided me out of the en suite. "How did you find out about the job opening? Duke doesn't usually post them, although he'd been searching for a bartender who won't leave after one night."

I could see how someone might call it quits. Amber alone was difficult to work with. So I dove in, explaining how Duke had ended up hiring me, and by the time we reached the bar, she and I had talked about several things, including the Hart of Hope gala and how excited she was that Duke was attending his first Thanksgiving dinner with the family.

Maybe Grace was the one I should be hanging out with. She was a wealth of information. Still, the second I was serving customers, I felt a weight lift off my shoulders. Being with Duke was all-consuming. I was starting to think that maybe I wasn't the right person for this undercover assignment, that Bruce was right. I was too green around the gills to pull off this op. Not only that, Duke had made the first move. For fuck's sake, that kiss. I hadn't been kissed like that… ever, not even by the drummer who'd broken my heart.

I tuned out Matt and Grace chatting as I served customers.

Matt nudged me. "Amber is calling you."

I laughed. "Maybe I'm ignoring her."

I wasn't. I hadn't heard her again. It was time for me to put my bitch hat on, though.

I glared at the strawberry blonde. "What do you need?"

Amber tapped on her tray with her red-painted nail. "It's about time you decided to work again."

"Let's get something straight," I said loudly because of the music. "Stop with the bitchy attitude. I'm not your competition with your beau, Vince. I'm here to make money. So if you don't cut me some slack, I'll make your life hell."

She took a step back then forward, hands on her hips, sticking out her tits. "You dare to threaten me?"

Grace intervened. "Amber, cool your jets. We all know you see Joy as a threat. She's not into Vince. Okay?"

Amber puffed out a breath. "Joy won't be here long anyway. Duke has a rule. He doesn't sleep with a woman more than twice. Then he kicks them out."

"And maybe I'm not like other women," I volleyed back with acid in my tone.

Matt spoke up. "Ladies, nix the drama. We're approaching last call. I'll help Amber. Joy, the bar."

The last time I had been a target of drama was in high school, but that wasn't why I was stomping away. I was annoyed with her comment about Duke. I shouldn't have been. I wasn't here to sleep with Duke. At least, my brain wasn't on board with that idea, although I couldn't say the same about my damn body.

"Matt just told me you used to work in California." Grace was throwing out empty bottles and wiping down the bar. "Are you from there?"

I made a cosmo and a dry martini. "All over, really." I wanted to be as aloof as possible. Not dive in too deep as to who Joy Whitlock was. "But my grandmother, who passed away a year ago, lived in Weston." Lydia Whitlock was buried in Linwood Cemetery and had died of sepsis from a torn bowel because of an obstruction, according to the research I'd done on her.

Grace's burgundy-stained lips turned downward. "You should spend Thanksgiving with us."

"I couldn't impose." I wanted to sneak away to spend the day with my dad—a dad that wasn't in my profile.

"Nonsense," she said. "We have plenty of room, and I know my sisters-in-law would love to have you."

After witnessing the bonds among Duke, Denim, and Grace, I wasn't sure I could handle any more of the lovefest.

You need to tuck your emotions away. You have a job to do.

"Please," she said. "I can see that Duke likes you, and you'll fit right in with us. Brian McCauley, maybe not. He's kind of an ogre sometimes. But his daughter will be there, and he's usually tame when Fran's around."

I'd had my introduction to him, but this might be the opening I was looking for to find out more about Jason's death. Maybe. "Can I think about it?"

Nodding, she smiled then dashed off to help a customer.

Matt had been close by, wiping down the bar. "Bad idea, Joy. Remember what I told you."

"I know. Don't mix business with pleasure, in so many words."

He gave me a wary look. "You'll get burned. I've seen it happen."

"Thanks for the advice. Truly."

This undercover gig was starting to rattle me in more ways than I cared to admit.

12

DUKE

The sound of Sam Tinnesz's music filled the gym as I mercilessly pounded the punching bag at five thirty the next morning. So many emotions were bottled up inside me, and all the liquor in the world couldn't take away the shitstorm that was my life.

With every jab, I pictured that fucker who'd roughed up Joy. I wanted to hunt him down and beat him to a pulp. What the fuck was wrong with men who battered women? I wasn't exactly innocent of the things I'd been accused of doing in my life, but hitting women had never been one of them. They should be treated with respect and kindness and like equals.

I laughed as pain shot up my arms from my assault on the bag. Joy had earned more than my respect last night when she challenged my threat to fire her. I'd been serious, though. She needed to know where I stood with men like that bald guy. I'd almost killed my old man several times when I found him beating Grace and my mother. I couldn't count how many times I'd grabbed a steak knife and tried to stab him, only to be stopped by my mom, when she'd been living at home, or one of my brothers.

Grunting, I continued to destroy the punching bag as my thoughts switched to Joy and that mind-blowing kiss—sweet, delectable, and addicting. What had I been thinking? I shouldn't have done that. Now I was hooked. I wanted to kiss her again and again.

The music suddenly stopped, and I jolted out of the haze I was in, whirling around, my gaze landing on her.

Sweat poured off me, my mouth slightly ajar, and I must have had a deer-in-the-headlights look.

But holy shit! It was like I was seeing Joy for the first time. I knew she was stunning and curvy, but damn.

"You didn't hear me," she said. "I didn't want to break your concentration. I was afraid if I startled you that you would turn around and punch me."

She was wearing a green sports bra and black leggings that hugged every part of her body. Her biceps were rather defined and perfect for her size. Her toned thighs could probably put a hurt on anyone if she did any kickboxing. But the best thing about the beauty with the golden-brown hair was her six-pack abs. Whoa!

I went over to the chair near her, snagged my towel, and wiped the sweat off my face and neck.

"Taking out your frustrations?" she asked.

She had no idea. "Something like that." I traded my towel for the bottle of Gatorade as I checked my watch. "You're early."

"I couldn't sleep."

"I guess we have something in common."

I'd stared at the ceiling the entire night, replaying that kiss in my mind over and over like a broken record.

Joy walked around the gym then over to the boxing ring. "Your sister is super sweet. She told me you're good in the ring."

Before Grace had left the club last night, she couldn't stop talking about how pretty Joy was. How cool she was. How Joy knew the best dress shops in Boston. Hell, my sister had even invited Joy to Thanksgiving dinner.

My first holiday with my siblings was turning into a match-making game. As much as I loved Grace for wanting to yank me out of the dark and bring me into the light, now wasn't the time to entertain a steady relationship. *No way. No how.*

"I can hold my own. Do you box?" I chugged the bottle of Gatorade and tossed the empty bottle into the trash can.

"I've done some kickboxing." She plucked a pair of gloves off the shelf where other workout gear was located. "I would rather use my fists than gloves."

I reared back. "Hardcore."

She shrugged. "Aren't you?"

"Come again?"

She gave me a ball-squeezing smile. "You seem like the type to play hard and take no shit from anyone, and the way you were attacking that punching bag looked as though you like things rough."

I almost choked. I didn't know how I felt about her reading me to a tee.

I strode over to her, needing a cold shower—or an ice bath, was more like it. My dick was enjoying her siren voice and her gorgeous body.

"Do you own this gym?" she asked.

I proceeded to tie a glove she'd tried on. "No, I would like to own a gym. A bigger one than this. My buddy Shawn is the owner. He doesn't open until late morning on Sundays. I have a key to come in whenever I like."

"I take it we're going in the ring," she said. "Can we not use gloves? Boxing isn't self-defense. If you want to see my moves, then we should use the mat and play out a real-life scenario."

I untied the glove. "You're right."

My mind wasn't firing on all cylinders with her in my presence. Even last night in my bathroom, all I could think about was kissing her, and I had. Such a big fucking mistake. Even now, standing this close to her as I took off the glove, I wanted to taste her again.

I was so fucked as my heart was skipping beat after beat. Hell, I even had butterflies in my stomach. What the fuck was happening to me?

My adorable sister had seen right through me too. "You like her." She hadn't asked but told me.

Joy's cold hand landed on my hot one. "Duke, where did you go?"

Everywhere and nowhere. Even her vanilla fragrance was causing those flutters inside me to freak the fuck out.

Blinking, I ground my teeth, thinking of strangling my enemies —anything to stop my speeding heart. "We should get started. I have a busy day."

She examined my knuckles. "It looks to me like you either punched someone or a wall. Why didn't you tape them?"

"Don't need to." That came out a little harsher than I intended. "Why don't you warm up?"

While I compose myself and think of death and war so I don't tackle you onto the mat and have my way with you. That just might happen before we left here today.

She wiggled her fine ass over to the mat while I tossed the glove on the shelf.

"If you can handle yourself like you say, why did you let that bald beast hurt you?"

She sat with her legs stretched out as she bent over to touch her toes. "I didn't see him until it was too late. The way he had me pinned left no room for me to attack."

I crossed my arms over my chest, settling on the edge of the mat. "Awareness is everything, Joy. You have to know your surroundings inside and out and right down to the people around you. You should always be looking for an outlet, an exit, a way to free yourself."

A former mentor of mine had taught me from day one to never, ever let my guard down. Always know where the exits were and how to read people. Keep my eyes wide open and my hearing sharp. That advice was partly the reason I hadn't been busted.

She puffed out a breath, sitting up before curling her legs underneath her. "How did you know to come to my rescue?"

"I saw the guy shove you into the hall," I said.

"Do you rescue every girl in the club?"

"No, I have bouncers for that. But when it comes to my employees, yes, if I see it happening. So, let's talk about a real-life scenario, as you put it. You're about to be attacked. What do you do?"

"Go for the vulnerable parts of the body first and quickly," she said.

I nodded. "Good. What are those?"

She assumed a downward dog pose. "Eyes, jaw, throat, groin."

I closed my eyes briefly, shaking off the ideas of what I wanted to do with her.

When I focused on her once again, she was in a cobra pose.

"There are other parts of the body, like the knees," she said. "A severe knee hit can cause intense pain, leading to temporary mobility to give me a chance to run."

She knew more than I had presumed she would, and relief had me breathing a little more easily that she might be able to fend off attackers. However, knowing and doing were two different animals.

"Do you carry a gun, knife, any type of weapon?" I asked.

She stood to her full height. "Gun in one boot. Knife in the other."

I raised my eyebrows, not expecting that she was armed to kill. "I'm glad to hear that, but is there a specific reason you're armed?"

Grace had a concealed weapons permit and carried. It was essential she did after escaping a sex-trafficking ring. I wanted her armed to the hilt, if need be.

"Crazy world out there," Joy said. "Living alone has its downside, if you know what I mean. Look, I'm sorry about drawing attention last night."

"You're not the first to be attacked, although it's mostly drunk guys who get testy either with the female help or other customers." I stepped on the mat. "If you're warmed up, we'll simulate an attack."

She hesitated. "Are you sure? I don't want to hurt your balls."

As if my nuts heard her, I could almost feel the pain. "You let me worry about that."

Grinning, she shrugged. "If you say so, I'll show no mercy."

I liked that she was bold and had the courage to take me down or at least to try.

"Ready?" I asked, standing behind her.

She rolled her eyes as she walked away.

In one stride, I had her by the arm. She spun around, her knee inches away from my groin. As I deflected her from my jewels, she threw an uppercut to the underside of my jaw.

Smiling, she danced on the balls of her feet, not showing any signs that she was in pain from that bone-on-bone hit.

I rubbed my jaw. "Nice." Then I waved her toward me. "Show me what else you can do."

She stepped toward me, left forearm in front of her, hand fisted while her right was ready to attack me. Then she rushed forward, her attention on my face, primed to throw punch after punch. Just when I thought she would ram her fist into my jaw again, she threw a snap kick, like an MMA fighter. The top of her foot connected with the side of my arm, feeling like a tap.

"Impressive." I was beginning to feel much better about her abilities.

She pursed her lips. "Why are you just standing there?"

"I want to see what you're made of, not hurt you. But try again. This time, I'll engage."

She lunged at me hard and fast, fists flying. We danced around each other, with me deflecting her jabs. I had every opportunity to tackle her and throw her over my shoulder, but I was enjoying this way more than I thought I would.

Until she did a sweep kick, knocking my feet out from under me. My back hit the mat, air whooshing out of my lungs.

Standing over me, she held out her hand. "Your feet weren't planted. What gives? You were lost in space."

Because I was thinking about kissing you again.

I inhaled deeply, managing to fill my lungs with air. "You're better than I thought." I accepted her offer, only to pull her down to the mat with me.

She giggled as she fell on top of me. Her vanilla scent filtered into my nostrils, seeping into my veins and down to my groin. I couldn't stop my erection even if I had a gun to my head.

I rolled us so she was beneath me then pinned her hands over her head, searching her face. My gaze finally landed on her lips. I couldn't kiss her. Not twice. A second time would lead to a third, then I wouldn't stop.

Man, back away. Walk away. Get the hell out of there. You can't fall for her. Look what happened the last time you let someone in. She died.

"Where did you learn how to fight?" I asked, not recognizing my own voice.

"Here and there," she said in a breathy tone. "Did I pass your test?"

"Not quite."

"Come again?"

"I have you pinned."

"You also have an erection."

I laughed. "So? That shouldn't stop you from fighting me off. Never hesitate. Do you hear me?"

She licked her lips. "Yes, sir."

The throbbing in my dick dissipated. "Don't call me that."

She knitted her eyebrows. "Why not?"

"'Sir' reeks of someone you respect, and I'm not that guy. I'm not good, Joy. I'm an asshole."

"I don't think so. You're taking time to help me today. You

bandaged me up last night. Not many bosses would do that. Your brother Denim even said you have men to do the work."

"Don't read into anything. If you do, you might be sorely disappointed to learn more about me."

"Like what? Are you a killer? Stalker? All of us have parts that are not good."

I pierced her with an empty look, my chest tight that her last line was spot-on. "And what part of you isn't good?"

She wiggled beneath me, and my erection was coming alive once again. "I guess you'll just have to stick around to find out."

I raised my eyebrows slightly. "Is that a challenge?"

"Call it whatever you like. It's clear you're going to." Her gaze lowered to my groin area.

"How do you figure?"

She rolled her eyes then squirmed once again. "There's fire between us, Duke. I feel it, and you're clearly showing it with that bulge in your shorts. Plus, that kiss last night says it all."

I ghosted my lips over hers. "Are you saying you want to fuck me?"

She sucked in air. "I think we need to. Maybe then we can alleviate the sexual tension and move on."

It was bad enough the kiss was messing with my head—and possibly my heart—but making love to her would surely be my downfall.

I trailed a finger down her neck to her cleavage. Her skin was damp and silky. Goose bumps trailed in the wake of my touch. "You think you can handle me?"

"There's only one way to find out."

With all the control I could muster, I left her on the mat. "We're done for today."

She rose up on her elbows. "What's wrong, Duke? Are you afraid?"

"Not at all," I lied as I went over to my bag. "I have the money for you to pay that bald beast."

"We should talk about *us*. That kiss," she said at my back.

I counted the bills then slipped them into the envelope. "Joy, you're beautiful, but you and I aren't going to happen. Last night was a mistake."

"I thought we had something." She came over and yanked a towel out of her bag on the chair next to mine.

I tucked the envelope in the front pocket of her gym bag. "We do, but the only thing to come from us being together is me killing any guy who dares to touch you or look at you. Do you know that I would've pulled the trigger last night if you had more than that surface wound on your head? I'm not good for you."

"It's probably best anyway. I have a habit of not staying in one place too long. I usually run when a guy wants a serious relationship."

She had me pegged wrong. I didn't do serious either. Maybe we should just have one night together then part ways. Yet I was lying to myself if I thought I would allow her to leave after one night.

13

———————

FALLYN

ALIAS: JOY

Later that day, dressed in running gear, vest, scarf, earmuffs, and gloves, I was jogging from my studio apartment to meet Gwen. After the little trysts with Duke in his bathroom and in the gym, I needed to blow off some much-needed tension. My mind was bloated with so many conflicting thoughts and emotions that I was afraid I might forget who I was supposed to be and blurt out the truth of who I really was.

There was no doubt that the lives of Fallyn and Joy were beginning to blur. All because of one freaking kiss that might've started a potential train wreck. If Grace Hart had her way, Duke and I would be locked in a bedroom or walking down the aisle to say, "I do."

That couldn't happen. *Never. Never. Never.*

Take away the criminal and peel back Duke's layers, and I would be certain he had some wonderful qualities. So far, he'd shown a side of himself with Grace that warmed my heart, but that was the conundrum. I couldn't allow that sweet side of him to overshadow the deadly side of him—the criminal mastermind, the one who dealt in illegal weapons.

I ran faster, trying to clear so many things from my head. His damn erection had had me blurting out that we should sleep together. Not to mention his kiss and the way he smelled—his sweat mixed with that Sauvage cologne was an aphrodisiac. The war between what was right and what was wrong was becoming shadowy all of a sudden.

He's forbidden. He's the enemy.

A horn jolted me out of my stupor as I crossed a street.

"Watch where you're going!" the driver yelled at me.

"Sorry." I slowed to a walk as I approached Boston Common, trying to catch my breath.

I rubbed the stitch of pain on my waist, taking in the streets teeming with traffic and pedestrians out and about.

Gwen was sitting on a bench along the wide stretch of road for pedestrian traffic, bundled in a black beanie and a winter jacket, with coffee in hand.

I dropped onto the cold seat beside her as couples strolled by. Others were walking their dogs, and joggers were out for their daily workouts.

"Sorry about the urgent meeting," she said. "We might have a problem. I wanted to be sure you were informed immediately. What happened here?" She pointed at my temple.

"You can thank that dude you sent in to give me a message."

"Why did he rough you up?" She sounded appalled.

"The dude thought if he tried to kiss me, I would knee him in the balls. He would be right. Anyway, he strong-armed me just to be safe. It's nothing. I should thank him too. That little incident caused Duke to make the first move."

"No shit. Tell me more."

I would if it weren't for the fact that I wasn't ready to tell any of what had happened during the last twenty-four hours between Duke and me. One, I was afraid it would become real if I did. Two, she would relay the info to the team, including my father, and I didn't want Dad to worry. Finally, I wasn't there to dish about my hots for the enemy. She had something urgent to tell me. However, I could throw her a bone.

"He's training me in self-defense after that incident."

She lowered her sunglasses on the bridge of her nose. "Nothing more?"

"Absolutely not. I'm not going down that road." *Liar. Only a few hours ago, I told Duke that he and I should fuck. Well, I blamed that suggestion on my body. My inner voices are continuing to have a grand old time.* "But if Grace has her way, Duke and I will be dating shortly. She invited me to Thanksgiving dinner with the Harts."

"Huh. You're really settling in. Good job. The team will be pleased."

"I don't have any intel yet. I mean, I've met Brian McCauley. He'll be at Thanksgiving dinner."

Her mouth parted slightly. "Maybe this op will be successful. Who knows? You might find out what really happened to Jason after all."

"One day at a time. I'm not going to lie. Undercover is harder than I thought."

"It always is," she said. "I've had buddies come out of long undercover assignments different people, and they've told me it was one of the hardest jobs anyone could imagine. Which is why the quicker we can gain concrete intel, the faster we can pull you out." She picked up her phone beside her, brought up a picture, and handed me her cell. "Have you seen that guy next to McCauley before?"

The man in the photo had military-style brown hair, brown eyes, and pockmarks on his face. He was dressed in jeans, leather jacket, and shiny loafers.

"I haven't. Is he part of a gang? Cartel?"

"Fed," she said, gaze directed at the pond in the distance. "DEA. Neal Fitzgerald."

I sucked in freezing air, my pulse going from seventy to one hundred in a second. "They look chummy. Does the DEA have someone inside McCauley's camp?"

"To our knowledge, no, but that doesn't mean shit. You know that agencies don't like to share their special ops assignments, afraid to compromise their subjects."

That was one issue we'd talked about before I'd gone in. Only key personnel on a need-to-know basis were privy to what we were doing. Agent Howard was adamant we didn't bring the FBI in on the matter, as was my dad. We hadn't discussed the DEA, only because Duke didn't deal in drugs. McCauley did, though.

"Does my dad know?"

"He's calling in some favors to find out what's going on. McCauley could be this dude's informant, for all we know."

"McCauley an informant?" I mumbled. "I don't believe that. Though it would be ironic for him to snitch on his own men or maybe his good friend Duke."

I didn't want to totally discount the idea. If McCauley was desperate to save his own ass, he might throw Duke under the bus. Or, maybe, Rosario Mendoza.

She pulled her hat down over her ears. "I agree with you. McCauley and Hart have been joined at the hip for many years. I highly doubt Brian would fuck one of his only longtime friends. My main concern is you. Keep alert."

"I will. Any updates on the stolen guns? Who might be involved?"

"My contacts within the gangs haven't heard a thing. Bruce learned that Mateo Alvarez was seen with a cartel member weeks ago, but no one is talking. But we know that the Alvarezes have been trying to gain leverage into the gun market way before Tito went to prison. We know Arturo Rodriguez wants a piece, if not all, of the market on illegal firearms for his Mexican cartel. They might be teaming up. Keep your ears open."

"So could we be looking at a coup to oust Rosario and gain control of both the gun and drug businesses in Boston?"

She bobbed her head. "Possibly. I wouldn't be surprised if they use Duke Hart as a pawn to get to Rosario."

"Or take Duke out altogether." I bounced my knee. "Anything else?"

"Be careful. If you see Neal Fitzgerald around, make yourself invisible. Until we know more about him, we don't want you compromised. As soon as I have info on him, I'll message you. So check your burner more often."

"Copy that. By the way, how's my dad?"

She plucked her cell from me. "I won't lie. He's worried."

I blew hot air into my cold hands. "Tell him I'll call on Thanksgiving. Also, please don't mention my scratch to him."

"My report will say that you have no intel yet but are making inroads with the Hart family. I don't know if I'm jealous or scared for you."

"Duke is a target, nothing more."

She pushed to her feet. "I know we've joked around about fucking Duke, but—"

"You don't have to say it." Tucking my hands into the pockets of my vest, I rose.

Her blue eyes were filled with worry. "I do. I wouldn't be doing my job if I didn't. It's easy for us as women to use our sexual charm to lure a man to trust us. I know your brain is all in on doing a kick-ass job and taking down the likes of the cartel, Duke, hell, maybe even Brian McCauley. But separating the enemy from the man isn't always possible when emotions take the lead."

It wasn't my emotions driving the ship but my physical attraction to Duke.

"I'm sensing that you speak from experience." I wasn't aware that she'd gone undercover.

"No experience. As I told you earlier, I had friends undercover. Just be careful. Also, if you find those lines blurring between your mission and your heart, call me immediately. I don't know if I can help, but I'll be there for you."

I'd been on the team for six months, and during that time, Gwen was proving to be a good friend. I just prayed that my heart wouldn't take the lead.

14

—————

FALLYN

ALIAS: JOY

I was feeling nauseated as I walked up to a twenty-story high-rise in an upscale area of Boston, where expensive shops were nestled below expensive apartment buildings. Grace had given me the 411 on Denim's place, formerly owned by Duke, who'd given Denim the penthouse suite not long after he'd been paroled from prison.

Shivering from the cold, I stood outside the high-rise, my mind waging war on whether I should go inside. Did I really want to spend the day with people I hardly knew and one I could arrest at some point?

I should hop into my truck and drive to Weston. Dad was probably alone in the sunroom, reading the latest thriller. I hated that I wasn't with him. Holidays sucked every year without Mom and Jason.

I kicked my legs into gear toward my truck that was parked around the corner and called Dad.

The line connected on the first ring. "Sweetheart," he said, surprised.

I probably should've used the burner cell or called him before

I'd left my apartment, but then I'd decided I would wait to talk to him after dinner with the Harts.

"I'm coming home," I said.

"Absolutely not," he replied in a soft-but-firm tone. "I understand you're spending the day with the Harts. That's what you need to do."

The job always came first with Dad. He would always tell Jason and me that criminals didn't sleep.

I scanned the somewhat-deserted street with the occasional car here and there. "I need a day to be Fallyn. I want to visit Jason and Mom at the cemetery too. I also don't want you to be alone on Thanksgiving."

Snow was falling, and with two inches on the ground, I imagined it was a perfect time to stay inside for the holiday.

"Sweetheart, I'm fine. Gwen tells me you're making inroads. That's great news. I'm not alone either." The sound of a dog barking came through the phone. "Did you hear that?" He laughed. "I have a new addition to the family. Her name is Rosie, and she's a golden retriever, two years old. I got her at the SPCA."

I started crying. We'd had dogs growing up, but after Daisy, our springer spaniel, died not long after we'd buried Mom, Dad didn't want any more.

I sniffled. "So you're replacing me," I teased through tears and laughter.

"Never, but I can't wait for you to meet her. I decided the house was too darn quiet. Plus, I needed a fishing buddy."

"That's great, Dad." I rested against the corner of the building, my truck in view to jump in and go meet Rosie.

Any ideas I had of seeing my dad were squashed when someone called for Joy. It took me a beat and a glance to my left to see that Grace was walking toward me,

"Dad, I have to go. Grace Hart is coming."

"We'll talk soon. Be careful," he said.

I met Grace halfway, feigning a smile that was painful at the moment.

Two military-type men I didn't recognize dressed in black lingered behind her.

Reality came roaring back along with the lie I was living.

She startled. "Are you crying? What's wrong? Did Duke do something to hurt you?"

I laughed. Otherwise, I might have bawled like a baby. "Not at all. The wind and cold makes my eyes and nose water."

"Then we should go inside."

She always looked put together in expensive clothes with her brown hair styled perfectly and makeup done artistically. The hummingbird tattoo on her neck stood out against the glittery gold top she was wearing beneath a long wool coat.

"I could use something warm to drink," I said. Or a stiff drink.

We walked into the high-rise, with her guiding the way.

"I can't wait for you to meet my sisters-in-law, Maggie and Jade. You'll love them."

Grace had shown up at the club two nights ago to make sure I was coming. We'd also had a chance to chat more, and she'd filled me in on who was who and what to expect.

I really liked Grace, and I had no doubt she would be devastated when she learned who I really was. I would be lying if I said I wouldn't be gutted as well. I didn't know how Jason had spent a year and a half undercover. I was approaching my two-week mark, and I felt as though I was becoming emotionally attached already.

A bellman rushed over from a desk near the elevator to open the door for us. "Ms. Hart," he said. "So good to see you again."

Grace gave the gray-haired man a hug. "Happy Thanksgiving, Dave. I'm sorry that you're here today. I'll be sure to bring you a plate."

The fifty-something bellman gave her the warmest smile. "You're so good to me."

Grace quickly introduced me to Dave as her guest, then he

hurried over to the elevator and inserted a keycard. "You're all set to go up."

After the doors closed, I felt a sudden wave of dizziness. I shouldn't be this nervous. I loved meeting people and hanging out with friends. Shyness wasn't a part of Fallyn Williams. Yet, it seemed it was for Joy Whitlock.

"You look great." Grace's light-and-airy voice zapped the fog from my brain. "I love those ankle boots."

I'd chosen a simple V-neck cream wrap sweater that hung just to the waistline of my taupe skinny-leg pants, which were tucked into my suede tan boots.

"I'm not too dressed up, am I? You said nothing fancy."

Her copper eyes swept over me. "Duke will go weak in the knees when he sees you." She fluffed up my hair. "Not that I'm setting you two up," she was quick to add with a shrewd smile.

A smile flitted across my mouth, one I didn't feel. "You love your brother."

The elevator seemed as though it was taking its sweet old time. I wasn't complaining. I could hang out with Grace all day. She was easy, free-spirited, and not wound as tight as her gorgeous brother, whose kiss was seared into my heart.

"More than you know."

I lightly touched the hummingbird tattoo on her neck. "I've been meaning to tell you that tat is badass. Any significance?"

Her shoulder twitched. "I just always loved watching them in our backyard when I was a kid. These birds washed away the bad times."

The car came to a stop, erasing that fleeting forlorn look she had.

After the doors slid open, the aroma of turkey rushed at us like a gust of wind in a brewing storm. Much like the way my stomach was tumbling and swirling as though I had my own storm raging.

Grace held my hand. "You're going to do great." She ushered

me alongside her like I was her new toy, a prize she'd won and wanted to show off.

The need to turn and run was poking at my senses, the banging in my ears competing with the buzzing voices.

Despite my anxiety, I felt as though I'd walked into a world of champagne and riches. Two pillars, round and wide, were erected on the edge of a cozy living room, with a fire crackling in the hearth. Couches and pillows and eclectic art decorated the walls around the fireplace, giving the space a bohemian vibe. Shiny floors wound through the open floor plan to a gourmet kitchen that my mom would've loved at this time of year for all the baking she'd done for charities.

A young blond girl ran up to Grace and gave her a hug. "It's so nice to see you again."

"Fran, this is my friend Joy," Grace said.

I shook Fran's hand. Her vibrant sea-green eyes had an uncanny resemblance to those of her dad, Brian McCauley.

"You're as pretty as Duke says," Fran said in an excited voice. "Are you going dress shopping with us this weekend?"

Out of nowhere, an average-height woman with silky black hair had her arms around me, cutting off my chance to answer Fran. "Joy, I'm Jade, Denim's wife. So happy you could join us."

Then a slightly taller lady than Jade ambled up. Her curly blond hair made a statement, but I knew who she was. We had files on all the Harts, but Maggie Marx was also a TV reporter.

"I'm Maggie, Dillon's wife." She held her wine glass, assessing me with curious intent.

I'd never been in the spotlight with so many people excited to meet me or regarding me as though they knew something about me that I didn't, but I hadn't been with the ATF long enough for news reporters to recognize me. Yet, the vibe Maggie was throwing my way told me she might have seen me before.

Just to be sure, I asked, "Have we met before? You look familiar."

"You've probably seen me on the news," Maggie said. "I'm a reporter for WBXC."

I bobbed my head. "That's right. Didn't you report on a gang bust about a month ago?"

"I'm mostly a crime reporter," Maggie replied.

Fran had dashed off.

"Maggie is up for an award this year," Jade gushed.

Grace seemed bored with shoptalk. "Isn't she perfect?"

I felt as though I should twirl around like a model as the knots in my stomach notched tightly. Again, I wasn't shy. I owned my shit but not at that moment.

Maggie brought the wineglass to her lips. "Grace, careful. You know matchmaking will not go over well with Duke."

"How can I play matchmaker if he already likes her?" Grace said.

"Very true," Jade agreed. "Maybe Joy can snuff out Duke's grumpy style."

That got a laugh out of me. "Is he always like that?" I might as well join the fray instead of fighting against Grace or maybe lying to myself.

"You have no idea." Jade rolled her eyes. "Let me take your coat."

"Can you point me to the bathroom?" I needed a minute to compose myself.

"Follow me," Jade said.

Shrugging out of my jacket, I had yet to glance around for the elephant in the room. A laugh broke out in my head. Duke wasn't an elephant, but for fuck's sake, he sure was the metaphorical animal.

With no Duke in sight, I felt less tense as Jade hung up my coat in the closet on our way into a wide hallway.

"This is a beautiful place," I said. "I understand Duke used to own it."

She closed the closet door. "That's right. You should've seen it when he lived here. It was cold and sterile." She wrinkled her nose. "You know how some men can be with no taste for design."

"Speaking of Duke, is he here?" I asked as she guided me farther down the hall.

"He and Brian are in Denim's man cave." She pointed at the door beside the guest bathroom. "Duke got an urgent phone call. Anyway, once you're done, you know the way back."

I tossed a look over my shoulder. "Pretty simple."

After I closed myself into the bathroom, which was almost as large as my studio apartment, I stood eerily still as I listened for voices. The man cave was on the other side of the shower wall, but I couldn't hear anything.

I checked myself in the mirror, running my fingers through my hair, breathing in and out. *Please let me get through this day.*

After giving myself a pep talk, I stepped into the hallway and lingered, admiring the watercolor painting between the man cave and bathroom while attempting to hear Duke and Brian's conversation.

"I might have a lead on who in our ranks leaked that meeting," a man with a Spanish accent said in a voice I could barely make out.

I strained to hear more.

"Gustavo, do you know who he's working with?" someone asked. I was pretty sure it was Brian.

"Not yet."

"Denim has been talking to the Southside Creepers. Their leader, Chris Vargas, is putting out feelers among the gangs." That was definitely Duke's voice.

"For now, enjoy your holiday. We'll be in touch," Gustavo said.

After a few seconds of silence, I stayed perfectly still, waiting to see if I could hear more.

"If you need my help, I'm in," Brian said.

"Nah, Vince will handle it with me," Duke said. "I don't want you involved. Besides, Fran's home."

"I'm available if things go south at any point," Brian said.

"Appreciate it. We should join the others."

The doorknob to the man cave clicked, and I sprang into action. I hurried into the bathroom and over to the sink to busy myself then realized that I hadn't shut the door.

Footsteps echoed in the hall.

"Joy?" Duke's voice was gritty and sexy. "Don't you close the door when you use the bathroom?"

Brian laughed. "I'll leave you two."

I turned off the faucet, grabbed a monogram towel, and wiped my hands, guilt keeping me from making eye contact.

"You showed," he said.

"It was hard to say no to Grace."

The heels of his shoes scuffed along the floor. "You seem nervous." He took the towel from me. "The Harts don't bite."

A jittery laugh barreled out as I focused on his shiny loafers. "Are you sure about that? Grace is sinking her teeth into setting us up."

He placed a knuckle underneath my chin. "Look at me."

The second we locked eyes, butterflies decided to flutter inside me. We stared at one another as the room began to fade, my heart started to beat faster, and the rate of my breathing increased.

He blinked, lowering his gaze to my lips then my eyes then my lips again.

If he kisses me, I might rip his clothes off this time.

15

———

DUKE

Fuck the war brewing with the cartel. I had one battling in my head. To kiss her or not. Walk away or not. I couldn't shake her. I closed my eyes at night, and she was the star of my dreams. I woke up in the morning, and I was jerking off in the shower to images of her full lips on my dick or those big hazel eyes that were yanking me to her like a horse drawn to water.

My fingers danced along her soft cheek, through her hair, and over her ear until my hand was seated at the base of her head.

The other night, she tasted like sugar and mint and oh, so fucking delicious.

My mouth watered at the thought of taking her right here on the sink or in the shower. Hell, there were three bedrooms in the suite, and one of them had our names on it.

She tucked her fingers into the waist of my pants as her chest rose and fell.

My heart was beating furiously, and my dick... Well, it was throbbing as fast as my pulse.

I rubbed my nose over hers, testing the waters to see if she would run. The other night, I had her caged between my legs. I didn't at the moment. She should beat feet if she knew what was best for her.

She moaned ever so lightly, a beautiful sound that massaged my soul.

"You should run, babe. Run like the wind from me," I whispered.

"I know," she said on an exhale. "I can't, and I don't know why."

My fingers were tangled in her silky strands, holding her in my grasp as she gazed up at me.

"One last chance," I warned her and myself, but I wasn't going anywhere. My feet were toe to toe with hers and glued to the floor. My body would beat the crap out of me if I walked away. My heart might stop if I did as well.

She didn't move, her tongue sliding out to lick her lips. As if that was her answer to engage, I pounced.

My mouth crashed to hers as I dove in and took what was mine. And whether she knew it or not, she *was* mine. I would destroy any guy who dared to lay a hand or even his damn mouth on her.

The second her tongue collided with mine, I was transported to another planet. Her and me. Wild and free. No guns. No cartel. No gang members.

She shook slightly in my grasp, tense and skittish.

I slid one hand to her lower back and pulled her to me.

She mewled, a sound that drove my dick to jerk in my pants.

I continued to tease, take, and devour the best thing I'd ever tasted, despite her unwillingness to engage.

"Duke," she said in a pained voice. "Is it terrible that I want what I can't have?"

I hedged away, inhaling her vanilla scent. "Not at all. Forbidden fruit is always decadent," I whispered, nibbling on the shell of her ear. "I want to throw you up against a wall, strip the clothes off you, and run my tongue over every inch of your gorgeous body."

She turned her head toward me until our mouths were aligned.

Then she struck. We were all tongues, hungry for one another in a kiss that was wet, wild, and sloppy. I hardly did anything like this with the women I slept with. The time in bed with them was nothing but cold fucking. No emotion behind the act at all. Yet a sensuous kiss was all it took to send me into the stratosphere.

I was fucked. My heart knew it. My body knew it. Even my damn brain knew I couldn't walk away from her after this.

There was something about Joy that affected me far more than even Savannah. Suddenly, guilt was a razor's edge, slicing my veins one by one.

Someone behind me gasped. "Duke?" Grace's voice was loaded with shock and a whole lot of excitement. Too much for my liking.

Joy and I froze, mouths fused, until Joy giggled, a sound that gave me goose bumps. What was happening to me?

Sighing, I pivoted on my heel, intent on kicking my sister out and picking up where I'd left off. But that glimmer in Grace's eyes stopped me. I couldn't allow her to think Joy and I would become a couple. On the surface, Joy was everything I liked in a woman—tough, tomboyish, beautiful, and not afraid to stand up to me. But I wouldn't dare risk her life with the shit I was caught up in.

"I knew you two had chemistry. You make the perfect couple," Grace gushed.

"Please don't get your hopes up." Joy took the words right out of my mouth.

"Why are you two fighting the connection you have?" Grace planted her hands on her hips. "I don't understand. It's clear you two like each other. So why deny it?"

I could feel my forehead creasing. Grace knew exactly why I couldn't or wouldn't start a relationship, especially after the recent debacle of the stolen guns.

"Fine," she huffed. "You're both missing out."

"Missing out on what?" Dillon asked as he waltzed in. "So, this is the pretty lady who snagged Duke's attention. I see why."

Joy hugged herself.

Dillon padded deeper into the bathroom, his dark eyes appraising. "Joy, I missed you when you came in. I'm Dillon, the good brother."

I muttered swear words under my breath.

After Joy and Dillon exchanged pleasantries, I said, "Grace and Dillon, leave. Joy and I will be out in a minute."

My siblings were giddy, closing the door behind them.

"If you don't want to go out there," I said, "there is an emergency exit at the end of the hallway. My siblings might be too much."

"Your family loves you. You can't fault them for that. I can handle them." She cinched the ties on her sweater more tightly. "But Duke? Once we walk out of here, we can't kiss like that again or do anything else, for that matter."

Her words felt like nails she was hammering into me, but she was right. I had my reasons to stay away, and I was more than curious about what hers were and why she'd changed her mind. After all, at the gym, she'd said we should fuck to break the sexual tension. But if I probed, then I might be obligated to share why she and I could never be.

I gave her a slight nod as we made our way to join the party. I felt like a dead man walking. I wasn't prepared for the curious stares or my sister's suffocating excitement.

I wanted to retreat, scoop Joy into my arms, and tear out of there. I didn't want to sit and make small talk. Or listen to Jade drone on and on about her sister, Savannah, like she had when I arrived. Or hear Grace titter on about how lovely Joy was for me. Or my brothers telling me to throw caution to the wind, that it was time I settled down.

Denim was all about throwing caution to the wind. During our talk the other night at the club, he'd encouraged me to go for it with Joy. "Tomorrow is never promised," he'd said. "No matter if you had a happy life or not."

A dining table separated the living room from the kitchen,

where nine plates were set, and everyone else was seated, leaving two seats open on the end, facing the fireplace.

I pulled out the inside chair from the end for Joy.

She gave me a knee-knocking smile. "Thank you."

Brian chuckled across from me with a knowing look. I refrained from throwing him the finger.

Denim rose at the other end of the fancy decorated table. "Now that we're all here, I want to say how grateful I am that we are finally together as a family." He stuck his gaze on me.

I was waiting for Grace and Dillon to chime in, but they didn't.

Instead, Jade joined Denim and snuggled up to him, her green eyes lasering on me.

Whatever she was about to say involved Savannah, and I was kicking myself in the ass for being here.

I bounced my knee, my body tense, my throat constricting, my jaw in pain.

Joy placed a gentle hand on my thigh as if to say, *I got you. It's okay.*

Then Jade spoke. "I wish Savannah were here. I know, Duke, you loved my sister in your own way. It warms my heart that you have a special place at Linwood Cemetery for her. I don't blame you anymore for her death."

I wasn't one to run, but I couldn't handle this. I was tired of Jade's constant reminders of Savannah. I'd been in my own hell since she was murdered. I had enough guilt to fill the three-thousand-square-foot penthouse.

Jade doesn't know that, asshole.

I excused myself and trudged down the hall, needing air, anything other than sitting at a table where I didn't belong. I made it to the emergency exit when heels clicked on the floor behind me before Joy came around the corner.

Pity was stamped on her pretty face.

I growled like a wolf in the wild. "I don't want consoling or for you to feel bad for me. Everything that happened to Savannah was my fault. I own up to that shit, but I don't need anyone shoving it down my throat for the last four years."

Joy kept her distance from me, watching in concerned fascination while I popped my head against the wall adjacent to the emergency exit.

Smart woman. If she touched me, I would devour her.

"It was wrong to come here today," I continued as though someone had turned on my emotional switch and I couldn't stop the words from coming out. "I'm fucking exhausted."

"Jade is hurting, Duke," Joy said softly, looking like an angel in that cream sweater that seemed to bring out the sparkle in her eyes. "But I think it's not just Jade who's bothering you. You're wound tight, Duke. Maybe that's your nature, but I don't think so. Whatever it is, though, you need to talk to someone."

I regarded her as if she were the one who was crazy. "A shrink?"

"A friend. Someone. Hell, get a dog and talk to him." Her lips turned up at the corners. "I hear animals help with emotional pain."

"A dog?" Growing up, I never had pets. My old man would've probably beat the poor animal to death.

Joy inched closer, her fingers laced together. "Or me. I'm a good listener."

"With you, the last thing on my mind is talking."

"You and me in bed is not the answer to your problems." She sucked her bottom lip between her teeth, looking sexy as fuck.

"Maybe not, but you did suggest we fuck to ease the sexual tension between us. But it seems you've changed your mind about that. Why?"

She giggled. "Seriously? You're doing the same thing. One minute, you tell me you're not good for me, and the next, you're kissing me like you're dying. Look, right now, it's not about us. Talk to Jade. You two need to hash things out."

As if on cue, Jade called my name.

"We're by the emergency exit," Joy said, raising her voice. Then she poked me in the chest. "Be nice." She gave me a pointed look before turning on her heels and leaving me alone with Jade.

I didn't move as Jade crossed her arms over her chest, those green eyes too familiar, even though Savannah had had brown eyes. It was the regret, the shame, the blame, and the hurt in Jade's glare that reminded me of Savannah.

"Well, tell me again how much you blame me," I lashed out like a whip of fire. "It's been four years, Jade. Four fucking years, and you still look at me like I'm the devil. I didn't feed Savannah's addiction. I tried to break her from her drug habit. All I did was give her a job at my club. All I did was fall in love with her. All I wanted was for her to get away from me. Leave my world behind. I pushed her away to protect her, not to get her killed."

Tears streamed down her cheeks. "I know." She swallowed. "But I didn't then. I had to blame someone other than myself. I was supposed to protect her, Duke. I was the older sister. For all Savannah's faults, I didn't want her to die. I can't help but think that if you had just gone to see her in jail, she would still be here today."

I pushed off the wall. "Do you know how many times I've thought the same thing? Jade, I can't even find it in myself to let the past go. But if I don't, if you don't, the guilt will eat at us forever." I pulled her in for a hug. "I'm so fucking sorry. That day she died and you came to beat my ass, I was ready for you to kill me. I was silently begging that you would."

She squeezed me and cried. "I'm sorry too. My sister was a handful. She was her own worst enemy." She sighed, her gaze climbing up to meet mine. "You really did love her?"

I nodded. "I never had the chance to tell her either."

She placed a hand on her heart. "Hearing you confess your feelings for her warms my soul, Duke. Thank you for that." She kissed me on the cheek. "I promise I won't be such a bitch anymore. Savannah will always be with us, and it's time for both of us to move on." She touched her stomach. "I just announced it to the family.

You're going to be an uncle. Denim is going to be a daddy." She lit up as more tears flowed.

"That's great news, Jade," I said with genuine happiness in my voice. "You and Denim deserve that big family you want."

She patted the wetness off her cheeks. "Would you do me a favor? I know you're caught in something horrible right now. Denim doesn't tell me anything, but he doesn't have to. I know when something is bothering him. I also watch the news, but can you please, please find a way out before you get yourself killed? I couldn't bear to see Denim suffer or Grace or Dillon. Please, Duke."

"I will." I had to. I didn't want my brothers and sister to agonize over my death like I had Savannah's.

"Are we okay?" she asked.

I draped my arm around her as we headed back to the table. "We're good."

With each step, I felt lighter, freer.

Everyone was eating, talking, and laughing when Jade and I returned. I nodded at Denim to let him know Jade and I were cool.

I sat next to Joy, who was smiling at me.

I would like to say she was next on my list to deal with, but first I had other important matters to tie up.

16

___

DUKE

Vince pulled into the abandoned manufacturing plant in Dorchester. Gustavo had called me this morning while I was at the gym training Joy—or rather, she was kicking my ass. He'd informed me that he'd gotten confirmation and found the mole within his camp.

I'd never been so relieved that my men hadn't been guilty. Vince had questioned them, and he assured me we had no rats among us.

"I hope we're about to finally put this problem to bed." Vince shifted into park. "I would like to enjoy the holidays. Amber is up my butt about taking time off for Christmas."

While I was making inroads with my family, I wasn't exactly ready to spend another holiday with them just yet, even though they were planning a big Christmas gathering, going as far to invite Joy as well.

Joy Whitlock? It had been two solid days since I'd kissed Joy in the bathroom at the penthouse and only hours since I'd seen her delectable body at the gym. I couldn't bring myself to resume that conversation we'd had in the hallway at Denim's place, only because I wasn't ready to tell her the truth about who I really was. And to a

112

certain extent, I didn't want to hear why she kept vacillating back and forth when it came to us. Despite that, I was dying to fuck her brains out.

I wondered endlessly if she had a man in her life. If so, was it serious? Jealousy was an emotion I wasn't accustomed to for the simple fact that I tried not to allow myself to fall for anyone. But with Joy, it was becoming increasingly difficult. Surely, love at first sight didn't exist. That was just a myth.

"You haven't seen that bald asshole in the club? The one who hurt Joy. Have you?"

I searched the crowd every night from my office window for that bald beast who'd touched her. I even asked her that morning if she'd seen him around. She assured me he wasn't a problem and that she'd paid him off.

"No," Vince said as we climbed out of the car. "I heard Grace last night at the club say Joy is attending the charity event with you. Will that be an official date?"

I shook my head. "Since when do I date?"

Dillon had invited Joy to the gala at Thanksgiving dinner. She gave him some pushback, but Grace wouldn't take no for an answer.

"You have to start somewhere," he said.

Preferably, bed would be my choice with Joy. No talking. All fucking. Then maybe we could both open up to each other.

At the mention of her name, I had butterflies in my stomach. For fuck's sake, that never happened, but I had to be honest with myself. Her radiant smile was like a vice grip on my balls, tightening with every passing moment. Her big hazel eyes were like a sledgehammer to my heart, shattering any semblance of control I had left. She was stirring something deep within me that had been dormant for far too long, and I could feel myself losing my grip on reality when it came to her, blocking my ability to concentrate.

It was time to buckle down and focus on the real issue—stolen guns.

Squinting in the bright sunlight that had been melting the fallen snow over the past two days, I did a quick sweep of the parking lot. Aside from three trucks parked alongside Vince's car, the area didn't have much activity. I didn't expect any for a Saturday, and this part of Dorchester wasn't exactly thriving with businesses.

We strode through the entrance, only to be stopped by two cartel soldiers. The one with his hair tied in a low ponytail, I hadn't seen before. The other, Kurt, who wore diamond-studded earrings, had been working for Rosario for as long as I could remember.

Kurt nodded his scarred chin at me. "Duke."

"I thought by now you would've gotten a promotion to a higher rank," I said.

"I like where I am," Kurt responded. "This is Joe, Gustavo's cousin. He's the one who got a promotion since we found the rat. Gustavo is through that door beneath the landing overhead."

I crossed the trash-ridden place past spent needles, torn boxes, and empty food wrappers. The stench of urine was heavy in the air.

If I thought the odor was bad, it was even worse when I entered the dilapidated former cafeteria, where Rosario's lieutenant was pacing with his phone to his ear alongside a set of cabinets to my right. In the middle of the room, an unmoving young man sat tied to a chair, his nose bloody, his eyes swollen and bruised, and his head hanging so that his chin hit his chest. And to my left, Chris Vargas had one knee bent, foot planted against the chipped painted wall as he read from his phone.

Vince beelined it across the cafeteria to the door as if he'd heard something.

"Chris, what are you doing here?"

Then it hit me. Denim had mentioned he'd spoken to the leader of the Southside Creepers and asked Chris to talk to the other gangs about a shipment of stolen guns and dead cartel members.

Chris, a tall, lean, and mean motherfucker with two sleeves of tats and a scar from his ear to his chin, rolled his eyes. "I'm as surprised as you are, but Gustavo wanted me here." He pointed at the prisoner. "I'm the one who learned this fucker is working with

Mateo Alvarez. He goes by Emilio and is a low-ranking soldier for Rosario."

"Figures that fucker is involved," Vince said, returning to join Chris and me.

"I'm not shocked, either," Chris said, "but this isn't my fight. My guys and I are not into illegal firearms. I hated when Tito started down that road."

In the grand scheme of things, whether it was drugs or guns, all of us were in the middle. We answered to the cartel. They were our suppliers, after all. Granted, people like Chris dealt with front men and not the cartel directly. That job was left to people like Brian and me.

"Do you know who else is involved?" I asked Chris.

"I don't," he said.

Gustavo's chilling baritone voice made me turn in his direction, where he was still glued to his cell. "Yes, Rosario. All parties are present. I'll put you on speaker."

That was our cue to join the fray.

"Gentlemen," Rosario started, "I understand that we're making progress in an attempt to find my guns." Her Spanish accent, coupled with her smoker's voice, reverberated through the barren space. "Chris, bring us up to speed on what you learned?"

Chris roughed a hand through his short blond hair. "There's not much to tell. I did some digging after Denim came to me and asked if I could put out feelers. Seems the right number of threats will get anyone to talk. I won't give you my source, but he ran into Mateo and two men huddled outside the Mills Tavern in Boston about a month ago. Mateo called one of them Emilio. I passed that along to Gustavo the day before Thanksgiving."

"Do you know where Mateo is?" I asked.

"I don't," Doug said. "He doesn't stay in one place too long. But before Denim came to me, I heard that Mateo has been visiting Tito quite frequently in prison."

I clenched my fists at the mention of Tito Alvarez. "I would put money that fucker is the mastermind."

Chris harrumphed. "I say this loosely, but don't underestimate Mateo."

"What's his motive?" Vince asked. "Surely, Mateo knows that fucking with the cartel has deadly consequences."

"Not if he's working for the cartel," I said. "Rosario, have you talked to Arturo yet? Because if I recall, Arturo was the one who Tito had been in talks with about a gun deal right before Tito was sent off to jail. That was four years ago when the Mexicans were trying to worm their way into Boston. So, I would suspect Tito is pulling the strings to have Mateo pick up where Tito left off."

"I agree," Rosario said. "But why steal from me?"

"To get your attention." Chris crossed bulky arms over his chest.

Rosario sighed. "You mean to fuck with me."

"I don't know," Chris said. "Unless Mateo wants revenge against Duke for sending Tito to prison. Maybe Mateo and Tito think by stealing from you, it hurts Duke in some way."

"But it doesn't," I said. "I don't pay Rosario until the client pays me."

"Mateo probably doesn't know the deal we have with Duke," Gustavo piped up.

"Arturo won't return my calls," she said. "But word from my guys on the ground in Mexico is Arturo has been in the States quite frequently in the last six months. I'm trying to confirm where."

I scrubbed a hand over my unshaven jaw. "Maybe Emilio can tell us."

Gustavo clenched his bloody fist. "I've already tried. I'm hoping Rosario can put the fear of God into him to talk."

"Gustavo, wake up Emilio," she said in a steely tone.

The hairs on the back of my neck stood at attention. We were inching closer to a full-out war.

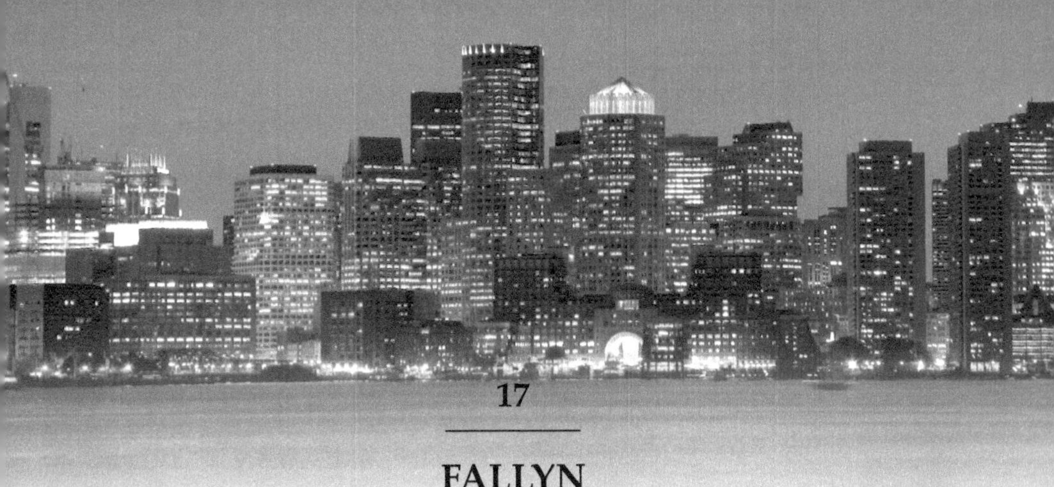

17

FALLYN

ALIAS: JOY

My heart was in my throat as I stood breathlessly outside the lunchroom and listened through the crack in the door. I'd done a lot of adrenaline-junkie feats but none as high-strung and death-defying as spying on the cartel.

I'd almost gotten caught when I heard footsteps coming toward me. I'd barely had time to hide in the supply closet that was on my left.

Nevertheless, as I listened to bits and pieces of the conversation interspersed with my pulse banging endlessly in my ears, my hands were trembling harder than they ever had.

I'd gotten a lucky break when I overheard Duke talking to Gustavo on the phone at the gym that morning. Duke had repeated the address where they were meeting as he asked Gustavo for key landmarks in Dorchester. I couldn't have passed up the opportunity to be a fly on the wall. After all, I was undercover to find intel any way I could.

The second I'd left the gym, I rushed over to the manufacturing plant to scope out the facility and the area before their meeting at noon. No one had been here when I arrived, which gave me a chance to walk the facility to locate the entrances and exits.

"Emilio, wake up," Gustavo said.

I'd been upstairs, keeping an eye out, when Gustavo and two men pulled up and dragged a passed-out prisoner inside. Voices carried in the empty facility, so I was able to hear Gustavo order the men to tie Emilio to a chair in the cafeteria, then they were ordered to guard the entrance and wait for Duke and some guy named Chris.

A chair screeched across the floor, sounding like nails on a chalkboard.

I glanced up and down the hall, my stomach tighter than ever as adrenaline poured through me like a fast-moving train at high speed.

"He's about to shit his pants." Vince laughed.

"Emilio, I'm going to ask you this once." Rosario's voice over the speakerphone sounded as if she had just smoked a box of cigars. "Just so we're clear, I have your mom and sister in custody. So I want you to answer truthfully for their sake."

"No, please don't hurt them!" Emilio cried out. "I'm sorry, Rosario, but I had no choice. I told them I wouldn't snitch. But they beat my brother, Juan, within an inch of his life. He's in the prison hospital now."

"Who's they?" Duke asked, calm, cool, and collected.

"Tito Alvarez and his gang in prison. They knew Juan worked for Rosario. They even knew I did too. Please, please don't harm my family."

"You should've thought about that before you opened your big mouth," Gustavo lashed out. "You took an oath when we hired you."

I held a hand over my chest, looking in both directions, my emotions tugging at me for Emilio. I prayed they wouldn't kill him for this, but I knew that was unlikely. I had to help him if I could.

"Calm down." Rosario's voice was soothing, like a mother consoling her child. "Where are my guns?"

Emilio shuddered and groaned loudly. "I don't know. I haven't seen Mateo since we stole the guns," Emilio cried. "Please don't harm my family, Rosario. Juan begged me not to do it, but I couldn't let him die."

This poor man was caught between two Mack trucks speeding down the highway in a race to see which one would splatter Emilio's body all over the road.

"Are the Mexican cartel involved?" Rosario asked.

"I don't know," Emilio said.

"How many men are behind this?" Duke asked.

"Mateo has a gang, and his right-hand man is Lou-Lou Ro-Romano," he stuttered. "He pulled out t-two of my fing-fingernails."

"Motherfucker." This from Duke. "I should've taken care of that bastard after he stole from me."

A door squeaked around the corner to my left, and I jumped a mile, sucking in air.

"Did you hear that?" Vince asked.

"It's probably my men," Gustavo replied.

"Just the same, I'll be right back," Vince said.

I darted into the supply closet next to the lunchroom and locked the door, breathing in and out as quietly as I could.

Heavy footsteps clobbered the floor, growing louder. Then the doorknob twisted, sending my pulse over the edge. The *boom, boom, boom* was so loud in my ears that I swore my head might blow off.

Breathe, Fallyn. If I didn't calm down, I would be a second away from passing out.

I pressed my ear to the door.

"Oh, it's you, Kurt," Vince said.

"Yeah, why?" Kurt asked. "I was using the head. Is there a problem?"

"Nah, I'm always on edge at meetings."

More footsteps passed by—then silence.

Sweat slid down my spine, and I felt like an inferno was burning inside me. After several minutes, I managed to regulate my breathing as my pulse slowed for the moment.

I'd known when I came here that leaving would be tricky. It was easy to get inside since no one had been here. Plus, the abandoned factory wasn't secure. It was clear that squatters slept in the building at night.

Still, my plan was to hide out until the coast was clear, even if I had to stay until darkness set in. I doubted Gustavo and his men would stay at the plant overnight, unless he decided to keep Emilio prisoner.

My conscience was tugging at me to try to keep Emilio safe.

I gingerly moved two empty boxes against the door to block out any shadows or the light from my phone that might escape beneath that thin strip between the floor and door.

I had to text Gwen. I needed someone to save Emilio.

Me: *It's Fallyn. I need your help. I'm stuck in a supply closet at an old factory on 45 Bay Street in Dorchester. Duke is meeting with Gustavo, who's holding a prisoner captive by the name of Emilio. I'm afraid that he'll be dead before dawn. He has info on the ambush. Not much but enough to know that Tito and Mateo Alvarez are behind the stolen guns and also a guy by the name of Lou Romano. No guns yet. Don't worry about me. I'm good for getting out of here, but I can't save Emilio without risking both our lives.*

Chewing on a fingernail, I fixated on my cell as I silently said, "Come on, Gwen, answer me."

Five minutes ticked by. Ten. Fifteen.

Nothing.

Knowing my dad was probably glued to his phone, anxiously waiting for any updates on my assignment, I reluctantly texted him.

Me: *Dad, it's me. There's nothing to worry about, but I'm trying to reach Gwen, and she's not responding.*

The three bouncing dots flashed on screen, and I almost cried.

Dad: *What's wrong?*

I copied and pasted my message I'd typed out to Gwen and hit Send.

Me: *Also, two men are guarding the entrances, and Gustavo, Duke, Vince, and another guy, Chris, are with Emilio. Again, I'm fine, and I have my gun and knife on me.*

Dad: *I'll call a buddy of mine who's with BPD. I don't want to risk ATF's involvement or blow your cover. The most we can do is have the men in blue break up the meeting to at least get you out safely. I'll call Gwen myself to fill her in. Hang tight.*

I would like to believe that I was good at practicing patience because, in my line of work, we couldn't allow our anxiety to drive our actions. Yet a life hung in the balance, and I was having a difficult time not reacting to the situation at hand.

Your life does, too, so don't be stupid.

I sat on the floor, resting my head against the frame of a shelf, and closed my eyes, willing my body to stop panicking and my patience to simmer down.

Instantly, I was transported back in time to this morning when Duke and I were in the boxing ring, sparring.

"You're not anticipating my moves," he complained after throwing a jab that caught the side of my face. "What's wrong with you today?"

"You," I replied. "You and me in a ring isn't working."

His six-pack abs were distracting. The thin, happy trail that disappeared beneath the waistline of his shorts was driving me insane, and his legs. Whoa! If I had to pick one feature that I appreciated in a man other than his good looks, it was toned and powerful thighs that shaped nicely from top to bottom, and Duke had that in spades.

"Come again," he said.

But I didn't have a chance to answer when his phone kept ringing. He'd brought it with him in the ring and mentioned he was expecting an urgent call.

My cell vibrated in my hand, zapping my lustful memory.

Dad: *My buddy isn't answering. When he does, I'll see what I can do. In the meantime, you can't worry about Emilio. I know that's not a good answer, but you need to leave as soon as you can. Do you understand?*

Me: *Yes. Did you talk to Gwen?*

Dad: *I did. She's hanging tight just in case. Text me when you're safe.*

Me: *Copy that.*

I couldn't leave the supply closet yet, though. The situation was still rife with danger, and I couldn't risk getting caught. An hour later, voices had me perking up.

"Make sure Emilio delivers the message to Mateo that I have something he wants." Duke's raspy voice carried in the hall.

"You think Mateo will bite and meet with you?" Gustavo asked.

"I'm beginning to think Tito and Mateo are trying to get my attention as a ploy for revenge. Plus, the Alvarezes are money and power hungry. At the very least, Mateo's curiosity will get the best of him."

"I just want this over with it," Gustavo said.

"Me, too, man."

"I need to clear out," Gustavo said. "Call me when you have something."

Voices and footsteps faded.

Hallelujah. It sounded as though Emilio was safe for now. I texted my dad to give him an update and tell him to call off the men in blue.

We were making progress, and while that excited me, the adrenaline was rushing out of me, making me feel jittery because I'd almost blown my cover.

18

FALLYN

ALIAS: JOY

L ater that night, I was counting the cash tips we'd hauled in while Matt ran a sales report from the computer, a routine he and I were responsible for before we clocked out.

Two waitresses were cleaning up tables on the second floor, and Amber was tidying up the bar tables scattered along both sides of the main floor.

While the printer was spitting out the report, Matt sidled up to me. "You seemed distracted and quiet tonight. Anything wrong?"

The young hottie with a man bun was the sweetest person. I could see why customers fawned all over him, including the men who swung that way.

"Stomach has been acting up," I responded truthfully.

Since I'd returned from the factory, I'd almost hauled up the protein shake I had that morning. Not to mention, I was on edge. I'd barely made it to work on time. I'd stayed in that factory closet for two hours after everyone had left to be sure Gustavo didn't have his men hang around.

"Are you sure everything is okay in your personal life?" He stole a glance at Duke's window. "The boss has been watching you

123

intently since you started but more so after Thanksgiving. Care to share?"

I gave him a warm smile, placing a twenty-dollar bill in one pile and a ten in another. "Is it that obvious?"

My other issue was Duke himself and the way he was affecting me. Oh, I'd seen him up on his perch all night, watching me.

"Sickening," he teased. "Remember my warning, though. Hearts have been broken by him."

With the club empty, voices carried through the room, causing Amber to sashay up to the bar. "Sorry, but I am eavesdropping." She pursed her red lips. "I am beginning to like you, Joy. You're still a bit slow for my liking, but you and Duke should just fuck and get it out of your system. I keep telling Vince to nudge Duke too."

My throat closed as my eyes popped wide. "One of you says protect my heart, and the other says go balls to the wall. Not helping."

Amber chortled, curling errant strands of her strawberry-blond hair behind her ear. "Why not just have a good time? He likes you. Totally obvious. I've been working here long enough to know that. Matt, you have too. Joy, it's clear you're all hot and bothered, always sneaking in a look upward while you're working."

I stopped counting the tips. "But didn't you tell me, Amber, that Duke only sleeps with someone twice then kicks them out? As in fires them? I need this job."

"He won't fire you if you're good at your job," she said. "But he does have that rule. So what? Sleep with him twice. Have fun. I think that's your problem. You're wound too tight."

Matt rolled his eyes, darting over to the printer. "You know my advice, Joy."

I had all the bills separated by numbers then counted each pile and jotted down the total. "Thank you both for the love advice."

"I hear you're going to Dillon's charity gala," Amber said. "I am too."

"Bad idea," Matt mumbled behind me.

Amber darted off to finish collecting empty beer bottles and glasses.

Matt slid the sales printout next to the tip money. "I know by asking this, you might think I'm encouraging you, but I'm not. Can you deliver this to Duke's office? I have a hot date who's waiting outside, and sometimes Duke asks questions about the night, how many bottles of liquor we went through, et cetera. At times, I end up leaving an hour later."

"Of course. Who am I to stop a young lady from all that?" I flicked my hand up and down his fabulous physique.

"You're the best. How much is the lot tonight?"

"Eight hundred." I divided his share and mine.

We still had more tips with credit card receipts, but each of us had our employee code we entered into the computer when cashing out a customer. Those tips would be added to our checks.

"Sweet." He pocketed the money. "Have a good night."

I folded my bills, collected the sales printout, and grabbed my purse, making sure I had my phone, then ducked out from behind the bar. I was exhausted and ready for bed. The stint earlier today had wiped me out. I had almost called in sick but thought twice. If I had, Duke might have sent out the cavalry to check on me. I didn't want to raise any concerns, whether innocent or not.

"Do you want to give this to Duke?" I held out the sales printout to Vince as he passed me on the stairs.

"No." His blue eyes sparkled as he smirked. "You can handle a simple task."

"What if I don't want to?" The question came out before I had a chance to think.

Vince let out a belly laugh. "I've been around Duke a long time, and most ladies want to run to him, not from him."

If he only knew. "Maybe I'm shy."

"Joy, you're far from that and different from what Duke's used to."

As much as I wanted to know specifics of what he meant by

that, I doubted he would tell me, at least not now with his hungry gaze on Amber.

I trudged up the steps, each footfall heavier than the last, as if I were climbing a steep mountain only to learn that I had no way down.

Vince called Amber's name as I knocked on the open door before inching inside. "Duke?"

His manly scent wafted in the air, but there was no Duke. I hurried and deposited the report on his desk, turned to leave, and got as far as three steps when the bathroom door clicked open and my name dropped from his lips.

"Joy." His damn voice, gravelly yet smooth, slid over me, and tingles burst free.

Inhaling, I pivoted, releasing a shaky breath. "I put the sales report on your desk. Have a good night."

He rolled up his shirtsleeves. "What is it with you? You're hot and cold. Fire and ice. I can't read you, and that's pissing me off, if I'm being honest here."

The conversation we'd had at the penthouse, in which we'd danced around why we couldn't just rip off each other's clothes and fuck the tension out of our systems, was still something I wanted to avoid. I'd thought a lot about throwing caution to the wind with him, but I had to keep my sights on the bigger picture. Although, if I was being honest with myself, I was on the verge of caving every time I set eyes on him or was in proximity to him.

"Are we really going to talk now about us?" I sighed. "Okay, here's my two cents. I'm tired. I'm going home, and I think we both agreed not to engage in anything other than an employee-and-boss relationship."

His eyebrows shot up. "I never agreed to that."

"You said yourself that you're not good for me." I tapped my mouth with my finger. "Mmm. I think your words were, 'You should run, babe. Run like the wind from me.' We both know we're wrong for each other. On that note, I don't want your help anymore in the gym."

He half grinned, making him look even sexier. "Maybe I've changed my mind. A person can do that."

My pussy was screaming for him. It didn't help that I'd felt his erection a few times already through the fabric of his pants or shorts.

"Do you want a drink?" he asked, going over to his bar.

I clutched the straps of my purse like I was holding on for dear life. Liquor could make me do stupid things, but I needed something to quell the jitters.

Ice clanged in one glass then the other. Then he filled both and returned to hand me a drink.

I wasn't a bourbon drinker. I preferred vodka, but when in Rome and all that.

He rested his butt against the front edge of his desk and sighed, undressing me with his gaze.

I stiffened as I stood in the middle of the room between a lounging area on one side and bookcases on the other, holding the glass—afraid if I drank, I might strip for him.

He set his glass on the desk and ambled by me to close the office door.

The sound of it snicking shut made me flinch. "What are you doing?"

"It's time we have a quiet chat."

I downed the whiskey, not caring that my throat was on fire or that an inferno was spreading through my chest. I almost choked as my eyes watered from the burn. "Just so you know," I said, sounding as if I'd lost my voice, "I prefer vodka."

He took the glass from me, unhooked my purse from my shoulder, and dumped both on his desk.

"What's next? My clothes?" I teased, my muscles loosening after that drink.

"Do you want that?"

I lifted my chin. "What do you want, Duke?"

He dragged a hand along his five o'clock shadow that added mystery and sexiness to him. "Are we being open and honest?"

"Of course." My stomach was doing somersaults.

Without warning, his lips were on mine. He kissed me like a man possessed—harder, firmer, hungrier than the last two times.

The delicious shudder made my body quake inch by slow inch until my clit was throbbing. I wanted him so badly, but I promised I wouldn't give in to my desires. I couldn't.

"Let go, Joy," the formidable criminal pleaded.

Oh, how I would love to hear my real name on his lips.

"I need you," he whispered. "You're like a drug I never had and want more of."

"We're wrong for each other, Duke. So wrong." My weakness was bad boys like him. Maybe not in the criminal sense but men who were confident, brave, dominant, and assertive. The problem with that type was they shattered hearts. Matt had even confirmed that very thing about Duke.

"Why do you think that?" he asked, pain in his voice.

"Your two-fuck rule. I'm afraid I would want more of you." I wasn't lying about that. I had to keep our relationship as employee and boss. Easier said than done when my body was steering the ship and telling my brain to take a hike.

"One night, Joy. That's all I'm asking, and anyone close to me knows I don't beg for anything."

His pleading tone was pulling at my heartstrings as my conscience battled with my desperate need to feel him on top of me, me on top of him, and him in me.

He captured my bottom lip between his teeth, tugging me against his massive erection.

As if that was my cue, I breathed out, "One night."

I had no doubt that my decision would ruin us both.

19

DUKE

My pulse raced like a thoroughbred in the lead at the Kentucky Derby as I ushered Joy into my room. My body screamed to be inside her, but I couldn't rush into sex. She deserved to be handled delicately, like a priceless work of art that needed to be admired and appreciated before I attempted to fuck her.

I wanted to see her stripped bare, to run my hand over every curve and dip of her body, to taste every inch of her from head to toe. I craved the sound of her moans and longed to see the way she would writhe under my touch.

I should wine and dine her. I should start there, but that wasn't me. I needed to feel her pressed against me, on top of me, smell her vanilla scent, and finally unleash that part of myself that had been locked away for far too long. The side of me that had a minuscule amount of love somewhere inside.

After locking my door and flicking on the bedside lamp, I said, "Please tell me that you want this too. No lies, and don't say yes because I'm your boss."

Sitting on the bed, she giggled, a sound that was a balm to my black soul. "I would never say yes because I work for you. You don't have that much dominance over me."

"And what do I have that dominates you?"

She started to take off her V-neck T-shirt.

I grasped her wrist. "Don't."

"I thought you wanted me naked?"

"Oh, babe. You don't know how much. But I want to unwrap you like a Christmas gift that I never got. One that has the best present inside." I knelt down in front of her, not sure if I could even say the words that were about to come out next. I never gave a crap about what others thought of me, but I was worried that she would think I was a loser.

"I'm scared, Joy, to be with you. I've never said that to anyone. I would rather burn myself than tell anyone how I feel. I didn't even share my feelings with Savannah."

She combed her fingers through my hair. "Tell me about her."

Not the time to bring up Savannah, not when I wanted to devour Joy, but I needed her to understand me. I felt I had only one shot with her. I agreed with Denim that tomorrow was never promised, and with tensions of a potential war mounting, I might not be around to enjoy the things I'd seen only in my dreams.

I smiled, leaning into her touch. "Savannah was beautiful and carefree and had a smile that made my knees weak. First woman to have that effect on me until you."

She searched my face. "That's who you were visiting in Linwood Cemetery when we met?"

"I go out there every year around the time of her death."

She cupped my face with a hand. "I'm sorry for your loss. I know how excruciating grief feels. I lost my mom and brother. But as much as we miss our loved ones, they would want to see us happy. Since I met you, you're the opposite—sad, angry, tense."

Oh, to tell her all my sins. She would definitely run if she knew what I did for a living besides running a nightclub, which was why one night with her was appropriate. Although I knew I wouldn't be the same after tonight.

She brushed her lips over mine. "Duke, what do you want in life? What would it take to erase the sadness in your eyes?"

"Redemption, family, a beautiful wife, maybe kids." Saying all that out loud to someone other than Vince or Brian felt freeing. My brothers didn't even know that. "I've only said those words to two other people."

She kissed me softly. "You can have those things."

I couldn't envision any of that in my future. "What I want right now is you."

"Then what are you waiting for? Unwrap your Christmas present early."

I quickly removed my shirt and carelessly threw it onto the nearby chair.

She removed her boots, watching me as I kicked off my shoes.

Then I helped her onto her feet and removed her T-shirt that had the Monarch emblem. When my gaze rounded on her black lace bra, I lost my damn breath.

I traced the curve of her jaw with my finger, down her neck to the swell of her breasts, my touch eliciting goose bumps along the way.

She held onto my waist, her body trembling, her breathing ramping up.

I moved her hair over her shoulder. "You're stunning."

Her hands skated up my bare chest. "Why are you being gentle? It goes against your hardcore exterior."

I chuckled. "Are you complaining?"

"Not at all. I haven't been with anyone who treated me like a delicate flower, and I like it."

"I'm just getting started." I peppered kisses to her jaw, her chin, her neck, and her cleavage then her stomach. "Best part so far is these six-pack abs."

She giggled. "Not my breasts?"

"Verdict is still out on that." I unbuckled her belt, and as she shimmied out of her jeans, I honestly felt like I was unwrapping gift after gift.

And the best present of all was her standing in my room in only black lace panties to match her bra, hair draping partly over one shoulder and behind the other.

I stepped backward to snap picture after picture to commit to memory because this was my only chance with her.

"Duke, are you okay?"

I nodded. "I've never seen anyone more beautiful in my life."

She blushed. "That means you like your gift."

I shook my head as I buried my hands in her hair. "I fucking love my gift, but I need to unwrap two more items." I snapped off her bra and faltered when her tits came free—nipples pink and hard, perfect in every sense.

I wasted no time in sucking on one nipple as she pushed against me, moaning, a sound that was making me impossibly hard. I gave the other nipple equal attention but didn't play long as I dropped to my knees and slid her panties down to her ankles.

She pressed on my head, lifting one foot then the other as the last of the garments were tossed aside.

My heart beat like a drum solo at a rock concert.

She opened her stance a little wider, seemingly telling me I had full access. Just the same, I ran my hands up the back of her legs to her ass while kissing my way up one thigh then the other.

She massaged her fingers through my hair, breathing heavily, and every so often, a whimper escaped her. But when my tongue finally flicked over her clit, she threw her head back and mewled loudly.

I guided her onto the bed. "Tell me what you want, Joy."

She spread her legs as wide as they would go. "I want your cock inside me, Duke. I want to feel the weight of your body on top of me. I want your tongue in my pussy. I want it all. If I don't get any of that, I think I might die." Emotions coated each line.

"You and me both, babe." I dragged her body closer to the edge. "But I need to taste every last drop of you."

I trailed my tongue along the inside of one thigh then the other, trying to remember every second of how she reacted, tasted, looked, and eventually felt with her gripping my cock. But I was afraid to go that far. Afraid I would become a different man, and right now, I had to be the asshole, criminal that I'd always been.

You will. You're not giving her your soul, man. One night, remember?

"Please, Duke. I'm seriously going to scream if you keep teasing."

Grinning, I hovered over her wet pussy for the briefest of seconds then flicked my tongue over her swollen clit. She bucked, screaming the word "fuck."

I settled in, licking and sucking. She tasted of heaven, blissful and sweet. I could stay here forever and pleasure her for an eternity if only to hear her whimpers and moans as she rolled her nipples between her fingers.

I wasn't going to last a second, inhaling her essence, tasting her juices, and watching her climb that crescendo.

She mewed more little noises, breathing heavily, moving her hips into me as though she needed more friction. So I slipped one finger inside then two, fucking her as I kept up my assault on her swollen nub.

She pressed her knees against my head. "I don't want this to end."

"Let it go, babe."

She rose on her elbows, locking her legs around my neck. "Look at me, Duke."

Without missing a beat, I lifted my gaze to hers.

"Roll your tongue around my clit, slowly," she begged, watching in lustful fascination. "I want this to last."

The dim light in the room cast a glow, showing a beautiful sight —rosy cheeks, lips between her teeth, hazel eyes seemingly more green than gold.

"That's it," she said between breaths, closing her eyes briefly. "I'm about to…" She lay down and moaned her release, clutching the blanket as her entire body tensed.

I grabbed my cock and squeezed, grunting as I kissed her pussy lightly while she rode out her orgasm. Another picture snapped and committed to memory.

I crawled on top of her, dragging my lips up her gorgeous body, stopping to play with her nipples before my mouth was over hers.

She opened her eyes and smiled at me, her gaze full of satisfaction and warmth. "Hi." She flattened her hands on my face. "That was amazing. You're nothing like I imagined."

I angled my head. "Tell me more."

"I pictured sex with you, rough and dirty. No emotional attachment at all."

My MO in the bedroom was rough and dirty. "You pictured correctly." I didn't handle my other bedmates the same way as Joy.

She kissed me. "I want to feel you inside me now."

For a split second, I thought twice about going any further. Only because that emotional attachment she mentioned just might break free, and I was frightened out of my fucking mind.

20

FALLYN

ALIAS: JOY

Duke climbed off the bed, unbuckling his belt, keeping his eye on me. I hadn't moved. My toes were still tingling, my mind mush, my body limp. The man was more than I imagined, both inside and out.

I smiled at him, tracing every sculpted muscle, broad chest, ripped abs, and bulging biceps with my gaze. But when he was finally naked, I swallowed thickly then blew out a breath as my internal walls clenched. I'd speculated he was big, but fully erect was another matter entirely. I'd had sex with a handful of men but none as large as Duke.

He stroked his cock, his gaze sweeping over my body while he grinned boyishly. I opened my legs, needy and ready to take all of him in.

If we only had one night, I wanted to make the best of it. I was trying not to think past the moment or the truth in his words that he was afraid to be with me. Or his confession that he wanted redemption, a family. Or most of all, how he'd pleaded with me for this one night. Duke wasn't the type of man to ever beg for anything. I doubted he would even beg for his life.

He snagged a condom from his nightstand, tore the wrapper, and rolled it on his long, thick cock with expert fingers as if he had done it a million times.

I wanted to say I was on the pill, but it was better to be doubly safe.

He crawled on the bed and braced his hands on either side of my head, his dick grazing my pussy. "Are you okay?"

I didn't want to ruin his happiness and tell him that I was emotionally distraught, that he was too much to absorb. After all, I was a gift he unwrapped. Fuck, he'd lit up like a boy at Christmas who'd never gotten a present from Santa.

I licked the seam of his lips, breaking them apart, pushing my tongue inside his mouth as my answer. He tasted of me, of us, of sin. He was the enemy, but I didn't see him that way. Not here. Not now. Not in this room that smelled of him.

"I want you, Duke, desperately." That wasn't a lie. I'd never spoken anything from the heart in a long time. I would have liked to blame my desperation on my lust, but I felt something far deeper than that. Nope, I wasn't going anywhere near my emotions.

He kissed me, hungrily, possessively, as he pushed his dick halfway inside me and groaned, a sound that sent waves of pleasure through me.

I was going to hell. My mind knew it, but my heart didn't. The damn thing was jumping up and down with glee as my inner walls squeezed around his cock.

"Fuck," he whispered, pressing his forehead to mine as he tensed.

I yanked on his hair. "I need more." I didn't recognize my own voice. That alternate reality I'd felt walking into his club two weeks ago was even more vivid. I'd become Joy, a different version of myself, and it seemed like she was taking over Fallyn's mind, body, and soul.

"No, not yet." He blew out a breath. "I'm about to lose it, and I can't. I feel like a teenager who just hit puberty."

I giggled for nothing more than to distract him for a beat and to shake the emotions out of my head.

He brushed his nose over mine, slowly pushing farther inside me. "You feel so fucking good."

I slid my hands down his sweat-slick waist and grabbed his ass, opening my legs as wide as they would go.

Then with one hard thrust, he rammed in his cock, groaning. The look on his face of pure pleasure and pain was priceless.

He nibbled on my bottom lip, my jaw, my ears, everywhere he could as he picked up speed—in then out, breathing heavily through grunts and moans. "I've never been with anyone as breathtaking as you."

Emotion clogged my throat as our tongues tangoed and we rolled around, me on top of him, him on top of me, hands in each other's hair, kissing, nipping, sucking, breathing heavily, making sounds of pure unadulterated pleasure.

I never wanted this night to end, but my orgasm spiraled down hot and fast, and I squeezed around him so hard that he stiffened.

I cried out his name as he shuddered, both of us reaching that blissful state together.

His cock throbbed inside me, and with a satisfied grin, he raised his upper torso, his mahogany eyes filled with something I couldn't quite put my finger on. "You okay?"

"Never better. You?"

He pecked me on the lips. "Perfect." Then he rolled off me. "Come on, let's take a shower."

"I should go." Leave and never look back. I needed to take myself off this case. Run far. Run fast.

He removed his condom and deposited it in the trash by the nightstand. "One night, remember? Plus, I would rather you not drive home alone at this hour."

I drove home myself every night after my shift, and four a.m. wasn't any different than two or three a.m. But a hot shower and another hour with him wouldn't hurt. The damage was already done. That wall around my heart cracked, and slowly Duke had seeped inside.

I acquiesced. "Fine, but I would rather not be seen leaving the boss's room."

"I have a back entrance, and no one comes in until the afternoon."

Sighing, I followed him into the bathroom as he turned on the shower. "Duke, everything you said to me tonight—was it the truth?"

I was fairly certain he'd been honest with me, judging by the emotion that had been in his voice and the expression on his face. But a tiny part of me felt that maybe that was how he lured women into his lair. I didn't exactly know why I cared because he and I could never be.

He held out his hand as he guided me into the gray-tiled enclosure that had a bench along one wall. Once we were under the hot water, he gently grabbed the sides of my head, lowering his lips until they were ghosting over mine. "Every word was from my heart."

Then he kissed me softly, and I knew when I left him that I wouldn't be the same person. I was beginning to understand the severity of what Agent Howard had said. "No one comes out as the same person they were when they went undercover."

Yet as Duke and I showered, taking time to touch and kiss each other while we did, I knew neither of us would be the same after my assignment ended. A part of me wanted to help him, to give him that redemption he craved, to make sure he didn't go to prison. Considering my team was involved, that seemed unlikely. After all, it wasn't just Duke we wanted.

21

———————

DUKE

The club was dark save for the dim lights over the bar and the ones edging the steps that led up to the second floor, where I'd left Joy snuggled in my bed, looking like Sleeping Beauty. Blood was pooling in my dick, just by me recalling the feel of being inside her.

Denim sat at the bar. "Every time I come in here, I'm reminded of that night Jade was shot right there." He stabbed a finger to a spot behind him. "Fucking Tito Alvarez. I'm surprised someone hasn't shanked him in prison."

"You woke me up at seven in the morning to tell me that?" I filled two glasses with Coke.

One of his eyebrows went up. "Since when do you sleep past four or five? Are you feeling okay?"

He had a point, but after my intimate time with Joy, I had actually slept soundly for the first time in ages until my phone kept vibrating on the nightstand. Denim had left me several messages that he wanted to stop by on his way home from his security job.

I set a glass in front of him. "Why are you here?"

"We didn't have a chance to chat after Thanksgiving dinner. I

139

wanted to thank you for working things out with Jade. You don't know how much that means to me, bro."

"She needed to come clean too. But she and I are cool. Also, congratulations again. You're going to be a dad. Who would've thought any of us would have kids?"

He toyed with a napkin. "I'm scared out of my damn mind about being a dad. How can any of us be a good father after what our old man did to us as kids?"

"This is what's bothering you?" I asked.

He puffed out his cheeks. "I can't sleep."

"You want *my* advice? I'm honored. But I'm the last person who would know how to be a father."

"Give yourself credit, bro. You raised Dillon, Grace, and me."

I pressed my hands into the edge of the bar. "All of us know that we don't ever want to be like our old man. That in itself is all you need. You also have Dillon to lean on for advice."

"Why are you sounding like you won't be around?" A glare of worry colored his face.

I pulled my T-shirt down in the back. "Come on. You have to know that as much as I want out, it's not that easy. The way things are going, too, it looks like Tito and Mateo might be driving the ship with the stolen guns."

He gaped. "They really aren't the sharpest knives in the drawer, are they?"

"If the mole in Gustavo's camp does his job, I might be meeting with Mateo soon."

"Please let me be part of that meeting," he said with too much eagerness for my liking.

"Fuck no. You're going to be a dad. I don't want anything happening to you. That would gut me, and Jade would have a cow."

Lines wrinkled his forehead. "I know the consequences, and no matter how much you try to keep me and Dillon out of this, you can't. Remember, the Alvarezes will use your siblings to fuck with you. Either way, we're in this with you."

My brothers were as stubborn as I was.

"Look, stay alert. I promise that I'll reach out if I need you. All the chess pieces are not set yet."

Denim drank his Coke. "If Mateo truly is involved, why don't we set him up like we did Tito? That might be the angle you need to clean up this mess."

I smoothed a hand over my hair. "Not happening unless I can keep Rosario out of the picture. I don't care if I go to prison, but I won't throw her or Gustavo under the bus." That was suicide. Not to mention, I owed her.

"Fair enough, but we could always use Detective Hughes to work with us. After all, Mateo has been high on his list forever."

"Duke, are you down there?" Joy's siren voice filtered into my ears, and all was right in the world for a moment.

Denim almost fell off the barstool. "Is that who I think it is? Bro? Way to go."

"Don't count your chickens and all that," I whispered as my eyes landed on Joy climbing down the stairs in nothing but one of my button-down shirts that was way too big for her. Thank fuck she was covered.

She flipped her long waves of caramel hair over shoulders, her attention on Denim. "Oh, hi."

My dick was having a fantastic time in my jeans at the sight of her, which was the best fucking picture this side of the Mississippi.

"Holy shit!" Denim whispered as his gaze bounced from Joy to me. "You should see the look in your eyes. I think you've fallen harder than ever before."

Ignoring him, I asked Joy, "Couldn't sleep?"

She sashayed behind the bar and snuggled up to me. "My heat blanket was gone."

Denim watched us with awe. "Joy, whatever you've done to this brute, you need to do more of it."

I wrapped my arm around her. Inside, I was losing my shit because, in a way, Denim was right. I was falling, and it felt like the best damn feeling ever. But Joy and I had agreed to only one night.

I kissed her head. "You should go back to bed. I'll be up in a minute."

Denim hadn't taken his eyes off us.

"Thanks for the lovely Thanksgiving dinner," she said to Denim in a sultry, sleepy voice.

I needed to be inside her again. Fuck, I needed more than that. I needed to see her beautiful face every day. I needed to feel her against me while we slept and hear the soft sounds of her snoring, like she'd been doing when I crawled out of bed.

But until I could give myself to her as a free man—free from the chains of Rosario and the bloodshed and wars—I had to keep her at a distance.

She peered up at me with doe-like eyes. "I'm starving."

I chuckled. "No food around here."

"Why don't we head to the Paramount near Boston Common for brunch?" Denim asked. "Jade loves that place."

I would rather go round three with Joy. Only this time instead of in my bed and in the shower, I wanted to take her on the bar.

"Or maybe another time," Denim said as if he knew what I was thinking. "I'm beat from my shift anyway. Thanks for the advice, bro. Call me later." He climbed off the stool, fishing his keys out of his pocket. "Joy, I'll see you at the gala."

When we were finally alone, I grabbed her hand. "Come on. The night isn't over yet."

"But it's the morning," she protested.

"It's dark in here," I teased.

"Duke, we can't."

She was right, but I had to ask, "Do you have a guy in your life? I probably should've asked you that well before now." I wasn't one to steal another man's woman.

"No," she rushed out. "It's just that working and sleeping together don't make for a healthy relationship."

"Then I'll fire you."

She swayed against me. "No! I need the money, and don't you even think of offering to help me financially. I am my own person. I don't need a man to support me."

My fingers danced in her hair. "Seems we're in a quandary, then."

"No, we're not," she said emphatically. "I need to shower and get on the road. I'm visiting my family at Linwood Cemetery today. I try not to miss Sundays."

At the mention of Linwood, I winced.

"Hey, I'm sorry. I didn't mean to—"

"No need to apologize." I lifted her and set her on the stainless steel counter. "Tell me about your family. How did your mother and brother die?"

She paled. "I'm not ready to talk about it."

I curled her hair around her ear. "I understand."

"Duke, will you be okay?"

"Honest answer?"

She worried her bottom lip. "Of course."

"I'm not sure I can stay away from you."

"Then let's discuss why we keep dancing around each other." Her pretty eyebrows rose.

Talk about chess pieces. She just checkmated me.

I considered her for pulse-pounding moments. She had mentioned the employee-and-boss thing, so I got why she had reservations. But she wouldn't understand mine—no way. She would run far and fast. While coming clean wasn't a bad idea to keep me from seeing her—she would be out of sight if not out of mind—I could still fire her. If I had to do the latter to keep her safe, I would, but to can her because I couldn't keep my hands off her would be an asshole move.

For now, I only had one recourse—walk away.

"You're right. A deal is a deal. Have a nice day off."

I left as fast as I could to keep from touching her, kissing her, or even carrying her up to my room. Or worse, spilling my guts to her. That I wasn't prepared to do.

As I trudged up the stairs to my office, I knew more than ever it was time to change shit up.

I dared anyone to stand in my way.

FALLYN

ALIAS: JOY

By six that night, I was turning into my dad's driveway, feeling conflicted, queasy, and nervous. My head was spinning like an F5 tornado.

Duke had walked away angry, not at me but at himself. I thought for a second he would share his secrets with me, especially after that mind-blowing sex.

In a way, I was glad that he hadn't opened up. I wasn't prepared to share my secret, but I assumed he thought that my reasons for not wanting a relationship stemmed from the employee-and-boss thing. Or his rule of not sleeping with a woman more than twice.

I checked myself in the visor mirror. Dark circles ringed my eyes, a telltale sign of the toll that the nightclub gig and undercover mission were taking on me. I'd tried to conceal them with makeup before leaving my apartment, but the shadows persisted. I didn't know why I was trying to hide them. My dad would surely notice, no matter how much concealer I used.

I scanned the immediate neighborhood to make sure I hadn't been followed. Duke didn't have anyone tailing me, but I needed to be sure. He hadn't been happy when I'd gone up to his room to change before I left the club.

A government vehicle was parked across the street in front of Mrs. Dannon's house. I suspected someone from my team was here, but I hadn't called anyone. Something must be up. I still hadn't heard any news about Neal Fitzgerald. That had to be it.

I'd texted my dad to tell him I would come to my childhood home in Weston to see him after my visit to the cemetery. He didn't think that was a great idea, but my alias profile indicated Joy lived in Weston. Duke knew that. After all, he and I had met at the cemetery.

Regardless, I needed to see my dad and meet Rosie. Since Thanksgiving, I had been feeling a tad homesick. I also needed a pep talk that only my dad could give me. He was an expert on undercover assignments. He'd seen many cases over the years with the Bureau.

Hushed voices, along with a dog barking, filtered into my ears as I entered the house. Rosie came running up to me, sniffing and wagging her tail.

"Hey, girl." I let her smell my hand. Once she gave me the all-clear sign, I petted her. "It's nice to meet you."

I already felt better. I laughed out loud, recalling how I'd told Duke to get a dog.

Dad came out of the kitchen with a smile only for me. "Fallyn."

I almost cried at the sound of my real name as I abandoned Rosie and hugged my dad more tightly than I had ever done before. "It's so nice to see you."

He pulled back and clutched the sides of my arms, examining me. "What happened? Did Duke hurt you? Is that why you're here?"

I shook my head vigorously. "I might regret saying this, but Duke would never hurt me."

He lost his smile. "Men like Duke don't care about anyone if their lives are on the line—unless he's falling for you."

"If he hasn't, he's close," I said truthfully. Lying to my dad wasn't an option. He was the best reader of people, especially his daughter. "His sister, Grace, is another matter. She's trying to set us up. I'm going to a charity gala for Dillon's Hart of Hope shelter in two weeks. That aside, can't a daughter come see her father?"

"A father isn't in Joy Whitlock's profile, Fallyn. Were you followed? Does he have a tail on you?"

My eyebrows pinched together. "No, I'm good at knowing if I have a tail."

His facial features relaxed.

"I'm just a little melancholy from knowing you had to spend Thanksgiving alone. I also wanted to come out here to visit Jason and Mom. Duke knows I'm in Weston anyway."

He reared back.

"Chill. Are you forgetting the cemetery is where I met him? I have to be honest on some occasions to support my alias."

I spied Gwen Holiday watching us from the kitchen as Dad and I lingered in the hall by the pantry—confirmation of the government vehicle parked outside.

He examined me, searching for something. "You're beginning to like Duke. I can see it in your eyes, sweetheart."

And there it was. "He's—"

"The enemy," Gwen said from behind Dad.

I sighed, skirting by my dad, not wanting to discuss how I felt for Duke. "He wants redemption," I said to Gwen, entering the brightly lit kitchen.

Dad harrumphed. "Is that so? How does he see that happening?" Rosie was right on Dad's heels, panting.

I set my purse on the table by the French doors. "He didn't tell me that part. But if I overheard him correctly, I don't think Duke cares if he ends up in prison. He won't narc on Rosario either."

Gwen rested against the marble island. "That's Duke's MO. He's loyal to the bone."

"I wouldn't go that far. He and Denim have been discussing a possible plan to screw Mateo."

Gwen adjusted the sidearm on her hip. "Mateo isn't Rosario, and the Harts might not admit to this, but they would seek revenge any way possible against the Alvarezes. Tito did have Savannah Kelly murdered in jail. She'd witnessed Tito killing his brother Hector. Since the text you sent me regarding your jaunt to the factory, we've pulled all the files on the Alvarezes, though it was like pulling teeth. The BPD gang unit is very territorial."

"Is that why you're here?" I asked Gwen, pulling out a chair from the breakfast table and sitting down.

Dad gave Rosie a rawhide bone then swapped a knowing look with Gwen.

My stomach pitched. "What's going on?" The last time I'd seen panic on Gwen's face was the other day when she warned me about Neal Fitzgerald. "Do you have news about that DEA agent Neal Fitzgerald?"

She pushed up the sleeves of her sweater. "Nothing on Neal as far as whether he's a dirty agent, but we're watching him. I came for two reasons. One, to see how you're holding up. I know it took a lot of guts to spy on Duke at that factory."

That was probably a coded statement that meant she was worried about me and the feelings I might be developing for Duke.

The sounds of Rosie chomping on her rawhide reverberated through the kitchen.

"The other reason?" I asked.

"Sweetheart, that man Emilio, who you overheard being questioned in the factory yesterday afternoon—his body was found this morning in South Boston."

A sharp pain spread through my chest. "What? No. I specifically heard Duke and Gustavo saying that they would have Emilio get a message to Mateo Alvarez. Duke wants to talk to Mateo. He wanted Emilio to pass that info along."

"Well, we're trying to track down Mateo," Gwen said. "Kyle—

or rather, Agent Howard—and Bruce are paying a visit to Tito tomorrow. We know he won't talk, but we can take his temperature. See if he drops any hints accidentally."

"I want you out of there, sweetheart," Dad said. "I know we talked about the assignment lasting up to six months, but if we suspect that Mateo is working with the Mexican cartel to screw Rosario Mendoza, I don't want you in the middle of that war."

"It's my job, Dad."

"Sure, but taking part in raids is far less dangerous than being undercover," he said.

"The best outcome is if we could get Rosario, Arturo, and Duke in a room and send all of them to prison," Gwen speculated out loud. "But I'm wishing upon a star. I doubt Rosario will leave Colombia. Still, we'll settle for Arturo and Duke, if we could catch either with the guns. Of course, Mateo, but he's small potatoes in this game of cat and mouse. I need to run." She regarded my dad. "Sir, thank you for the tea. Fallyn, can you walk me out, please?"

Dad busied himself with Rosie as Gwen and I left. The freezing temperatures made me shiver. Luckily, I hadn't taken my coat off yet. She and I strolled down the brick path from the porch to the sidewalk.

"I sense something else is wrong," I said to her.

"I got my ass chewed by Howard. Nothing I can't handle."

I stuffed my hands into my coat pockets. "Was it about me?"

"He had a conniption because I panicked and sent my guy into the club to give you a message to meet me. He thought it could wait. I didn't."

"I'm sorry. As I told you, that incident brought me closer to Duke. I'll alert you if I hear anything of substance."

"How are you holding up with Duke?" she asked.

I shrugged. "I'm trying to stay away from him, if you want the truth. As you heard me tell my dad, Duke might be falling for me."

Her blue eyes pinned me where I stood. "Are you feeling something for him?"

My stomach recoiled. "It doesn't matter, Gwen. He and I aren't going to jet off into the sunset. Regardless of how I feel about Duke, I'll do my job. That much I promise."

From her frown, it appeared she didn't believe me. "Then you need to continue your dance with Duke. How else will you gain intel? You won't get much behind the bar."

She had a damn point. "I might be too late for that."

She fastened her hands on her hips. "Then find a way to do your job, Fallyn. Also, have you forgotten about your brother?"

Frustration was a bitch. So was this assignment. I wanted to scream.

"The last thing you need, Fallyn, is for Bruce to say I told you so."

I laughed, but it wasn't a nice sound. "Are you trying to rouse my competitive side?"

"Is it working?"

"Fuck, yeah." I glanced at the house to be sure Dad wasn't lurking. "I'm at my wit's end with Duke. I want to be the same Fallyn I was before I became Joy, but those lines are seriously blurred. Duke made the first move and kissed me. Then he avoided me. Then he kissed me again at Thanksgiving. Last night, he all but begged me to give him one night with me."

"You obliged?"

I could give her all kinds of excuses why I had, such as I'd given in because he would have fired me otherwise. But that wasn't the truth. Nor would Duke even do something like that to get his way.

"Let's just say it was more than I was ready to handle."

Her lips puckered as if she were about to whistle. "That good?"

"I feel sick to my stomach, knowing I'm lying to Duke, Grace, even his brothers. I feel heartbroken when I see the Harts having a good time together. I won't ever have that with Jason again. I know everyone warned me about undercover work, and while I'm learning that it's one of the toughest jobs I've done yet, I'm not going to fail. I also haven't forgotten about my brother. He's in my thoughts constantly. But most of all, I want to puke that I'm lying to myself. I'm embarrassed that I like Duke. I'm not supposed to like my target."

She searched my face. "Fallyn Williams, no one will fault you for how you feel. There aren't many people in this world who can turn their feelings on and off. Humans are not programmed that way."

"Bruce might be," I mumbled.

"Fuck Bruce," she said. "I bet he would react the same as you if Duke was a hot-as-fuck female. I would put my life savings on the fact that Bruce would fuck her brains out too. But if we're telling the truth, mine is this. I didn't volunteer for the assignment because—"

"You have friends who didn't come out the same."

"Yes, but one other reason. I know I would've fallen for Duke the second he kissed me. Whereas you? You had this determined look that nothing would stop you from taking Duke Hart down and finding info on Jason's death. That's why Howard recommended you, but he's also not naïve. Look, you can have it all, Fallyn, though you might not like the outcome."

"What you're saying is I can bring down Duke and the cartel and find answers on Jason, but I'll have a broken heart in the process?"

"Something like that," she said. "Love is about sacrifice. Read into that however you like, but I highly encourage you to do your job. The faster we can put this op to bed, the quicker you can come home." She hugged me. "You got this. I'm here if you need me." She pressed on her key fob, and the *beep beep* resonated in the quiet neighborhood. "We'll talk soon."

I watched her dart over to her car, my mind a mass of confusion. I had a lot to unpack after that conversation. Right now, I wanted to curl up by the fire and spend time with my dad and his new dog.

DUKE

I was watching the crowd from my office window. For a Wednesday night, the club was jam-packed. Our two-for-one specials and half-off ticket prices at the door drew in the midweek crowd. Even the VIP section was filled to the brim.

I roughed a hand over my close-shaven beard as my gaze diverted to Joy behind the bar. She was hustling alongside Matt as they made drinks and served customers. I would go apeshit if someone put a bullet in her. In a way, I was glad I'd left her at the bar that morning and hadn't looked back. If my enemies found out that she was special to me, Joy would be another pawn to fuck with me.

It had been ten days since she'd rocked my world. I couldn't stop thinking about her, though. My mind replayed that night with her over and over like a video on repeat. I was torturing myself, and that felt worse than having a gun to my head.

My thoughts shattered when I spotted Grace climbing the stairs, her big brown eyes smiling at me. I loved my sister, but I had a feeling I knew why she was here.

I moved away from the window as Grace breezed in, looking

as pretty as ever, with her hair in a high ponytail and wearing a tight outfit that no doubt drew the wandering eyes of every guy in the club. I was tempted to throw my coat over her, but I had to ease up on the big-brother attitude. She was a grown woman who knew how to handle herself. At least I had to keep telling myself that.

She kissed me on the cheek. "You look like you lost your puppy."

"Maybe I did," I teased, infusing a smile on my face that actually hurt.

She placed her purse on the bookcase along the wall adjacent to the door and twirled an imaginary circle around my chest. "You only wear a black T-shirt and jeans when you're making a deal. Do you have a job tonight?"

"What brings you to the club?" My tone was colder than I intended for my sister.

"I wanted to talk to Joy to be sure she's planning on attending the gala this Sunday and see if she bought a dress yet. But she's super busy right now. You're going, right?"

I wasn't in the mood to rub elbows with Boston's elite citizens, like the mayor, a few of Maggie's cop friends, and her foster dad, Detective Ted Hughes.

Grace snapped her fingers. "Duke."

I blinked. "I'll be there, Grace." Unless the shit hit the fan, as in Mateo finally having the balls to meet with me. That was, if Emilio had delivered the message like we instructed him to.

I wasn't holding my breath, though. Less than a day after we had cut Emilio loose, his body had been found. Gustavo had nothing to do with his murder, but I would bet money that Mateo had. If I was right, it was clear to me that Mateo was telling me to fuck off and that I wasn't getting the guns back.

Gustavo and I had our men scouring the streets for Mateo. Chris Vargas and his gang were helping as well.

"Good." She sank into the couch. "Have you and Joy gone on a date yet?"

A dark laugh came out of nowhere. "I love you, Grace, but we are not discussing this."

"Funny, I overheard Denim telling Dillon that Joy was here with you in the wee hours of the morning the Sunday before last."

Fucking brother. "You shouldn't be eavesdropping. Again, not talking about this."

Vince knocked before he entered.

Thank fuck.

But my breath lodged in my throat when Mateo Alvarez and his right-hand man, Lou Romano, strutted in with Vince. The shock quickly wore off, and I grinned, rationalizing that Mateo had the balls I'd known he had all along.

"I found these two sitting at the bar," Vince said in a rip-roaring, deathly tone. "Lou was playing with his pliers. They're both clean of bugs and weapons, even the pliers."

Lou liked to torture his victims by pulling out toenails, fingernails, and teeth with his pliers.

Two of my bouncers were standing at the doorway, ready to pluck Mateo and Lou by the scruffs of their necks and throw them to the crows on my command.

Mateo swung his gaze around my office. "Do you have any bugs in here, Duke? The last time Tito was in your club, your brother was wearing a wire."

"Do you honestly think I would be working with the Feds? My boss would snip off my dick."

He chuckled, his beady eyes rounding on my sister. "I'm surprised Rosario hasn't already."

"What's that supposed to mean?" My jaw flexed.

"You lost her shipment." Mateo was drooling at my sister and peacocking. "You must be Grace Hart." His skinny, denim-clad legs ate up the large space of my office as he swaggered toward her.

I was primed to throw him over the balcony outside my door if he even shook hands with Grace.

My sister, with her courage and defiant attitude, was on her feet, fisting her hands at her sides. "You're Mateo Alvarez. Number one asshole in Boston."

"Grace," I warned her. "Leave us."

Mateo stuck out his chest, holding up his chin that had a soul patch below his bottom lip.

Grace and Mateo squared off, and for a second, I didn't move, curious to see what Grace would do and itching for any reason to ram my fist into Mateo's ugly face or throw him over the balcony. But if I did, I would only be igniting the spark of war that we were trying to prevent.

I clutched my sister's tense bicep. "Vince, watch these assholes for a minute. Grace, come with me."

She yanked her arm from me. "No, I want to talk to Mateo."

"She likes me," Mateo bragged.

Grace shoved him. "I hate you. Do you like pimping out women? Is that your new role in Boston now?"

Mateo faltered.

"You're a pimp?" I asked Mateo. It was the first time I was hearing that.

"For now, but I'm moving on up." He was proud of what he was doing.

Since Grace's sex-trafficking ordeal, she went off the rails with men like Mateo.

Once again, I strong-armed my sister. "Grace, this way."

She stomped in front of me toward my private quarters.

"What are you doing?" I laid into her.

She spun around, breathing fire. "I hate the Alvarezes. They've fucked with our family for far too long. But recently, Mateo beat up a gal who came into the shelter. Something needs to be done, Duke."

I swallowed what felt like sandpaper in my throat. I could taste her derision and revenge as if they were my own. "He will be dealt with by me. Not you. Please, go down and see Joy. I'm not asking either."

She stabbed a painted-blue nail into my chest. "Do you know if he continues to pimp women, he'll be selling them to the sex traffickers? He has to be stopped." Tears pooled in her eyes.

My gut churned at the remembrance of what she'd gone through when she'd been sold to the highest bidder. "I know, Grace," I said softly. "I know." I hugged her tightly.

She shook in my arms. "I still have nightmares, and every time I see someone like him, my PTSD gets worse."

My body felt as though it had broken into tiny pieces as I held back my own tears. "Vince," I called, my voice cracking.

"Yes, boss?"

"Have one of the bouncers take Grace down to the bar." I eased away from my sister. "We'll talk when I'm done."

She blinked away a tear. "I want the Alvarezes out of our lives. I'll take matters into my own hands if you don't."

I stiffened. "Whoa! Are you saying what I think you are? Because I don't put contracts on people's heads. That's not my style. Never has been, and like hell will you do something like that."

I'd never intentionally killed a man because he pissed me off. That wasn't my MO.

"Then find a way to make Mateo suffer." She stomped off into the club.

Lou and Mateo were lounging on the couch, like we were childhood friends and they were here to catch up on our life stories.

"Your sister is quite feisty," Mateo said. "I like that in my women."

I snarled like a lion about to pounce. "I don't want to hear you talk about my sister or say her name."

Mateo lifted his hands. "I'm just giving her compliments."

Lou, creepy as fuck with oily hair, dirty nails, and soiled jeans, sucked his lips between his crooked teeth. "She is a fine piece of ass."

In four strides, I had Lou by the throat, his short legs dangling over the couch. "I've been wanting to pluck out your nails and every tooth you have with your pliers. I just might do that before you leave, if you so much as make one more remark regarding my sister."

Lou's leathery face turned red as he tried to grin through the pain.

Mateo just sat there. "Lou is quite the fuckwad. I don't know what Tito saw in Lou to hire him. But he serves my purposes."

I tossed Lou on the couch. "You're next." I turned to Mateo. "Now, instead of trying to rattle my cage, let's talk business."

"What? You're not going to offer us a drink while we chat?" Mateo asked.

I needed one for sure.

Quiet pounded through my office as I served them their beverages. Too bad I didn't have strychnine to sprinkle in their bourbons.

Vince stood by the door, hands in pant pockets, eyes on our enemies.

The burn of the alcohol sliding down my throat was exactly what I needed to deal with these assholes.

"I heard that you have something I want," Mateo said. "I'm dying to know what that is because I can assure you that you don't. You lied to flush me out."

Maybe he wasn't as stupid as Tito. "Then why are you here?"

"Can't a guy come to a club to drink and have a good time?" he asked sarcastically.

"Cut the bullshit, Mateo." My anger was rising fast and furious.

Mateo regarded Lou, who had a cheeky smirk on his face. "Lou tells me that before you linked with Rosario, you were making deals with Arturo Rodriguez. Lou even told me he stole money from you." Mateo whistled. "I want to know why you kept Lou alive?"

"Do you want to tell him, Lou? Or should I?" I asked.

Lou's nostrils flared. "Fuck you, Hart."

Vince was grinning. "Oh, come on, Lou. I want to hear how you can't satisfy women anymore."

Mateo's jaw dropped so far, it approached his lap. "The fuck. You cut off his balls?"

I pushed my tongue against the back of my teeth. "You see, Mateo, dead men in our business bring a lot of attention to us. That's something neither you nor Tito understand, which is why Tito would've never been accepted in my organization. So if your motive is to steal something that doesn't belong to you, like Lou did, then I suggest you return what's not yours. Otherwise, you might be the one without a dick and balls. Because in the end, I will get what I want. Isn't that right, Lou?"

He flipped me off.

"That's just wrong," Mateo mumbled, seemingly scared out of his mind.

It was fucked up that men who weren't threatened by a gun to their heads were desperate to keep their manly parts. I wouldn't lie. I was one of those men.

"In the end, Lou returned my money," I said smugly. "So start talking, Mateo. Because the way I see it, Emilio already told Rosario who he was working with before you whacked him. You did, right?"

Lou grinned cunningly. "Emilio was fun to kill."

Mateo growled at Lou. "Shut the fuck up."

Lou didn't seem fazed by Tito at all.

"Rosario knows that you have her guns," Vince chimed in. "The question is why?"

"Are you working with Arturo? Tito? Is this Tito's way of fucking with me?" I asked. "Or are you trying to do what Tito couldn't?"

Mateo played with the flavor savor on his chin. "For the last year, Tito and I have been planning on how to exact our revenge on you. You're the one who gave Tito the finger. You're the one who snubbed him. If you hadn't, he wouldn't be in prison." Mateo's knuckles were white around his glass. "When I stole the guns, that was to fuck you over, Duke. Without weapons, you'd have angry customers, and you would have to pay Rosario regardless, or she would kill you. Either way, you're out a lot of money or screwed with the Colombian bitch."

I was willing to give him a small amount of credit. We certainly would lose customers if we couldn't deliver.

I pressed on the cap of a pen I'd picked up off my desk as I leaned back in my chair. "You didn't do your homework, Mateo. Rosario and I have a different business arrangement. No money exchanges hands until I sell the goods to our clients. I hear a 'but' coming, though."

"The game has changed," Lou said. "Two of Rosario's men in prison shanked Tito."

"Bullshit," Vince said.

Lou wasn't blowing smoke up our asses. The rage and sorrow on Mateo's face was clearly evident.

"Is Tito dead?" I wanted to be sure I was reading Mateo correctly.

Mateo's Adam's apple bobbed. "Yes, so you tell Rosario if she wants her guns to come and get them herself."

I would give anything to be on a tropical island fucking my brains out with Joy. Joy? Not the time to be thinking of her. Or maybe it was. She certainly had a way of taking my mind off shit I didn't want to deal with.

I tossed the pen on my desk. "Did you honestly think your plan would work? You murdered two of her men in cold blood. Just by doing that, you started a war—and not with me." I wagged a finger between us. "You and I are soldiers in this game, Mateo. Now, you either hand over the guns to me, or you better run—leave the state, leave the country. That's your only option. Rosario isn't coming to Boston to deal with you. She has men on the ground here. She has me and my men as well, but I'm going to give you a chance to rectify this load of crap."

Mateo slammed his drink on the coffee table, and bourbon splashed everywhere as he pushed to his feet. "She'll meet with me.

In addition to the guns, I have something that she'll want, but it will cost her more than her guns."

I felt my face twist. "What?"

Mateo's lips curled into a cocky grin as he skirted the table. "I'm not about to show my cards. Just pass the message along. She'll figure it out."

I rounded my desk and got in Mateo's face. "Whatever you're planning will only end with you in a coffin next to Tito."

His nostrils flared, his cigarette breath washing over me. "Or maybe *you'll* be six feet under."

"You know I don't scare easily."

He bumped his chest into mine. "Oh, I know how to do just that."

Mateo strutted to the door, making it clear from his stride that he thought he had the upper hand.

Vince opened the door.

"One more thing, Mateo," I said. "Is Arturo behind this with you?"

"I don't need that fucker's help." He held his middle finger high in the air on his way out, with Lou sniffing up his ass.

"What is going on?" Vince asked.

I snagged my cell off my desk and punched in Rosario's number. "No clue. Lock the door. Don't let anyone in."

Rosario answered on the first ring. "Duke, I was just about to call you."

"I have you on speaker," I said. "Only Vince and I are in the room."

With the bass of the music reverberating outside my office, no one would be able to hear us.

"I spoke to Arturo," she said. "He's not behind stealing my guns. He was also in LA, not Boston."

"I'm figuring that out. Mateo just left my office. Did you have Tito Alvarez killed?"

I asked. *Please say no.* Not that I was distraught over his death.

"No one fucks with me," she shouted. "I had to send Mateo a message."

I pressed my fingers over the spot where I thought I had an ulcer. "You need to get on a plane to Boston if you want your guns."

"That's your job and Gustavo's." Her tone permitted no argument.

"Apparently, not this time," I growled out. "Mateo is confident he has something of yours that you'll pay top dollar for."

"He has nothing of mine. Unless…"

Vince's blue gaze was fixed on the phone as he sat across the desk, seemingly holding his breath.

Complete silence on her end.

"Rosario?" I asked.

She snapped her fingers. "Maria, call my daughter," she said, addressing somebody who was with her in Colombia.

Rosario's daughter, Alexa, was attending college at Penn State on an exchange program for two semesters.

My blood gelled, more at the prospect of Mateo using Grace to get to me than at the thought that Rosario's daughter might be in danger. Mateo knew how to scare us, for sure.

Vince paled, and I was pretty sure I had too.

"Duke, I need to call you back," Rosario said. "Alexa isn't answering." She hung up.

I could almost feel Rosario's rage and panic as if they were my own. I tore out of my office and down to the main floor, pushing people out of my way in the process. My fucking heart was about to burst out of my chest until I laid eyes on Grace. She was sitting at the end of the bar, talking with Joy.

As if Joy sensed my presence, her gaze darted in my direction. Then she said something to Grace, who in turn followed Joy's line of sight.

I made my way over to my sister and sat on the stool beside her.

"It looks like you've seen a ghost," Grace said. "Does your panic have anything to do with Mateo?" She snarled. "I hate that guy."

"Joy, double shot of Maker's Mark, please." I pinched the bridge of my nose. "Grace, I'm putting more men on you, and I need your word that you won't do something stupid regarding Mateo."

She flashed her brown eyes at me. "I'm sick of men guarding me. You, Dillon, and Denim are suffocating me."

Joy set my drink down. "Is everything okay?"

I gave her a nod because I wasn't about to tell her shit.

Joy lingered, swinging her gaze from me to Grace.

"Can I have a moment with my sister?" I asked Joy nicely.

Amber waltzed up to the waitress station on the other end of the bar, and Matt shouted for Joy.

I watched Joy until she was safely out of earshot. "Grace, I promise, once Mateo is out of the picture, I'm done."

"Really?" she asked. "How is Rosario going to take that?"

"You let me worry about her. I need to hear you say you'll let me handle Mateo." After her outburst in my office, I was worried Grace would take matters into her own hands.

"I'll let you handle Mateo. Satisfied."

"Thank you. Vince will drive you home."

"When I'm ready," she said, climbing off the stool. "I need my phone. My purse is in your office."

As she stomped away, I sat, fuming and worrying as I ogled Joy making drinks. What I wouldn't give to be balls deep inside her right now. To take my mind off my problems. To have one more night with her. What was I saying? I wanted, dare I say, forever with her.

24

———

FALLYN

ALIAS: JOY

I couldn't believe I'd been undercover for a month. I had mixed feelings about the length of time. In some ways, the days dragged on. I operated in a vacuum on other days, especially from Wednesday through Saturday nights when the club was hopping.

It had been two weeks since Duke and I had sex, and during that time, we'd managed to keep our distance but not without tense moments.

I'd missed something big between Grace and Duke the other night at the club when Mateo Alvarez and Lou Romano had shown up. I'd tried to pull it out of Grace, but she wasn't talking. As far as Duke, that man had a metaphorical muzzle over his mouth.

But Gwen had sent me a message that Tito was dead. That was a turn of events the team and I hadn't seen coming. No one would confess to Tito's murder, but the prisoners who shanked him to death were rumored to be foot soldiers in Rosario's organization.

I flattened a hand over my chest, hoping to calm my racing heart as I entered the Boston Harbor hotel where the charity event was taking place.

An usher was directing traffic for the guests in black-tie attire toward the ballroom at the back of the hotel.

I shuffled along behind couples excitedly chatting about the holidays. Christmas was only fifteen days away, and I was hoping I would be done with my assignment and able to relax with Dad and Rosie.

Soft melodies and chatter drifted from the ballroom as I stood in line to check my coat. Through the doors and wall of windows, I could see the glistening waters of Boston Harbor in the distance, illuminated by the city lights surrounding it.

I hadn't been to a black-tie event since prom. Grace had filled me on the guest list, which featured the who's who of Boston's elite society, including the mayor and other city officials. So far, the event had raised thirty thousand for the Hart of Hope shelter, and that didn't include the auction that would take place after dinner.

It was unfortunate that Duke wasn't more like Dillon, who was doing good things for the world. It still hurt to think about how emotional Duke had been when he expressed his desire for redemption. I couldn't even begin to comprehend the hardships he'd faced in life or why he hadn't sought redemption sooner. However, despite my empathy toward him, I couldn't allow my emotions to interfere with our mission. I'd been constantly reminding myself not to get attached to Duke Hart, but it wasn't easy when I saw him night after night watching me from his perch above the club.

Focus, Fallyn.

I hadn't gotten any intel since I forced Duke to walk away from me, and as Gwen had told me that night outside my dad's house, I had to rectify the situation. Ideally, tonight was the perfect opportunity to get chummy with Duke.

After handing my coat to the nice older lady, I steeled my nerves and entered the ballroom. Poinsettias adorned tables. White Christmas trees were positioned in key spots around the ballroom and at both ends of the stage. Donors were gathered in groups around tables, and others were already seated, while the bar was packed with folks either drinking or waiting for drinks.

I'd barely had a chance to gain my bearings when someone called my name.

I turned to find Dillon striding up to me, dressed to impress in a tuxedo he wore with a red bow tie. His brown hair was slicked back, and there was a spark in his brown eyes.

"Thank you so much for coming. Duke is at the bar," Dillon said.

I didn't have a chance to respond before Maggie Hart, wild blond curls in a beautiful updo secured with a ruby hair pin, walked up to us. She wore a silk red dress that fell to her ankles, and her emerald eyes glimmered.

Dillon kissed his wife. "Can you show Joy where we're sitting? I need to talk to the event coordinator for the hotel." He dashed off.

Maggie held a fluted glass of champagne. "He's a nervous wreck. I'm so proud of him."

I had a myriad of questions for the news reporter. If anyone was in the know, both about the Hart family and current events, it was Maggie. But it seemed I couldn't catch my breath.

Grace rushed over. "Joy." Her smile was blinding. "Duke is at the bar with Brian McCauley. Come on. I'll take you over to Duke."

"Grace," Maggie said in a firm tone, "let Joy breathe."

Grace responded with a pointed look at her sister-in-law. "Duke just asked if I'd seen Joy."

A waiter with a tray of champagne was heading in our direction.

"I'm parched," I said to defuse the tension between them.

I had a feeling that Duke and I had been a topic of discussion around the Hart family dinner table.

The waiter offered me a drink, and I couldn't grab it fast enough. I gulped down a mouthful. "I think I'll check out the auction table before dinner."

Grace frowned. "Fine. Just so you both know, Duke is miserable." She rounded on me. "I know my brother is a difficult man, but he has a huge heart. He needs someone like you. Sure, you two just met. There are kinks to be worked out, but be the bigger person. Duke is—"

"Grumpy," Maggie finished for Grace, sounding unnerved. "This isn't the time to play matchmaker, and I'm not getting in the middle. But I will say this. Duke has two expressions you can always count on, blank and grumpy. Tonight, he's brooding, which is a first. That's neither here nor there. For this event, it would be nice if there wasn't any drama at our table. I want my husband to shine tonight. I don't want Dillon to feel anything but the high he's walking on right now. He's put blood, sweat, and tears into his shelter from the ground up. So, Grace, ease up on Joy. Forcing a relationship never works." Maggie addressed me. "Joy, I agree with Grace. Can you be the bigger person, at least for tonight? Act as though you and Duke like each other?"

A mixture of anger and understanding had me gripping my glass tightly. "My purpose here is to support the charity, nothing more. As far as Duke and me, our business is our own." I swung my gaze between the two ladies. "Having said that, I wouldn't act any other way except cordial and polite. Now, if you two will excuse me."

I took one step then another, finding it difficult to walk in high heels when my legs were shaky.

I adored Grace, but she was too much to handle.

"Don't, Grace," Maggie said behind me. "Where's Dominic?"

I was curious about Dominic but didn't hear the rest as I weaved through the crowd, looking for no one. The only familiar faces belonged to members of the Hart family. I hadn't spotted Duke or Brian yet, and frankly, I needed air. I was about to head outside and walk down to the pier to collect my thoughts when I spied Duke out of the corner of my eye, and my body decided to stop short.

I lost the air in my lungs.

Duke in a suit was hot. Duke in a T-shirt and jeans—sexy. Duke in a tuxedo—rip-roaring panty melting.

Those mahogany eyes raked over me slow and sure, and I felt as though he was licking every inch of me. My pussy thought so, too, because it was throbbing faster than the beat of the music filling the room—or maybe that was my pulse.

Lord, please help. My determination not to give in to my desires was wavering. I knew he was the enemy, but why did he have to be so heart-stoppingly handsome?

Brian McCauley, a nice-looking man, big and blond, leaned close to Duke and whispered something in his ear. Then Brian clapped Duke on the shoulder and came toward me.

I kick-started my saltwater-taffy legs in Duke's direction. *Be the bigger person.*

"Joy, good to see you," Brian said in passing with a cheeky grin.

I couldn't say the same. I was tempted to follow Brian. Tonight might be my best opportunity to chat with him. I knew he wouldn't share his secrets, but I had to start somewhere in getting to know Brian, especially if my assignment went on for months.

But Brian became a distant memory as Duke straightened and gave me his most thigh-dampening smile that was reserved only for me.

"Hi." My greeting came out sounding strangled and odd.

He kissed me on the cheek then lingered near my ear. "You're absolutely breathtaking."

Heat pinched my cheeks and soaked my panties while goose bumps popped up along my arms and neck. "Thank you."

God, he smelled wonderful. Even the butterflies freaking out inside my stomach thought so too.

"We need to act like we are friends and be nice to each other. Otherwise, Maggie might put us in time-out if there's any drama between us during dinner."

He chuckled. "Is that so?" He sighed. "I can do that. Can you?"

"Of course, but there will always be tension between us."

"Sexual," he mumbled.

I rolled my eyes. "Is that the only thing on your mind?"

"Not at all." He covered my hand with his. "I can't read the future, but I know one thing whether you know it or not." His lips found my ear. "You. Are. Mine."

Despite the wedge between us—criminal versus federal agent—I believed him.

25

____

DUKE

With Joy by my side, the night was turning out to be one big blur. I hardly touched my chicken. It had been rubbery anyway. I couldn't think with Joy beside me. I'd managed not to reach over and slide my hand up her dress during dinner. And that dress? Fuck me. The backless sheath had me draping my arm over her chair and, every now and then, running my finger over her neck or shoulder. She hadn't protested or flinched, which surprised me. Probably because Maggie wanted us to be nice to each other.

As I listened to Dillon on stage, telling his guests about his life story and how his idea of a shelter for battered women was born, I was still tracing circles on Joy's neck and playing with wispy strands of her hair.

"I thought by now you would've stopped me from touching you," I whispered in her ear.

Her flirty smile made me lose my breath. "Shh. Your brother is talking."

I was listening. I was so fucking proud of Dillon. When he'd returned from his time in the Merchant Marines, he turned his life around. No more involvement in gangs. He stayed away from selling drugs, unlike Denim. However, Dillon had dabbled in selling a gun or two, which surprisingly began before my own involvement.

As he addressed the audience, with confidence in his delivery and excitement in his voice, he was inspiring me more and more to become a better member of society myself. From a quick sweep of the crowd, it was clear that everyone was equally affected in some way by Dillon's speech, especially his wife, Maggie, who sat next to me.

I abandoned Joy for the moment, leaning close to Maggie. "He's turned out the best in the family."

Her green gaze flickered my way, honor and love washing over her. "I know. You should take notes."

I could tell her that I had plans for the future that didn't involve the cartel or the weapons trade, but until I was actually out, she wouldn't believe anything I said.

Dillon's speech ended, and he thanked the guests.

Applause erupted around the room as guests gave him a standing ovation, and I was one of them.

"The auction table will be open for another hour," Dillon said. "In the meantime, enjoy the festivities, dancing, and bidding on the auction items. There are some high-end items on several tables throughout the ballroom."

Grace rose from the seat beside Denim. "Excuse me, I need to use the ladies' room, then I'll be at the auction tables. I have my eye on a Christmas gift for someone."

Dominic, Grace's date, said something to her that I couldn't make out.

I had respect for Dom. He was an ex-military soldier who'd been instrumental in helping Grace when she found her way to Boston after escaping her sex-trafficking captor. The two had had an on-again, off-again relationship for the last several years.

"I'm fine," she said to Dom. "I don't need anyone to hold my hand." She glared at Denim and me.

So far, Mateo hadn't made any attempts on Grace. Maybe because he already had the Holy Grail of prizes—Alexa Mendoza. Rosario was freaking out that Mateo had kidnapped her daughter. The former gang-member-turned-nutjob had actually snagged Alexa when she was coming out of a mall in Pennsylvania. Her roommate told Rosario that Alexa had gone shopping and never returned. But the roommate hadn't been worried since Alexa slept at her boyfriend's house most of the time, something Rosario had been unaware of.

"You guys are suffocating her," Maggie mumbled as Grace left the table. "I really wish you would—"

"Don't finish that sentence, Mags," I warned, knowing Joy was listening. "It's critical right now that Grace is not alone. Dom"—I tipped my head at Grace's retreating form— "move."

The band started in, and couples converged on the dance floor in front of the stage.

"Would you like to dance, Duke?" Joy asked, probably trying to keep the drama from escalating.

Dom obeyed my command, following Grace through the ballroom, as I got up from the table and held out my hand to Joy. "Sure."

After we blended in with other couples on the dance floor, Joy started in. "What's going on? You seem irritated with Grace, just like you did the other night at the club."

"I would rather not talk about it." My tone was not as measured as I would've liked.

I placed my hand on her lower back while my other one tangled in her hand.

As the band played a rendition of James Taylor's "Fire and Rain," I relaxed for the moment and got lost in Joy— the feel of her heated skin against my palm, her vanilla fragrance drifting into my nose, and the way her big hazel eyes sucked me. Nothing else mattered. Not even Mateo Alvarez or the meeting that was taking place next weekend. Rosario was scheduled to arrive in town on

Thursday, and Friday was D-Day. Mateo wouldn't give us a location yet.

"My mom loved James Taylor." Sorrow coated her voice. "God, I miss her, especially around this time of year." A tear cascaded down her cheek. "I'm sorry I'm getting all emotional."

"Hey, don't apologize. Grief is difficult to deal with. Look, I owe you an apology. I was harsh a moment ago, and I shouldn't have ditched you that morning at the bar."

Another tear fell. "What's happening between us is maddening. I'm not sure what to do anymore."

"I don't know either, babe." I held her tighter as we were barely moving in a sea of couples, the band still playing James Taylor. "What I do know is when I hold you, the world makes sense, Joy," I whispered to her.

She squeezed my hand that she was holding as if she felt the same way.

"I need you," I continued, her emotional outburst driving me to tell the truth. To tell her who I really was. "I'm a mess without you. You're constantly in my thoughts. I have no appetite. I can't even sleep in my own fucking bed. I smell you on the pillows. I see you naked, us making the best fucking music ever. Tell me you feel the same way."

"What if I do? Then what?"

Dominic rushed up to me, pale with fear. "I need you out in the hall now, Duke."

It took me a second to comprehend the severity in his expression and the panic in his words.

"Is it Grace?" Joy asked.

Dominic gave a curt nod.

My body went ramrod straight. "What the fuck?" I mumbled just as the song ended.

Dominic ran off.

Joy and I hurried behind him. Every muscle I had was as taut as a violin string. The best-case scenario was that Grace was beating the crap out of Mateo, but I hadn't seen him at the gala.

The whole Hart family was gathered near the restroom, all wearing forlorn expressions.

"I'll find Ted," Maggie said to Dillon.

Fuck. I did not want to tango with Detective Ted Hughes. He would blame me, no doubt, and he wouldn't be wrong. I would take full responsibility if Grace was truly AWOL.

"Fill me in," I said, acid rising in my throat.

Maggie held out Grace's phone. "I found this on the floor over there." She pointed at a spot by the restroom door.

"She could've just dropped it," I said. "We need to search the entire hotel."

"Grace mentioned she would be at the auction tables," Joy said.

Dom nodded. "I've searched the hotel lobby, the other restrooms, and even the lobby bar. A waiter thought he saw her leaving through the side door that the employees use. He caught a glimpse of a dark-haired guy, average height, with a patch of hair below his chin."

"Mateo," I gritted out as I got in Dom's face. "You were supposed to be watching her."

"I was. She went into the ladies' room, and I had to take a piss myself." He bared his teeth.

Dillon stuck his hand between Dom and me. "Step off, Duke. Dom is right. It's impossible to be with Grace every single second."

I sneered at my brother. "Not with that fucker lurking around. Mateo has Rosario's daughter as well."

Everyone paled.

"Well, if you weren't in the business you're in, Grace's life wouldn't always be in jeopardy." Jade's words were like daggers to the heart, despite the truth she was wielding.

"Who's Rosario?" Joy asked.

Several swear words blared in my head. "No one."

I fished my phone out of my tux and headed outside and away

from the damning looks my family was launching at me left and right.

The cold air filled my lungs, giving me a moment of reprieve to think. Valets were hustling to either help incoming or outgoing customers.

I paced up and down in front of the hotel along a brick side-walk lined by two ornamental trees when my phone rang from a number with a Boston area code that I didn't recognize. It had to be Mateo.

"Yeah," I barked into the phone.

"Duke." Mateo's voice was reserved.

"Where's Grace, Mateo?"

He let out a derisive laugh. "Do I have your attention now?"

"You motherfucker."

"I see you pacing like a madman," he said.

I glanced around the city street—up then down several times. "Where are you? You want my attention? Take me. Hold me until Rosario comes in. Torture me. Do whatever the fuck you want with me. You said you wanted revenge against me."

For all we knew, Mateo was setting up both Rosario and me to take the fall with the law. Eye for an eye and all that.

He clucked his tongue. "Tempting offer, Duke. I wouldn't mind snipping off your balls, but I like your sister a lot better. Oh, the things I could do to her. The things I might do to her."

I was gripping the phone so fucking hard that either I would crush it or break the bones in my fingers. "What's your game, Mateo?"

I was still searching the immediate area but couldn't spot a car or a van with people inside. Then again, the rage consuming me was probably blinding me.

"Grace is my safeguard," he said. "To ensure you don't bring the Feds to our meeting."

"Stop with the Feds crap. If I wanted to throw you to them, I would've done that already."

"Oh yeah," he said. "Then why is Detective Ted Hughes walking out of the hotel?"

Sure as the moon was high in the sky, Ted strutted out in his tux, smoothing a hand over his mustache.

"He's not FBI," I told Mateo. "Let me talk to Grace."

A moment of silence passed while Ted stared directly at me. I walked away from him.

"Duke," Grace said over the phone, sounding fine.

"Are you okay?" My pulse rate lowered a notch.

"Nothing I can't handle." Her voice was soaked in confidence.

I hadn't forgotten about her need to hurt Mateo. "Please don't do anything stupid."

Grace sighed. "I know what I'm doing. I guess I'll see you on Friday."

"Duke." It was Mateo again. "I will text you a location where to meet once you give me confirmation Rosario is in Boston. Oh, and don't forget the ransom." Then the line went dead. After a moment, I started to walk back to the ballroom, passing Ted in the process.

"Was that Mateo?" Ted asked.

"Don't get involved. This is not gang related."

He clutched my arm as if he were about to arrest me. "It is if Mateo Alvarez is involved."

"Then find him." I shrugged out of his hold.

He would be doing me a favor if he found Mateo before Friday. Maybe then Mateo would be caught with the guns. That would get Rosario and me off the hook.

"I have no problem taking you into the station," Ted said. "I also have no problem crossing lines with the Feds. Maggie would be distraught if something happened to Grace. I would be too. Grace is just as important to me as she is to you. I would do anything to protect her."

I pinned him with a glare. "You have nothing on me to take me in. If you want to help, then drop your cop hat. Only then will I work with you."

His dark eyes skated over my face as we stood glaring at each other. "You know I can't do that. Let me help you, and I promise I will fight for a reduced sentence for you. Or would you rather end up in the morgue? How would that make Grace feel?"

The longtime detective was trying to fuck with me psychologically, and it was working. Grace would never recover if anything happened to me.

"You don't even know if I've broken the law." I couldn't help but laugh.

A deep crease formed between his bushy eyebrows. "You think that I don't know you work with Rosario Mendoza? I know these streets just as well as you do. I have informants. I know what goes on in this city."

"Is that supposed to scare me?"

"You've been one lucky motherfucker all these years. Don't think that your luck won't run out."

I was more afraid of Grace taking matters into her own hands if I didn't do something about Mateo. She had already killed once to save herself. Murdering Mateo out of pure hatred because he was a pimp was something entirely different. Grace would be the one going to prison. But I couldn't snitch on Rosario. I wouldn't do that.

"Grace is fine for now," I said, walking away. "I appreciate your concern, Ted, but I can handle my own shit."

"You're making a mistake, Duke." He raised his voice over the truck's loud engine as the driver pulled up to the valet.

I was probably fucking up, but until I could think clearly, I wasn't making any move to bring Ted into the fold.

26

FALLYN

ALIAS: JOY

My ears were still pounding after a jam-packed night filled with partygoers and drunks. I was exhausted as I climbed the stairs to Duke's office. Every step required more effort than the previous one. Physically and emotionally, I was one big fucking mess.

I was still processing everything that had happened at the charity gala. I'd been on edge the entire week. If I was serving customers at the bar, I was on autopilot. Too much was happening at once.

I'd heard enough at the gala to know that Mateo had kidnapped Grace Hart and Alexa Mendoza. The BPD gang unit was out looking for Mateo, Rosario was officially in Boston, as of last night, and Duke had made himself scarce.

We knew that Duke and Rosario planned to meet with Mateo, but what we didn't know was the date, time, or location of the meeting.

On the flip side, I was trying to reel in my emotions. Duke had said a lot to me on the dance floor at the gala, indicating he had deep feelings for me. But we never had the chance to talk about it further. After Grace had been taken, it was like I didn't even exist to Duke.

Sighing, I knocked on Duke's open office door then entered.

Sitting on the couch, Vince glanced up from his phone.

I held up the sales report. "It seems Matt gave me the permanent job of being the messenger." I deposited the paperwork on Duke's desk next to a sticky note with some scribbled words—*two exits, junk, S. Boston.*

Vince cleared his throat. "How were sales tonight?"

"As usual for a Friday," I said. "Is Duke around? I haven't seen him since the gala."

"He's in his apartment. I would leave him alone. He's been quite ornery all week."

I anchored my hip against the desk. "Any news on Grace? I understand the BPD is on the hunt for Mateo."

"Nothing yet." His nonchalant attitude was a dead giveaway that he knew something. Of course he did.

"I'm sick over Grace's disappearance. I hope the police find her soon."

He was cataloging my features, as though trying to read my mind. "We have many folks scouring Boston for her."

I didn't want to pepper him with too many questions, or he might become suspicious.

I flicked a thumb over my shoulder, stealing a look at that note again and for anything else on Duke's desk that might give me a clue. "Do you mind if I see Duke before I head home?"

Vince loosened the knot on his red tie. "Make it quick."

I wound my way down a somewhat dark hallway, not sure what I had in mind. I knew Duke wouldn't tell me about Grace or Mateo or anything about his business, but I had to try. Not to mention, I was worried about him. I knew he would go to the ends of the earth for his sister, even die for her, and I wanted to help him. I wished I could come clean and tell him I could help.

I poked my head into Duke's contemporary bedroom, which

had a manly feel and was designed in reds and blacks, from the art on the walls to the bedding.

"Duke," I called, stepping inside.

A noise sounded in the bathroom before the door opened.

Duke strode out, his bare chest showing toned abs. His hair was wet and his jeans zipped but unbuttoned, showing that thin line of hair from his navel to his beautiful cock. With him came a cloud of steam and the scent of the Sauvage cologne he wore.

Instantly, my tongue stuck to the roof of my mouth, and my memory of why I was there lapsed.

He gave me a boyish grin that erased my nerves and made me tingle with delight.

I rubbed my hands down the sides of my legs, thinking of what to say. "I haven't seen you all week. Everything okay? I mean, I know Grace is on your mind. I'm worried about her, but I'm concerned about you too. You said a lot to me at the gala, then I didn't see you or hear from you."

"Forget everything I said to you that night. I didn't mean any of it."

I felt as though he had punched me in the stomach and ripped out my heart. "So everything you said to me on the dance floor was just a come-on?" He was lying through his straight teeth. "To what? Fuck with my mind?" I dug my nails into my palms, my chest constricting.

I shouldn't care. I was here to find evidence to put him away. Yet I wasn't sure I could do that anymore.

Silence dropped like a boulder between us.

"Well, say something," I demanded, itching to stomp my foot like I'd done many times to get my way with my dad.

"We're no good for each other, Joy," he said with no emotion in his tone.

Unshed tears were on the brink of spilling over, but I refused to cry. He was right. He was so flipping right. How would we work with him in jail, in a morgue, or on the run? I upheld the law. He broke the law.

"I guess it doesn't matter that I have feelings for you that I haven't had for any other man." I blinked several times to dry my tears, the truth setting me free. "Talk to me, Duke. I know you meant those words on the dance floor. I'm not an idiot. I know you're pushing me away. I also know you're into some bad shit with Mateo Alvarez."

My pulse slowed to nothing as something dawned on me. Had he figured out who I really was? Was he pushing me away to save me? Because if the likes of Vince, Brian, and Rosario found out, then I would be dead.

"I've had a lot of time to think during the last week." He was talking as if he really didn't give two flying cents about me.

Gwen had been wrong when she said humans weren't programmed to turn their emotions on and off on a dime. She hadn't met Duke.

Without taking those mahogany eyes off me, he continued, "I don't want you in my life. I made a mistake with you. Tomorrow night will be your last shift at the Monarch. I'll give you a month's salary to tide you over until you find another job." The lack of emotion in his voice and expression was maddening.

My brain's synapses froze one by one, cutting off my ability to think or speak.

The cold, calculating thug was showing his true colors that were detailed in his case files. That thought was so chilling it felt like someone had thrown me into the waters off Antarctica, and I came out of the haze I'd been in.

Gone was that blurring line between Fallyn Williams and Joy Whitlock, and so was that spell he'd had me under.

Vince came in. "Boss, it's time."

"Time?" I mumbled. "To get Grace?"

"Go home, Joy. Nothing good will come from us being together. We're over." Duke just added more fuel to my fire.

No matter how much I tried to get through to him or told him that I could help, he wouldn't listen. No matter how I felt about him, I wouldn't compromise my morals for love. I couldn't. That wasn't who I was. Gwen's words blared in my head. *"Love is about sacrifice."*

I held my head high and squared my shoulders. "You can't end something that never started in the first place. Oh, and I won't be working tomorrow. Keep your month's salary and my last paycheck."

I brushed past Vince, bumping my arm against his, ready to scream to high heaven as I pulled out my phone. My undercover assignment was over but not before I finished what I had started out to do.

"Your car is free of bugs and trackers," Vince told Duke, his voice carrying down the hall as I entered Duke's office.

If only we could have planted bugs, then the assignment would've been much easier. But we knew Duke swept for listening devices almost daily. Since he and Detective Ted Hughes had spoken at the gala, I suspected Duke was even more paranoid now.

I checked the hall before I went over to Duke's desk, scanning the sticky note once again and looking for anything else that might give me a clue.

Footsteps padded in the hall, and I hurried out. By the time I reached the main floor, Amber was hiking her purse over her shoulder by the bar.

I growled under my breath. My handbag was locked in a safe behind the bar.

"Joy, do you want to go to breakfast with Vince and me?"

Vince was going with Amber. That meant he wasn't accompanying Duke. Maybe D-Day wasn't happening after all. Maybe I assumed wrong.

I unlocked the small safe beneath the stainless counter. "You never invite me anywhere."

Amber and I had built a better relationship since I was hustling more in making drinks, and she thought Duke and I fit well together.

"Well, I am now," she said. "I think we need to stick together. You know. Vince and me, you and Duke. We could double date and all."

She must be wanting to live her teenage years over again. Who the hell double dated anymore?

I collected my handbag. "Is Duke going to breakfast?"

"No, he has something to do," she said.

Bingo.

But why wouldn't Vince accompany Duke? Unless Duke wanted to go alone. Or he'd decided to work with Detective Ted Hughes after all. At the gala, Maggie told Dillon that Hughes offered Duke his help, but Duke had declined.

I frowned at her. "I hate to break the bad news, but Duke fired me."

She gripped the edge of the bar. "Why?"

"I guess as you said, he has that two-sleep rule." I had only slept with him once, though.

"That's not right." Her lips thinned. "I'll talk to Vince. I see how Duke looks at you. I saw you guys on the dance floor too. It appeared to me Duke is in love with you."

A shudder rocked its way down my spine. "If he is, he has a funny way of showing it." I swallowed my emotions. "Thanks for the invite, but I'll pass. It was nice working with you, once we got over our differences." I circled the bar.

"Wait, Joy." She blocked me from leaving. "Duke is overly worried about Grace. Once he brings her home, he'll change his mind about firing you."

"Do you know anything about where Grace is?" I probed, praying she knew something that would at least give me a clue.

"All I know is by this time tomorrow, Grace should be safely home," she whispered.

"He's going to get her now?" I held my breath. *Come on, Amber. Give me more.*

"Maybe. Vince isn't going. Duke needs him to take care of the club and other matters." She glanced up at the second floor.

"Do you know where Grace is?"

She pressed her lips into a thin line. "It's not like you can do anything."

I had to ease up on my interrogation. "You're right. I'm just really concerned about her."

"I am too. Because if Duke was to bring the cops with him, Mateo would crush Grace and the other woman to death."

My eyebrows felt like they rose to my hairline. "Crush? That's awful. What do you mean?"

"Amber?" Vince called. "Are you down there?"

She blanched. "It doesn't matter if you know now that you're fired," she whispered. She raised her voice, calling to Vince, "I'm counting my tips, Vince."

"I need to do a few things," he said. "Come up when you're done."

Amber addressed me again, still in a low voice. "Vince doesn't open up much about the other business he and Duke run. But between the sheets, he will on occasion if something is truly weighing on him. He's worried that he'll lose Duke and Grace. She's being held at a junkyard. I don't know where, though. I just pray Mateo doesn't crush her with that equipment they use on cars."

I slapped a hand over my mouth to swallow my horror. Duke couldn't go out there alone. Though I suspected that Rosario would be with him and maybe even Gustavo and Rosario's foot soldiers in Boston.

"I know," she said. "That was my reaction too."

That's what the scribbles on the Post-it note meant—junk for junkyard in South Boston.

She'd been a wealth of information, and I didn't want to seem cold and blow her off.

"I pray Grace comes home safely," I said. "I won't be returning, so maybe you can call me and let me know what happens."

She nodded.

"I should go." I gave her a hug. "Be well, Amber."

I jogged out as fast as I could.

"Night, Joy," Craig, the bouncer, called. "Careful driving in this thick fog."

I didn't even notice the fog, but he was right. It was soupy as hell. I hated driving in it. I'd almost crashed one Christmas Eve on my way home from a party because I couldn't see but a foot in front of me.

I hurried to my dad's old and dark Ford Taurus. The last time I'd been home, he asked to swap vehicles to make a run to the dump since he'd been cleaning out the garage.

Once behind the wheel, I regulated my breathing as I started the engine. Then I Googled junkyards in South Boston. There were three listed, but one was a towing service. The pics didn't look like a junkyard. The second and the third appeared to be true junkyards, but it was hard to tell from the images.

I could wait and follow Duke, but because of the fog, that might be tough. I threw the car into drive and wheeled out of the Monarch. If I could barely see, then Duke would have a problem as well, which meant it would take longer for him to get there. That would give me time to investigate each facility.

As I navigated the streets of Boston toward the highway, I called Gwen—and prayed that whatever happened over the next several hours, Grace and Duke would come out alive.

27

DUKE

Normally, I would be speeding down the highway at ninety miles an hour, but I couldn't because of the fog. It was as thick as the pea soup I'd made for my brothers and sister growing up.

Rosario, sitting in the passenger seat, was gripping the console with one hand while she clutched the door handle with the other. "You think we ditched those men outside my hotel?"

I hadn't seen Rosario since she was in Boston four years ago. She hadn't changed—short black hair cut into a bob, her signature red lipstick, thick eyebrows, and long pointy nails that could slit a person's throat.

"They're not following us," I said, fingers glued tightly to the steering wheel.

She'd disguised herself, leaving the hotel through a side exit and walking two blocks to meet me. The fog was acting as a shield of sorts.

"Panic is not your usual flair. Gustavo and your men will be there. Alexa and Grace will come out alive." I prayed those things would come about anyway.

She and I knew the risks of what we were facing. I was surprised she was prepared to die for her daughter. Rosario was all about her business, her seat at the top. Not many cartels could say they had a woman in charge who could run a billion-dollar illegal empire and succeed.

I liked the way she ran things. She was loyal, shrewd, and intelligent and had a master's in business education. She was also a fourth-generation cartel member, so she learned the ropes from those before her, including her father.

"Why don't we go over the plan again?" I said, trying to take her worries off the impending doom.

"It's easy. I kill Mateo, and you rescue Alexa and Grace." One of her flaws was that she let her emotions get in the way of her decision-making at times.

"Rosario, that's not the plan. We give Mateo the million-dollar ransom in exchange for Grace and Alexa. Once we have them, then your men will drive the truck with the guns through the back gate, if it's on-site. When Mateo leaves, my brothers will follow him and call Ted Hughes to arrest Mateo for kidnapping."

In a perfect world, that was the plan.

I'd decided not to include Vince and my team. In the event something happened to me, I needed Vince to continue to run things. He'd protested but knew I was right. He also knew I had Rosario's army, which was larger than mine.

I thought to ask Jeremy Pitt for the help of his army, but this wasn't his fight.

"I don't like that you included that detective," she said. "You and I could go to prison."

"We knew that," I tossed out. "We talked about this. Alexa is more important to you than your freedom, right?"

"Of course." Her thick voice cracked. "I'm not a bitch of a mom. I've been grooming her to handle the business, which is why she's at Penn State. We planned for this."

"Then we need to make sure our plan goes smoothly," I said.

"Involving Ted looks as though we're helping the law, which could make any sentences handed to us less severe."

If we were caught with the guns, that was. If not, Ted didn't have much cause to arrest us.

She pushed out a long-suffering breath. "I want to murder that bastard Mateo."

"You can, but you'll definitely end up in jail."

She gave me a sidelong glance. "Why are you calm? You love Grace. I would've thought you would be more nervous."

I chuckled. "Oh, I am. But I've been in enough life-and-death situations that I've learned to channel my energies inward and not let anyone see me sweat. You know this. Plus, whatever happens next, I'm okay with it as long as Grace comes out of this alive. As we discussed, it's time, Rosario, for me to hand the reins to Vince. It's time for me to step down. If that means a grave, so be it. If that means prison, I'll deal. I can't keep putting my family in harm's way. I'm going to be an uncle, and I would like to be a father someday."

The phone rang, the sound coming through the speakers, and Gustavo's name appeared on the car's monitor. I hit the answer button.

"Gustavo, are you there?" Rosario asked.

"The team is in place," he said. "There are two grunts at the gate, two outside the building, and a handful patrolling the junkyard. Our men are scattered throughout the yard and hidden among the piles of crushed metal. Our truck is here as well. I'm assuming the guns are in it."

"We're coming off the exit now," I said. "The fog slowed us down, but we're still early. By the way, are my brothers in the area?"

"I talked to Denim," Gustavo said. "They parked a block down from the junkyard."

I'd tried to keep my brothers from getting involved, but they hadn't listened to me. If the tables were turned, I would've been here, without a doubt. Our sister meant the world to them too.

Still, I'd met with my brothers a couple of days after the gala, after I started ignoring Joy, after I knew what I had to do if I wanted a new life and redemption—and for my sister and brothers not to be threatened every time a deal went bad or an enemy wanted to fuck with me. The conversation the night we'd met at Dillon's house had been tough.

"*Bro,*" *Denim said,* "*this is about to change your life and not in the way you planned.*"

"*Look, it's time for a new chapter for me, whatever that will be. Rosario is on board with the plan. Brian and Vince are, too, though they have argued otherwise. You both know what to do if anything happens to me. Vince will run things with the club until it sells.*"

"*We have your back,*" *Dillon said.* "*But whatever happens, know that I love you. You've taught me so much growing up. You kept our old man from beating us to a pulp. You kept food on the table any way you knew how. Denim, Grace, and I are alive because of you.*"

I wasn't an emotional man, but Dillon's comments sparked so many deep-seated issues.

"*Joy kind of knows what's going on,*" *Denim said.* "*Have you talked to her since the gala?*"

"*I can't. I'm walking away from her. She deserves better than me.*"

"*You're in love with her,*" *Denim said.* "*I see it in your eyes.*"

"*Doesn't matter.*" *I would never ask Joy to compromise her morals for a thug like me. No amount of love was worth sacrificing one's beliefs.*

Rosario clapped a few times, knocking me out of my reverie. "Where did you go? Did you hear what Gustavo said?"

"Sorry, man." I moved my neck around. "I was just going through the plan in my head." *Liar.*

"I haven't seen any sign of Mateo. Stay alert," Gustavo said. "Once I see Alex and Grace come out of the building, I'll grab them and head out. I'll keep Denim informed through my comm."

Denim had suggested earpieces for Rosario and me, but Mateo was nervous that I might bring the Feds, and earpieces would only set him off. So I'd nixed that idea.

"I'm coming off the highway now."

Two minutes later, I spotted Denim's Explorer and pulled up next to the driver's side and rolled down my passenger window.

"Bro," Denim said.

Dillon leaned over slightly in the passenger seat of the Explorer. "Ted should be here in five minutes."

"I still don't like having a cop here," Rosario complained.

"You agreed," Denim lobbed her way.

She mumbled under her breath. I didn't care whether she agreed. I was saving Grace at all costs.

"Are you guys ready?" I asked.

Both my brothers were dressed in black and wore skull caps, the same as me.

Dillon bit his lip. "Mateo is going down tonight."

"Stay safe, bro," Denim added.

After a quick nod, I drove away, ready to end Mateo once and for all.

28

FALLYN

It had taken me forty minutes to drive the five miles to South Boston. The damn fog was dangerous. I had to keep my speed at thirty miles an hour and sometimes less to ensure I didn't crash into a vehicle in front of me.

To make matters worse, the soupy air was thicker the closer I got to the water, which was where the third junkyard was. I'd driven by the first but didn't see any activity. Nor did it look like a place where metal was crushed. The second junkyard did indeed belong to a towing service, but I had hit pay dirt with the third because two men with assault rifles were guarding the gate.

I dumped my dad's car on the side street of a small business park, grabbed binoculars that my dad had in his trunk, and secured the pouch around my waist like a fanny pack. Then I tucked my service weapon in the small of my back, pulled out my smaller gun from my boot, and booked it on foot. There was a road that led to the back of the junkyard. I had no idea if Mateo owned the property, although Gwen was checking out all three junkyards.

The team was also scrambling to engage, but considering the weather, nobody would be here anytime soon. Apparently, Agent

Howard had gotten stuck in DC because of the fog in Boston, so he was calling in backup. I'd told Gwen during our phone call after I left the Monarch to reach out to Ted Hughes.

My phone vibrated against me as I approached the north side of the yard. I checked to be sure it was Gwen before I pressed my earbud.

"Fallyn, the team watching Rosario says she hasn't left the hotel," Gwen said. "Are you sure the meeting is today?"

"Yes, Amber told me Duke was going to get Grace today. It might not be right now, but it's going down today. Maybe Rosario decided not to come. She could be wary that we're lurking. Did you call Ted Hughes?"

"He's not answering," she said. "Bruce and I have backup. We're packing up now."

"I found the right junkyard, I think. I'll text you the location."

"Don't engage until we get there," she said adamantly.

"I'll do my best." I tapped my earbud to end the call and sent her a quick text.

As I was walking up and down the perimeter, examining the fence for any openings, I spied movement and stilled.

The figures were coming my way. I slunk backward in the tall brush and tripped over something. I couldn't stop my fall. Luckily, my ass hit the ground—or rather, a pipe, I thought.

Pain careened up my spine as I swallowed a grunt. I quickly adjusted my body, lying on my stomach, thanking whoever was listening for the fog.

"Anyone out there?" a male voice called.

"Sheesh, it's probably rodents running around out there," another man said. "Come on. Gustavo will have our hides if we fuck this up. We're supposed to keep an eye on the truck and be ready to drive away with the guns."

I didn't move. Didn't breathe. Didn't even blink.

I texted Gwen.

Me: *The address I sent you is the one. Shit is going down now.*

The three bouncing dots flashed.

Gwen: *I'm still trying Ted Hughes. We've left the facility. Not sure of ETA. Will text you when I know more. Do. Not. Engage!*

I slowly stood upright and grabbed the binoculars from the pouch, not sure they would help with the fog. As I adjusted the focusing ring, I couldn't see a thing.

Returning the binoculars to the pouch, I headed farther down the perimeter from where I had spotted Gustavo's soldiers. At the very end of the fence, before it angled at ninety degrees, the chain link was bent outward, as though someone had tried to use the spot to gain access into the yard.

The problem was that I could hear the guards talking. So they were close.

"Mateo is waiting for you in the building up ahead," a man said.

I imagined he was speaking to Duke.

I pulled the fence backward as far as my strength would allow then shimmied through. I couldn't wait for Gwen and the team. They wouldn't be here for at least an hour because of the fog and their distance from South Boston.

I crawled around a heap of metal, debris, and other blunt objects digging into my hands and knees. The adrenaline was keeping me from feeling too much pain as my pulse blasted in my ears.

Once I was hidden between stacks of metal, I stood up and practiced my yoga breathing, sweat sliding down my back one slow inch at a time.

The sound of tires crunching over gravel was ominous through the dark, foggy morning hour, which according to my phone was five a.m.

I needed to find a spot to hunker down, one with a bird's-eye view. I kept my senses open as I went to the edge of the stacks of metal and peeked around them.

Brake lights illuminated the surroundings as the vehicle turned in to a spot in front of what looked to be a two-story cement building. It was a bit hard to tell. The fog was both a blessing and a curse.

Regardless, my goal was to get into the building.

I looked both ways, took a deep breath, and ran across the expanse of the open gravel road as fast as I could.

29

———

DUKE

The damn fog was freaking me out. I couldn't scan the yard for threats. Ted had assured me he wouldn't call the Feds, at least not until he had Mateo in custody. For all we knew, federal agents could be hiding among the piles of metal—if Mateo was using the law to fuck with us.

"This weather is not helping us, Duke," Rosario said, exiting my SUV only to be stopped by the grunt with an assault rifle.

"Touch me, and I'll scratch out your eyes." She held up her cat claws. "They're sharper than you think."

"I need to check for weapons," he said. "So if you don't want me touching you, then hand yours over."

Rosario's laugh was laden with evil. "I am not walking in there unarmed. Mateo!" she shouted at the top of her lungs. "We do this outside. Bring my daughter out. Now!"

I collected the briefcase of money from the back seat. I preferred that we did the deal indoors. Not being able to see my surroundings was giving me a bad itch in my side.

I touched Rosario's shoulder. "We go in. I got you covered."

I left my weapon in the SUV.

194

She handed hers to the grunt. "You better return it when I leave."

The dude had no expression as he frisked me. "I need you to open the briefcase."

I did as he instructed. Once he was satisfied, Rosario and I went inside.

The second she crossed the threshold into the cement building, she swore like a drunken sailor at a bar during happy hour.

I held my tongue as I clutched the aluminum briefcase, looking around the space, which was empty except for a large crate butted up against the wall. Stairs led up to a landing that split to the right and left, with offices or rooms in view behind the metal railing.

No sign of Grace or Alexa. No sign of Mateo.

I walked toward the back of the building while Rosario rushed up to the second level.

I found shelves filled with old and oily car parts, boxes, and other junk. A desk beneath posters of half-naked women on the wall was by the entrance to the bathroom, and there was a side door. I checked the bathroom to be sure it was empty, and a shitty odor hit me when I poked my head inside. At least whoever had taken a crap had had the decency to open the window.

I backtracked, set the briefcase on the desk, and pulled out the two guns I had stored behind the velvet cover inside. The moron grunt hadn't bothered to inspect the case in detail. I hadn't expected him to. All he'd seen was money, and that was what I'd been banking on.

I tucked my 9mm in my back beneath my shirt.

Rosario came down, holding her nose, obviously smelling the stench filtering out of the bathroom. "Nothing upstairs but metal and boxes and trash."

I handed the other weapon to her.

"Never let anyone tell you that you're not intelligent." She pocketed the Glock. "Where do you think Alexa and Grace are? Or that bastard?"

I shrugged as she removed her phone from her front pants pocket and called Gustavo. "Mateo and the girls are not here. Are they out there somewhere?"

"I think he's walking in now," he said.

She returned her phone to her pocket as the door squeaked open and Mateo strutted in with a grin the size of California—gun in one hand and clutching Alexa with the other. "I see you brought the money."

"I don't see Grace." Panic clawed its way up to settle in my throat. "Where the fuck is my sister?" There was a bullet with his name on it.

Mateo's smirk was cutting my insides to shreds. "Patience."

I scrubbed a hand over my chin, keeping my anger simmering.

"Alexa, *mi querida*." Rosario's pained voice turned to rage when she lunged at Mateo.

Alexa wasn't exactly coherent, stumbling against Mateo for purchase.

I caught Rosario before her nails scored Mateo's face. "Easy."

I would have loved to see her gouge out his eyes, but any stupid move on our part could make things worse for Grace and Alexa.

Mateo laughed as he pushed Alexa down on the floor. The poor girl hit her head against the wall, the impact waking her up as she winced. When she finally set her eyes on her mother, she said, "Mom?"

Rosario was blooming red and oozing venom. "Sit tight, Alexa. Mateo, I'm here. Now what? You want to kill me? Give it your best shot."

He waved his weapon in the air as if he were wagging his finger at her. "Not yet. I have big plans for us this morning. But before we start, show me the money."

I sneered. "Show me Grace. And if there's a scratch on her, you won't be getting squat."

"I'm the one in charge, not you, Duke."

I craved to strangle him, hang him up by his ankles, slit his throat, and watch him bleed out.

"Where are my guns?" Rosario asked.

"In that crate," he said, not taking his eyes off me as if he knew I was up to something.

Oh, I was, but I was waiting for the right time.

"Where are the rest?" she asked. "That truck was loaded with them."

Mateo offered her a casual shrug. "You know, Duke here thinks Tito and I don't have the brains to sell guns." His sarcastic tone was scraping along my nerves. "But I'm on my way to success. I sold all but that crate. I wanted to save a handful for you." He pouted. "After all, I'm a man of my word."

Boiling-hot rage seared my veins. "If what you say is true, where's Grace?" My voice was matter-of-fact.

Mateo stared at me, as though I was too calm for his liking.

I could feel Rosario's eyes on me. She laughed. "Mateo, one thing I've learned about Duke Hart over the years is you should be afraid of how even-keeled he is right now. Kind of reminds me of a snake, perched with its neck high, biding its time before it attacks its victim."

"Duke isn't about to do something stupid." Outwardly, Mateo was exuding confidence, but the small crack in his voice said otherwise. "Because if he does, he won't see Grace again."

"Where is she, Mateo?" I asked, swinging the briefcase around my back, with my free hand joining the action, prepared to go for my gun.

Mateo aimed his Glock at me. "Hands where I can see them."

"Your men frisked me." I held out my arms. "See."

"Throw the suitcase over to me," Mateo ordered, losing his bravado.

Alexa moaned. "Mom, I have a headache."

She probably had a concussion.

"We're almost done here," Rosario assured her.

"Not happening until I see Grace." I stood my ground.

Mateo pressed the gun to Alexa's temple. "Rosario, tell Duke to slide the briefcase over to me, or I'll put a bullet in your daughter's head."

"You want the briefcase? Then go get it." I threw it in the direction of the crate.

Mateo ran for it like a drug addict needing a fix.

His momentary lapse of attention gave me ample time to whip out my gun at the same time Rosario darted over to her daughter.

I swung my Sig Sauer 9mm at Mateo as his eyes widened at something behind me.

Motherfucker. His ghostly look told me someone was here. Whoever it was had rendered him speechless, so it must be either someone who had returned from the dead—or the law.

I spun around, swerving my aim and stumbling when I saw a woman wielding two guns in her hands like she was some vigilante out of a Marvel show. One gun pointed at me and the other at Mateo.

I lost my breath.

"What the fuck is your bartender doing here?" Mateo asked.

I tried to speak, but nothing came out. My tongue froze. My mind lost all thought.

"I'm Special Agent Fallyn Williams," Joy said. "Put down your weapons."

"You brought the Feds with you, Duke?" Mateo's voice pitched. "I fucking knew you would pull something like this."

The word *Feds* shook the marbles from my brain as I backed up toward the front entrance, my gun still drawn, with Rosario to my right, protecting her daughter.

"Duke had no clue," Joy said, trying to keep her attention on Mateo, Rosario, and me.

Ted Hughes had assured me he wouldn't call the Feds. I didn't think he had. I'd been conned. She was undercover. She was fucking undercover. Shock transformed into anger. Not at her. At me. I was the idiot. I should've figured it out. Then again, Jeremy Pitt's tech team was always thorough with its background checks, and the government was always savvy in cloaking its agents.

"I am not going to jail like Tito," Mateo said through a tight jaw, his gun still raised, his aim at Joy resolute.

"I wouldn't do what you're thinking, Mateo." Joy's voice was as calm as a warm summer day.

I kept my arm steady, my finger on the Sig's trigger, my gun aimed at Joy, my attention on her unwavering, although the words *shock and awe* didn't begin to describe how I felt.

Rosario was mumbling, but I couldn't comprehend anything she was saying.

I thought back, trying to pinpoint signs I should've noticed, but there were none. Joy and I had met at the cemetery. Had she followed me there? No, I had no tail that day. I shouldn't berate myself. Brian had been none the wiser with an undercover in his ranks for more than a year, but I wasn't Brian. I usually pegged a Fed a mile away.

Yeah, a male undercover agent. Not a beautiful female.

The pulse in my ears grew louder, catapulting me out of my haze.

Joy could pop both Mateo and me, one after the other. Rosario didn't seem to care as she blocked her daughter, her hands shoved in her coat pockets where her weapon was stored.

I wouldn't be surprised if Rosario shot Mateo before Joy could.

Joy set those ball-squeezing hazel eyes on me for the briefest of moments. "Lower your weapon, Duke. You don't want to kill a federal agent."

Then everything clicked—or maybe it didn't. She wanted me then didn't. That day in the penthouse bathroom, she'd said, "Once we walk out of here, we can't kiss like that again or do anything else, for that matter." She'd tried to keep her distance, push me away. But like me, she'd failed.

This wasn't the time to analyze shit, and I hadn't come here to kill anyone, least of all her.

"I'm putting my gun down. Mateo, I suggest you do as well."

I quickly checked on Rosario, who was watching things unfold while Alexa was shaking beside her mom.

Once my 9mm was on the floor, I raised my hands, studying Joy then Mateo.

He lowered his arm, fixating on Joy.

"That's it," she said to him. "Put the gun on the floor."

That arrogant look he sent Joy's way sent chills down my spine. He wasn't about to give up so easily.

My reflexes kicked in as Mateo raised the gun, and I threw myself between him and Joy.

Gunshots rang out through the room.

One bullet hit my chest, the other my arm.

Alexa screamed.

Suddenly, I was falling as a burning pain careened through my body. I landed hard on my left shoulder, hearing a bone snap before my head bounced once off the concrete floor.

My vision began to blur as I thought of Grace. Where was my sister? She was all I could think of besides Ted's words about how Grace would feel if I landed in a morgue.

Then another gunshot blasted in the room.

I managed to stand, swaying in the process as blood seeped through my T-shirt, my left arm immovable.

Mateo was on the floor with blood pooling around him.

"Grace," I whispered, staggering to the door. "I have to find Grace."

Joy was calling my name, but she sounded far away.

I pulled open the door with my good arm, but it felt like the damn thing weighed a ton. I opened it just the same. "Grace!" I shouted.

I could barely hear what the grunts at the door were saying.

The cacophony of sirens and tires crunching over the gravel sounded distant yet loud.

I squinted as if the fog was the sun shining in my eyes. "Grace," I shouted again.

She had to be here somewhere. I staggered to the end of my SUV then leaned against it to catch my breath.

"Duke." Joy rushed to my side. "You're losing a lot of blood. You've been shot twice. You need to sit down and wait for help to come."

Lots of voices shouted nearby, saying things like "Put your guns down" and "I don't want to shoot you."

I winced, rounding on Joy, swaying. "Help. You want to help? What? By sending my ass to prison? I thought you were the one. I was about to give you my heart." Her pretty face was blurring in and out. "My sister adores you. My brothers too. Stay away from me. I don't need you or your help."

Headlights shone my way, car doors opened, and Denim and Dillon shouted at me.

"Holy shit" dropped from Denim's mouth.

"Motherfucker" came out of Dillon's.

"Find Grace," I said to them. "She has to be here somewhere."

"Bro, you're losing a lot of blood," Denim said.

"So I've been told. It's nothing," I assured them despite the excruciating pain clutching my body and how I felt colder by the minute. "Find—" I pressed my hand into my chest, wincing again, dizzy.

Then I heard Ted's command. "Round them up."

"We need the paramedics," Joy said.

"I'm going to look for Grace. Dillon, stay with him," Denim ordered as if he were in charge.

"I'll help." Joy took off with Denim.

I slid down to the ground and popped my head against the bumper. Darkness encroached on my peripheral vision as I tried to focus on Dillon. "I'm sorry I couldn't save Grace." The words came out garbled.

"Hang with me, man." He slapped my face.

"I want you to know that I love you. I only pushed you guys away to keep you safe. I should've gotten out when Grace came home all those years ago."

He tore off his shirt. "You're losing a lot of blood." He pressed the fabric to my chest. "Ted, we need an ambulance."

"One is on the way." I barely heard Ted as Dillon's face faded.

Then blackness took me under.

30

———————

FALLYN

I ran around the junkyard with Denim, looking for Grace, my mind reeling that Duke had thrown himself in front of a bullet that had my name on it. The man had saved me, yet I shot him. He'd taken one bullet from me and the other from Mateo.

If the adrenaline wasn't keeping me on my toes, I probably would've puked my guts out by now from the look of betrayal on Duke's face.

If Duke died, I would be responsible for his death. I shouldn't have been on-site. I'd disobeyed protocol and hadn't waited for backup, but I couldn't. By the time Gwen and the team arrived, the meeting would've been over.

Even now as I scanned the yard, I didn't see Gwen or any members of my ATF team.

Gustavo walked up to Denim. "I've been searching for your sister. I can't find her."

"Have you checked the building?" Denim asked Gustavo.

I hadn't seen Grace inside on the ground level, although if she had been on the second floor, then Duke wouldn't have run outside to look for her.

"Joy, why are you here?" Denim asked. "Duke would never bring someone he was in love with to a fight."

Cue the nausea. "My name isn't Joy. It's Fallyn Williams, and I'm an ATF agent."

No reaction whatsoever from Denim, as if he already knew. Gustavo, on the other hand, swore.

But I wasn't hanging around for the million questions. Grace's life was at stake.

A whirring noise filled the air, and the three of us took off toward the far end of the junkyard.

As we jumped over metal parts and skirted around car seats that had been left on the ground, Amber's words flashed in my mind. *"If Duke was to bring the cops with him, Mateo would crush Grace and the other woman to death."*

I didn't know much about junkyards and scrap yards, but I did know they used different types of crushers to flatten the shells of cars.

I prayed like a nun that Grace wasn't about to be crushed, but as we drew closer to that high-pitched whirring sound, the hackles on the back of my neck rose.

Dawn was on the horizon, and I hoped the morning light would cut through the fog, enabling me to see better.

A plane coming in for a landing at Logan Airport drowned out the sound of the machine as we searched the aisles of metal for what I was assuming was a crane operating the car crusher.

"Over here," I shouted as the plane's engine faded and the hydraulics of the crane became clearer.

The grabber—or claw, as it was sometimes called—was opening to pick up the car directly ahead of me.

Denim skidded to a stop to assess the situation.

I rushed over to find Grace passed out in the back of the doorless vehicle that had been stripped of seats. Grace's hands were tied, her mouth was taped, and her ankles were bound.

For fuck's sake. "Stop the crane!" I shouted to Denim as I dove into the car. "Grace." I checked for a pulse, which was extremely weak, then tapped her face. "Honey."

Denim glanced into the car and froze.

"Stop whoever is steering that thing," I snapped harshly.

The grabber had already latched on to the vehicle's roof, its claws sharp and ready to mangle us.

Denim darted away.

I moved Grace to the opening. If I had to push her out of the car, she might break bones in the fall, but she would live.

I blew out a breath, managing to move her to the edge of the metal floor.

The car swung violently from one side to the other. I wrapped an arm around Grace's waist, but that didn't stop us from swaying from one side to the other in sync with the movement of the car.

I repeated my Sunday prayers as the movement died down, giving me a chance to steal a look in Denim's direction. It appeared from my vantage point through the fog that he was fighting with the driver.

"Joy! It's Dillon."

I glanced down to find Duke's other brother positioned below the dangling car and realized the car was higher than I thought. "Grace is out cold," I called to him.

"Throw her to me," Dillon said.

"We're too high up."

Once again, we were swinging, like Jason and I used to do at the park. My brother loved to push me on the swing, and I would always tell him to go higher.

Right now, I wasn't a kid in a park, and I wanted to live. I wanted to see my dad again. I wanted Duke to forgive me. I wanted answers on Jason's death.

As we jostled around, I held onto Grace as if she were my lifeline. But fate decided it wanted to give me a big fuck-you finger when we were thrown to one side, close to the opening. I lost my grip on her, and she fell out of the car.

Holy mother of all moments, please let her live.

I managed to lie on my stomach, latching onto the outer edge of the floorboard. I peered down and saw that Dillon had Grace in his arms.

Thank you, Lord.

Suddenly, the car began to lower, but my pulse rate didn't.

I sighed loudly, almost screaming as I hung my head.

The car finally touched the ground, and I didn't move, my mind processing what my next move should be. I needed to see Duke. I needed to make sure he was okay. That talk with Gwen began to seep into my synapses. The one in which she'd said I could have it all but wouldn't like the outcome. I didn't have it all. I hadn't found answers on Jason's death, but with my assignment officially over, I never would. On top of that, I hadn't brought Duke and the cartel down. I didn't see a truckload of guns. No evidence. No jail time.

The only thing I'd accomplished was falling for the enemy.

"Joy, are you okay?" Denim was suddenly beside me.

I lifted my head. "I'm fine. Go see your sister." I needed a moment.

"Lou Romano is staked to a metal pipe. He fell out of the cab." He pointed at an area near the crane. "Look, about your—"

"Fallyn," a familiar voice shouted.

Denim's brow furrowed at the sound of my real name. Whatever he was about to say would have to wait. I was sure the Harts would have words for me at some point.

"Seems my team is here," I mumbled as I climbed out of the shell of the car on shaky legs.

Denim jogged off as Gwen ambled up in full ATF gear.

Her blue eyes assessed me. "You look like hell."

"I feel like it too." I sat on the edge of the car's floorboard. "I couldn't wait for you. I had to be a fly on the wall for that meeting. But after I climbed through the bathroom window and listened in, the situation started to grow out of hand. Mateo had a gun to Rosario's daughter's head. I had to do something."

She hooked her thumbs in her bulletproof vest. "You'll have to answer to Kyle for that. I'm not here to scold you. I was worried about you, though, when you didn't answer my calls."

"I think I dropped my phone when I fell over a pipe on the back side of the building. Did you see Duke? Grace?"

"Paramedics are taking them both to the hospital, along with Rosario's daughter."

"Is he alive?" I held my breath.

"So far. Hopefully, they can get him to the hospital in time. It seems he lost a lot of blood."

"I shot him," I said. "If he dies, I don't know what I'll do." I dug my nails into my palms, swallowing my emotions. "He saved me, though. He threw himself between Mateo and me just as Mateo and I pulled our triggers."

She cocked her head. "So who killed Mateo?"

"Rosario. When I broke up the meeting, she didn't have a weapon in sight, but she had one in her coat pocket. Everything happened so fast. Duke was the only one who dropped his gun. Do you have Rosario in custody? I ran out of the building after Duke, leaving her inside with her daughter." Something I shouldn't have done, but I was concerned about Duke.

She nodded. "Ted has Rosario in the back of his cruiser."

A shudder racked my body as I pushed out a sigh.

"Duke planned all this with Detective Hughes," Gwen said. "The one thing Duke didn't see coming was you."

That had clearly been evident by the shock on Duke's face when he'd whirled his weapon in my direction. "We don't have the truckload of guns. I recall Mateo saying he sold them."

"What happened here will have consequences for Duke and Rosario," she said. "It might not be the prison time we'd hoped for, but there is a crate of guns in that building. I would suspect Duke is probably looking at five years or less, considering he brought Detective Hughes into the mix. Rosario, on the other hand, might be brought up on charges for Mateo's death."

"Her lawyer could argue she was stopping Mateo from firing his weapon again. If he had, I might be dead. I lost all thought when Duke went down."

"You did your job, Fallyn. What happens from here is out of our hands. We should get you checked out."

Dawn was breaking as we headed in the direction of the red-and-blue lights cutting through the thinning fog.

"I never found answers about Jason's death," I mumbled, my body beginning to feel the effects of the night. "I hate that I failed."

"This assignment was never about that, Fallyn."

"It also wasn't about falling for Duke. Yet here I am. I'm heartbroken, angry, and confused and feel like I didn't do my job to the best of my ability."

She came to an abrupt stop. "You can be hard on yourself. I get that. But you didn't compromise your morals. If you ask me, I think you helped Duke see that he needed to change. Or maybe you were the catalyst to force him to. The Duke I'd been chasing during my years with the ATF in Boston would've never worked with the cops. He would've never put his gun down. He would've never walked out of that building alive."

"That wasn't because of me but rather his sister."

She laughed. "Partly, I agree. But did you know that there are pictures posted on the Hart of Hope shelter's website and a few of them are of Duke and you? One in particular is of you and him on the dance floor. Now, it's clear to me from that photo that he's in love with you. I would bet my job that you played a role in making him see the light."

"It doesn't matter. As you said, 'love is about sacrifice,' and a federal agent and a lawbreaker are not a recipe for a long-term relationship."

Besides, I was a thousand percent sure that Duke would never want to see me again.

31

FALLYN

Later that day, after I'd debriefed my superiors on my assignment and, in particular, my actions at the junkyard, I chomped on my fingernails as I entered the hospital where Duke was being treated.

Special Agent in Charge Howard wasn't thrilled that I hadn't waited for backup and had given me a slap on the hand. I had yet to see my dad, but I had talked to him by phone. He was relieved I was alive, still the daughter he knew, and that my mission was over.

I had mixed feelings. Part of me was glad I didn't have to keep lying to Duke and his family. The longer I stayed undercover, the easier it would've been to become Joy Whitlock. The easier it would've been to fall into Duke's world. I would like to think I was resilient, and while I knew right from wrong and understood the consequences, my heart was a different matter.

The other part of me was going to miss Duke terribly. The way he looked at me as if I was the only one who made him happy. The way he made me feel as we enjoyed the best lovemaking I'd ever experienced. I kept replaying his words and confession at the gala as he held me in his arms.

A doctor nodded at me as I walked by him on my way to the information desk.

I didn't know how Duke was doing. No one had contacted me yet. After Gwen and I had talked to Detective Hughes and tried to round up Rosario and Mateo's men, I'd returned to the field office.

The body count from earlier that morning totaled two. One of the dead men was Mateo, and the other was Lou Romano. He'd been the one in the crane operating the car crusher. Denim had been questioned by Detective Hughes about Lou's death, but unless the DA wanted to prosecute, Denim was off the hook. He'd fought Lou to save Grace and me, and during the struggle, Lou had fallen out of the crane and onto a sharp object.

Rosario and Gustavo were behind bars for the time being. Rosario's soldiers and Mateo's gang members had fled when Detective Hughes and his unit converged on the junkyard.

The lady at the information desk was typing on her computer and had yet to acknowledge me.

A couple went into the gift shop. Two nurses strolled in behind them. For seven at night, the lobby was rather quiet. Visiting hours were until nine p.m.

A woman was on the phone in the hall, near a bank of elevators. It took me a moment to realize the head of blond curls belonged to Maggie Hart. I suspected that she might be covering the story for her news station.

I abandoned the information counter and beelined over to Maggie.

She pocketed her phone, her expression dour as she gave me the once-over. "Federal agent." Her green gaze flitted to the badge on my belt and my sidearm then up to my face. "I knew there was something about you that I couldn't put my finger on."

"Could that be why you weren't as accepting of me as Jade and Grace or the Hart brothers?"

She was an investigative reporter—sharp, intelligent, probably suspicious by nature, and not exactly the type to roll out the red carpet unless she knew you inside and out.

"Funny," she said. "I just got off the phone with a source of mine. I did some digging on the Williams family for nothing more than to satisfy my curiosity. Well, that and the name was familiar. I did a story on your brother, Jason, right after his death."

I reared back.

"That's right. It wasn't a big one because no one within the FBI would give out details." Her voice was even and businesslike. "But an FBI agent found overdosed on drugs could've been a meaty news segment. At the time I was pulling the facts together, I asked if Jason was undercover. Of course, no one would tell me. But he was, right?"

"That's correct." I had no reason to lie, and the circumstances of his death weren't exactly classified either.

"Did you go inside to find out what happened to him?" she asked.

"Who's asking? Maggie Hart, Dillon's wife? Or Maggie Marx, the news reporter?"

Her lips twitched. "I like you, Fallyn—or do you want to stick with Joy?"

"Fallyn," I said. Joy was a pretty name, but I had no reason to pretend anymore. "Learning the facts of Jason's death wasn't my priority. The stolen guns were, as well as taking down the cartel along with Duke. I'm ATF, not DEA. Did you know that Duke dealt in illegal weapons?"

She adjusted the green scarf around her neck. "Who's asking? Joy or Fallyn?"

"Touché," I replied.

"Bottom line, I don't go near Duke's business. I don't ask. I don't want to know. If Dillon was aware, he didn't tell me. My husband knows not to discuss Duke around me, although he did recently. He shared that you slept with Duke. Was that a ploy for information? Is that why they sent in a woman undercover?"

I snorted. "I volunteered. Duke and the cartel need to be stopped. Do you know how many murders take place because of illegal firearms?"

"Too many," she said. "I understand, Fallyn. I'm about upholding the law, but Duke isn't my responsibility. Nor is he Dillon's, Grace's, or Denim's. Since Dillon and I got together six years ago, I can count on one hand the number of times I've seen Duke. The last thing that man wants is for his family to be dragged into his mess. So if you're looking for people to testify against him, you're barking up the wrong tree."

"I'm not here to gather witnesses. I'm here to see how he and Grace are doing."

The middle-aged couple who'd gone into the gift shop strolled toward us. We waited until they passed us and got into the elevator.

"I don't think you're welcome in the Hart family right now." She sighed. "They're in a private waiting room while Duke is in recovery. Doctors pulled a bullet out from behind his left shoulder and another from just below his clavicle." She touched the area above her heart and below her collarbone. "He also had a dislocated shoulder from falling, it seemed. Not to mention the blood transfusion."

"And Grace?" I asked.

"She had a hefty dose of drugs in her system. But she's alert, angry, and worried. If I were you, I would give the Harts space."

I crossed my arms over my chest. "So Grace knows about me?"

"I'll put it this way," she said. "The brothers are taking the news about you better than Grace. Look, if it's any consolation, I was a rival gang member of the Hart brothers growing up. We fought against each other. And look at Dillon and me now. We're married and happier than ever. Of course, we were teenagers then. You and Duke are playing on an entirely more dangerous stage. But my point —I know he loves you. I would go out on a limb and say you have feelings for him. Otherwise, you wouldn't be here."

"It doesn't matter how I feel. I'm a federal agent."

"Is there a law that says you can't date a criminal who is turning his life around?"

It wouldn't look good for my career if I were dating a front man for the cartel. However, if Duke had been serious about redemption and was turning his life around, maybe there was a chance for us. After all, I had promised my dad I would leave the ATF when my assignment was over. But I'd joined the ATF because of Jason's death, and I still didn't have closure.

Ignoring her question because the answer wasn't simple, I said, "Your story on Jason—do you still have your files and notes that you could share with me? My brother didn't overdose intentionally, but the evidence we have tells us that he did. I know my brother wouldn't commit suicide."

"It's been a while since I did that story, but I'll look in my files."

The elevators dinged, then the doors opened. Grace Hart breezed out, and her expression was dark and dangerous.

The devil was about to pounce.

Maggie tossed a look over her shoulder. "My cue to run. I have a deadline anyway. I'll be in touch, Fallyn."

"Thank you," I said.

"Dillon is looking for you, Mags." Gone was Grace's light-and-airy voice. In its place was a sound that was rough and gritty, as if she'd shifted into a different person.

She stomped over to me like a soldier ready to do battle. If she'd been drugged, it wasn't evident.

I braced myself for impact, grounding my stance and straightening my spine. I would take my licks. I deserved whatever she had to dish out.

She pointed at my badge and gun. "Are you trying to shove that in our faces? Or think that you're better than us?" Tears welled up in her eyes. "Duke adores you, and you stabbed him in the heart. He took a bullet for you, and you shot him."

"How do you know that? It doesn't matter." The information wasn't classified. "You're right. I shouldn't have worn my badge and gun. It's a habit. I just came from work." I wasn't trying to excuse my actions. I should've thought before I came in.

"I heard Maggie talking to Ted on the phone about what you did." She shivered. "I should thank you for saving my life." No sincerity in her tone.

"Grace, I adore you. I never meant to hurt you. When it comes to your brother, well, it's complicated. What Duke was doing was illegal, and no matter how much I… care for him, I won't apologize for doing my job. I lost a brother undercover."

She didn't need to know that Jason had infiltrated Brian McCauley's organization. Or maybe she already knew that. She certainly seemed privy to information, if only because she listened to others' conversations.

"Is Duke going to jail?" she asked, slowly losing the attitude.

"That's not up to me," I said. "Look, I would like to see Duke. I understand he's not awake yet."

If it weren't for him, I might be the one in a hospital bed or in a morgue. Although I should thank Rosario as well.

More importantly, Duke and I had unfinished business. Whether he wanted to hear what I had to say, I had to get some things off my chest. I hadn't found closure on Jason, but I had a chance to say my piece to Duke.

"If he wants to see you."

"I'll check back later." I had nothing else to say to Grace. She needed time to process who I really was, her brother's situation, and the hell Mateo had put her through.

I pivoted on my heel, and when I reached the end of the hall where the information desk was, Grace called, "Duke loves you, you know."

"People keep telling me that," I tossed over my shoulder. "Except Duke."

After my big reveal, I wasn't counting on hearing those three little words from his mouth. Even if I did, I didn't know if it would make a difference.

32

DUKE

I slowly opened my eyes, wincing at the pain in my body and an annoying beeping sound. I blinked several times as the blur began to fade amid the harsh lights.

"Duke." Denim's voice was somewhere nearby.

I jolted upright, pain gripping my left side. "Where am I? Grace?"

He placed a hand in front of me. "Easy. She's fine. You're in the hospital."

I grunted as I examined myself. My chest felt heavy, as though a weight were pressing on it. I had one of those oxygen tubes in my nose and pads stuck to my chest along with an IV in my right hand. I tried to move my left arm but couldn't.

Then everything came screaming back. Joy. Fallyn. Bullets. Mateo on the floor. Me falling on my shoulder. Grace in danger. The heart monitor beeped like it was on steroids.

"Water," I said in a gravelly voice, trying to move saliva around in my mouth.

Denim poured water into a cup that was on a table beside the bed. "You're lucky you're alive." He brought the cup to my mouth and stuck the straw in.

I sucked it down as if I'd been in the Sahara Desert for weeks.

I choked on the last of the water, and some dribbled out the sides of my mouth.

A nurse, a petite brunette in pink scrubs, breezed in carrying a tray with a syringe on it. "Mr. Hart, you're awake. How do you feel?"

Denim moved out of the way while Ariel, as her name tag read on her scrubs, set the tray on a rolling table. "From one to ten, with ten being the worst, what's your pain level?"

"Seven," I said. "My left side. I can't move my arm either."

She fiddled with my IV then added the contents of the syringe into it. "That's because you dislocated your shoulder and we removed a bullet from your bicep. Not to mention the other bullet we removed from below your clavicle. You lost a lot of blood too."

"You coded, bro," Denim said on my left.

"How long have I been out?"

"Three days," she said. "I'm giving you a mild sedative. But if the pain gets worse, press this button." She placed a remote device on my lap, then she typed on a computer. "The doctor should be in to see you later this afternoon."

A cop poked his head in, and the heart monitor went crazy.

"That's one of Ted's guys," Denim said as if he knew why my pulse was going haywire.

I didn't see any cuffs on my wrists.

Ariel finished typing then left as though she was in a hurry.

"Why isn't a Fed standing guard outside?" I asked.

"Ted is in control at the moment." Denim sank into the chair beside the bed. "He's gone to bat for you."

I had made a deal with him that once Grace was rescued and safe, he could bring me in.

"He's been arguing with the Feds," Denim continued. "They're pissed that Ted didn't contact them."

That was another stipulation I'd had in exchange for Ted's help. The pain began to dull even more. "Is Grace okay?"

"She is, thanks to Joy—or rather, Fallyn."

The names were like acid on my brain as images bombarded me of her pointing a gun at me. I felt like she'd yanked my heart out of my chest. But I couldn't process what had happened or who she truly was, and frankly, I didn't want to. I'd been a fucking idiot.

"So she saved Grace?" I asked through clenched teeth.

"It was a team effort." Denim crossed one leg over the other. "But yeah. Lou Romano was about to crush the car that Fallyn found Grace in. I had to fight him off that crane. Things got a little hairy. Thank fuck that Dillon was there to help. Because of the efforts of the three of us, Grace survived. On top of that, Lou fell to his death."

My sigh could probably be heard throughout the hospital.

"Our sister is home resting. Also, Fallyn has been trying to see you," he said. "We're all shocked about her. Well, some more than others. Maggie had a feeling there was something off about her. Grace is hurt and angry."

"Fallyn." I liked the name better than Joy. "She was only doing her job."

He harrumphed. "You don't sound like you mean that. I can see the hurt on your face, bro. I know you love her. I knew that morning she came down to the bar. If I were in your shoes, I'm not sure how I would react. But at some point, you'll have to deal with her."

"No matter my feelings, she and I could never be. I'm pissed at myself."

He leaned his elbows on his knees. "You're usually spot-on in detecting frauds and bullshit. I would like to think I am as well. But I wasn't around her long enough. But did you see any signs, hints?"

Daylight spilled through the slats in the blinds as I thought about his question.

"She was nervous around me at times. She was indecisive about her and me, but she had valid reasons, like the boss-and-employee relationship." The incident with that bald guy who had roughed her up came to mind. Was that a show to get my attention? It had to be. I'd already determined that she hadn't followed me to the cemetery since nobody had tailed me that morning. She had to have been there visiting her mom and brother. That was where they were buried. "Bottom line is her beauty, grit, and smarts blindsided me from the moment I met her."

"You might want to add your dick to that list." He chuckled.

Detective Ted Hughes's throaty voice echoed in the hall as he said something to the cop outside my door, then he strutted in and up to the foot of my bed.

He smoothed two fingers over his thick mustache. "You're one lucky bastard, Duke."

"So Denim tells me," I retorted.

"Have you told him yet?" Ted regarded Denim.

I couldn't tell by his even tone if he had good news or bad, but he had agreed to go to bat for me if any charges were brought against me.

"Just that you're in charge and not the Feds," Denim answered.

Ted crossed his arms over his chest, grinning like a bastard. "Feds are livid with me that I didn't clue them in. Like I give a fuck. Anyway, I managed to cut a deal with them on your behalf."

"To keep me out of prison?" I asked as the sedative seemed to be kicking in.

"I wouldn't go that far," Ted said. "But for the time being, I vouched for you that you won't be a flight risk. So until they contact you for questioning, you won't be held in a jail cell. So don't fuck me, Duke. But just in case, I've put a man outside your door, and one will be with you when you're released from the hospital."

"I told you, man," I said. "I'm not running. I'm done."

"I suggest you find a good lawyer," Ted added. "But since you worked with me, that should help your case. They probably can't pin the guns on you. Actually, only three were found in a crate inside the building. The truck was empty."

"Mateo sold the guns."

"Well, Rosario killed Mateo," Ted said. "And most of his men fled the scene. Not sure we'll find any guns."

"You probably won't." My eyelids were heavy.

"The Feds are holding Rosario," Ted continued. "She'll probably be brought up on murder, among other charges, as will her lieutenant."

Denim sat up straighter. "Rosario is claiming she shot Mateo to protect you and Fallyn."

Wrinkles ringed Ted's dark eyes. "The woman probably will get off on a technicality. But as promised, I told the Feds she was working with me to save her daughter and Grace. In the end, Duke, you still have a big hill to climb with the Feds. Conspiring with the cartel to sell illegal firearms comes with some heat. You'll need a good lawyer."

"Dillon hired Kelton Maxwell to represent you," Denim announced. "Don't protest or whine about him, Duke. He's a great lawyer, even though you snarl whenever you hear the Maxwell name."

Thanks to Dillon. He'd shoved that family at me any chance he got, talking about how the Maxwell brothers were tight and we should be more like them. But the lawyer I'd had on my payroll had moved out of state several months ago, so I didn't have anyone else ready to go to bat for me.

The pain meds sank in even more.

"Denim is right. Kelton has made a good name in the criminal lawyers' circles in Boston," Ted confirmed. "I'm happy you're okay and that we saved Grace and Rosario's daughter, although we did lose two in that debacle."

"Lou and Mateo," Denim mumbled.

"I need to run," Ted said. "Get some rest, Duke. I'll be in touch." He started for the door. "Oh, and you should thank Agent Williams. If she hadn't broken up your meeting with Mateo, we probably would've had more dead bodies, as in yours and Grace's."

I growled—or tried to. All that came out was a strangled sound. Whether he was right about that, I was thankful nothing worse had happened to my sister.

Once Ted was gone, Denim chuckled. "I like Ted at times, and at other times, he can be a narcissistic asshole."

"He's got to get his digs in whenever he can," I said. "He's probably not wrong, though."

"Well, you saved Fallyn's ass. That also has to count for something."

I wasn't worried about what would happen to me from here.

He pushed to his feet. "Not that I want to pile more shit on your plate because it looks like you're about to pass out from the meds, but you should know that Fallyn's brother died while undercover in McCauley's camp."

Bells dinged in my head, or maybe that was the heart monitor. "You mean Jason Williams? Why didn't I connect that before now?" I asked myself more than Denim. "He overdosed, if I remember correctly."

"Fallyn doesn't think so. She thinks her brother was murdered."

"Was that why she was undercover?"

His head moved back and forth. "Yes and no. She's working with Maggie now. Mags did a story on Jason right after his death, and she offered to show Fallyn the files she compiled for the news segment. Did Brian have anything to do with Jason's death?"

"No." I swallowed the dryness in my throat. "I don't know the whole story. Brian said it was a dirty agent who was responsible."

His jaw came unhinged. "No shit?"

Silence dangled for a long moment as the room began to fade.

Denim was talking about Fallyn, but I couldn't keep my eyes open any longer.

33

DUKE

Kelton Maxwell, in his expensive Armani suit, smoothed a hand down his light-blue tie as we stood outside the ATF field office. "Today is just about questioning. If they're going to charge you with anything, then they'll have to take your case to the DA before they get a warrant." His blue eyes glinted in the daylight. "Are you prepared to discuss Agent Jason Williams if asked?"

I fidgeted with my cufflinks, nodding.

A week had passed since shit went down at the junkyard, and during that time I'd met with Kelton and bared my damn soul about my role as Rosario Mendoza's front man. On top of that, I shared what I knew about Williams's death. I'd brought up the topic only because I knew there was a chance that the Feds would ask since Fallyn was still on the hunt for answers about her brother.

I had to inform Brian McCauley that I might have to answer questions about Jason Williams. He would be cool with it if the Feds brought him in for questioning. After all, he wasn't guilty of Jason's death.

"Also, Christmas is in three days." Kelton looked around as people came in and out of the government building. "If the Feds end up arresting you, it probably won't happen until after the holiday, although they might jump through hoops to bring you in ASAP. But Detective Hughes has put his job on the line to assure them that you're not a flight risk. If it comes down to it, though, I can call in some favors."

"I'm not going anywhere," I felt compelled to say for the fifth time. Yet I understood how Feds operated, wanting that big win to fuck with the BPD because of territorial lines or whatever the government types fought over.

Kelton checked his watch. "We have twenty minutes. I need to make a quick phone call. There's a coffee shop on the second floor. Why don't we head that way?"

I had no desire to eat or drink anything. In fact, I'd hardly touched food since I'd woken up in the hospital.

As we entered the building, I rubbed my sore arm. Aside from the tiredness, I was slowly on the mend and could actually move my shoulder around.

"I'll wait in the lobby for you," I said.

I wanted to call Vince. He and I had met during the past week to go over scenarios of what could happen to him. He would definitely be questioned. He also had gotten Kelton to defend him, as had Brian. The immediate issue was closing down the Monarch for the time being and making sure my employees were compensated, at least during the holidays.

As Kelton darted off with his phone to his ear, I reared back when I spotted Dillon, Denim, and Grace seemingly admiring some artwork.

Grace ran up to me with that smile that always warmed my heart. "We're here to support you. We don't want you to go through this alone."

I'd never been so fucking happy that Grace had survived her kidnapping ordeal without injury. I'd actually shed tears when I finally saw her with my own eyes. Even now, my emotions were bleeding through my steel exterior.

Denim and Dillon came over to us, both wearing concerned expressions.

As brothers, we'd talked for hours about the what-ifs of me in prison. I laid out a plan and instructed them to take care of my personal belongings, which weren't many. The big one was the Monarch. Originally, I had wanted to hand the club over to Vince, but considering our predicament, Kelton suggested that I put the club in one of my brothers' names. Denim volunteered since Dillon had the shelter and was busy moving it to a larger space.

"We'll be here waiting for you," Dillon said. "Oh, and Maggie wanted me to tell you that Fallyn won't be in the room during your questioning."

Fallyn had been pouring over Maggie's notes and the news story she'd done on Jason Williams.

"I'm still angry with her." Grace wrapped her arm around my waist on my good side. "She doesn't deserve you, Duke." Betrayal weaved through her tone.

I was severely conflicted with a mix of emotions—humiliation, hurt, deception, and anger. I'd opened up to Fallyn. I'd even begged her, about to spill my soul as to how I felt about her, something I hadn't done with any woman. For hours on end, I couldn't resolve the battle between my heart and my mind. The crazy thing was if I saw her today, I wouldn't be able to stop myself from pulling her into my arms and kissing the fuck out of her.

"As I told Denim, Fallyn was only doing her job. I do need to thank her for saving your life." I squeezed Grace.

I also should probably thank her for busting up the meeting with Mateo. Like Ted had said, if she hadn't, there was a very high probability that the outcome could've been a lot worse.

Grace nudged me out of my haze. "*She's* here."

I followed my sister's line of sight to the elevators, as did Dillon and Denim.

Fallyn was with an older man who I would guess was her father since the resemblance was uncanny. The former FBI director glared in our direction, but the second my gaze landed on Fallyn, the damn butterflies in my stomach decided to come alive. Even more when she smiled, albeit sadly.

Suddenly, I was transported back to the gala, mental images of her in that sexy dress and of us on the dance floor assaulting me. The way she felt in my arms was perfect in every way. The way she made me feel calm and content, despite the chaos in my life, was something I hadn't known I needed yet craved to feel again. Even if I tried to forget her, to push her out of my mind, I couldn't. I saw her, and my resolve crumbled.

I took a deep breath and gathered my composure. This wasn't the time to air our differences—or for me to take her into a nearby room and have my way with her.

The elevator dinged, ending the emotion-filled look she and I were locked in.

My siblings were talking, but I wasn't registering anything they were saying.

As soon as Fallyn and her father were out of sight, I shook off the effect she'd had on my mind, body, and soul. It was time to dig deep to find that asshole in me. The one who wasn't bothered or swayed by anyone, no matter how beautiful or alluring she might be.

Ten minutes later, after leaving Denim, Duke, and Grace in the lobby, Kelton and I were sitting in a conference room rather than an interrogation room.

He busied himself in jotting down notes on a legal pad while I took a moment to glance out of the seventh-floor window, taking in Boston's sharp skyline.

A sense of bittersweetness hit me in the chest. The city had been my home for as long as I could remember, and its vibrant energy always kept me on my toes.

But now faced with a possible prison term, I couldn't help but think of all things I would miss—the delicious food at places like Yvonne's, the peaceful moments spent in museums when I needed to think, and even the chaotic sounds of the busy streets.

The door opened and zapped my nostalgic moment. Even more so when Fallyn sashayed in, that government badge glinting on her belt—a reminder of who she really was.

Alongside her was a clean-cut man in a suit, who appeared too eager for my liking. But his demeanor wasn't what sparked my nerves to make me bounce my knee. I never fidget. I never squirm. Yet there I sat watching every step Fallyn took as she looked everywhere but at me.

I leaned into Kelton and whispered, "It looks like they have hard evidence on me."

He swung his hand over to my leg that felt like it was moving faster than a speeding train. "Don't get ahead of yourself."

I came mentally prepared to accept the consequences. I came knowing that I was facing a possible prison sentence. I came prepared to answer every question truthfully. However, I suddenly felt uneasy sitting across from Fallyn, who was avoiding eye contact with me at all costs, while the man next to her dropped a folder on the table and settled into the seat next to her.

"Duke, I'm Special Agent in Charge, Kyle Howard. You already know Agent Williams. Let's begin with where were you on Saturday, November 4, around midnight? I'll add that was the night two cartel members were found dead outside a container yard near Boston Harbor."

Fallyn kept her gaze on her lap as she rubbed her hands down her legs. Come to think of it, she'd done that several times in my presence—a tell that she was nervous. Her trepidation, for whatever reason, seemed out of character from the badass, beautiful, gun-wielding agent I'd seen at the junkyard.

"What is Agent Williams doing here?" I asked. "She's acting like she's the one who's being questioned."

She lifted her chin quick as a whip and narrowed her eyes.

There you are. There's that defiance I like.

"Mr. Hart," Agent Howard said, "I'm the one leading this meeting, and we'll get to why Agent Williams is here in a moment." His egotism was showing. "Now, answer my question."

Feds always thought they were better than people in my line of work, and while Agent Howard should be applauded for upholding the law, he didn't need to act like a pompous fuck.

"I have a feeling you know where I was," I responded.

Kelton was jotting something down on his legal pad. "Were you staking out the area, Agent Howard?" His tone could cut ice.

I liked Kelton's cockiness, self-confidence, and composure. His attitude screamed that nobody should fuck with him or his clients. I could see why my brothers liked him.

Agent Howard studied Kelton and me.

"Duke is here to come clean," Kelton said. "So cut to the chase, or we can go to court."

Howard's face turned red. "I'm running this investigation, Mr. Maxwell. I call the shots. I'm also not the one with his feet to the fire."

I swung my arm in front of Kelton. "It's fine. I was near that container yard, but you were there too."

I threw out that last line to take his temperature, to confirm that I was right about that feeling I had that night of someone watching Vince and me.

Agent Howard regarded Fallyn, as if he thought she'd told me.

"Then you know I didn't kill those cartel soldiers," I continued.

"But you were there to pick up the guns that had been in the truck," Agent Howard said.

Fallyn hadn't taken her eyes off me. Maybe this was the perfect moment to ask her some questions.

"Did you follow me to the cemetery?" I asked her. "That bald guy in the club, was he a ploy to get my attention?"

"Mr. Hart," Howard warned.

Fallyn straightened. "I got lucky running into you at the cemetery. As for the bald guy, he was there to give me a message from another agent."

"Mr. Hart, I'll ask again. Were you at the container yard to pick up guns?" Agent Howard's abrasive tone was like nails on a chalkboard.

"I was," I said, glaring at Fallyn.

"So you admit that you're a front man for Rosario Mendoza," Howard said.

"I admit I was there to pick up the guns," I said. Kelton had counseled me to stick to the recent incident and nothing more.

"Do you know who ambushed the truck?" Fallyn asked.

"Mateo Alvarez."

"Why?" Howard took the lead.

"First, revenge. He thought by stealing the guns, it would create tension between Rosario and me to the extent that she would kill me if I didn't pay her."

"But instead she killed Tito," Howard added.

I shrugged. "Don't know." She had never explicitly spelled that out. I also wouldn't add more shit to her plate. "But Mateo thought so. He kidnapped her daughter. Then he took my sister."

"Why Grace?" Fallyn studied me like I was a science project.

I was beginning to think she was in the room to rattle my cage. In a way, she was doing exactly that. I was yearning like a mother-fucker to jump over the table and shake her until Joy came out. I was beginning to like Joy more than Fallyn.

"He thought I might bring the Feds in, set him up like my brother Denim had done with Tito. So he took Grace as assurance that I didn't." My tone was even. "But I guess the joke is on me. Right, Fallyn?"

Her upper lip twitched like she was about to bare her teeth.

I wondered what I had done to piss her off all of a sudden.

"Where are the guns that were in that truck?" Howard asked.

"You'll have to ask Mateo that." I infused sarcasm into that line.

Kelton straightened his posture. "My client has answered your questions. He has nothing else to give you. Besides, you have

Rosario Mendoza in custody. I hear she's cooperating, so what more do you need?"

Howard stabbed a finger at me as if it were a dagger. "I want this thug in jail. He's been selling illegal firearms for years."

"Can you prove that?" Kelton asked. "Because all you have is what you saw that night at the container yard. My client didn't pick up any guns. And if Agent Williams overheard anything while undercover or had any listening devices, I doubt any of it would hold up in court."

"Who killed Emilio Vazquez?" Fallyn's fingers were interwoven so tightly that her knuckles were white.

Kelton regarded me, silently asking who Emilio was. I'd forgotten about the low-ranking soldier of Rosario's who had become a snitch for Mateo. "After Gustavo and I talked to Emilio, we let him go."

"You did with orders to get a message to Mateo," Fallyn said, not asked. "I was at the factory that day, listening."

I should be surprised, but I wasn't. "Okay, then you know it wasn't me who killed him. I was at the club all night with you."

Howard whipped his head around to look at Fallyn, his expression kind of priceless, as if he was jealous.

Fallyn's cheeks reddened as she pursed her lips. "Mr. Hart, do you know anything about the death of Jason Williams?"

Howard leaned close to her ear and whispered something that made Fallyn tighten her jaw.

"I might," I said.

Howard snapped his spine straight, darting his brown gaze my way. "You do?"

I was ready to blow this joint. "Just come out and ask whatever it is you need to know."

Feds and their secrecy made me want to jump out of the seventh-floor window. I was already about to explode, since I had to keep looking at Fallyn while I thought about her naked, me deep inside her, and the fact that she had outsmarted me.

Fallyn opened her mouth, and I held up my hand. "Jason Williams, aka Steve Montgomery, worked for Brian McCauley as a mechanic at one of his dealerships and befriended a coworker, who got him hooked on drugs. Then one day he was found dead from an overdose. Police questioned Brian and his employees but had no evidence to charge anyone for the death."

"That's public knowledge," Howard said.

Kelton nodded at me.

I rested my forearms on the table. "Here's what's not. You should look within your ranks for the answers you're seeking."

Fallyn and Howard exchanged a knowing look.

"Do you know who Duke is talking about?" Kelton asked.

Agent Howard opened a folder and slid a photo over to Kelton and me. "Have you seen this man before?"

In the photo, Neal Fitzgerald and Brian were talking—or rather, arguing. I knew why. When Brian had learned what Neal had done to Jason, he'd almost strangled the DEA agent because Brian knew he would get blowback. The law had been watching him like a hawk for months.

"Once," I said. "At Brian's dealership. He's DEA. Neal Fitzgerald."

"Did he kill my brother?" Fallyn's hazel eyes were filled with tears.

"As far as I know, yes. But you'll have to ask Neal yourself. My information is secondhand."

"Mr. McCauley is my client as well," Kelton said. "He's willing to testify to what he knows to be true."

Brian could be setting himself up for other charges, such as drug trafficking, but he was prepared to accept what came his way. With Rosario in jail, her drug and gun businesses were dead in the water.

"Did Neal confess to murdering my brother to Brian?" Fallyn asked, muscles tense.

"I believe so, but again, you'll need to go to the source."

"Are you willing to testify as well about Jason's death?" She brushed a tear away.

Kelton cleared his throat. "Ms. Williams, I'm very sorry for your loss, but we're here about my client's involvement with that stolen gun shipment and nothing more."

"Talk to Neal," I said to Fallyn. "Also, Brian has witnesses who saw Neal and your brother arguing outside Brian's dealership. That's how Brian found out that Jason was an undercover operative. Brian planned to fire your brother, but then he was found dead."

Fallyn tore out of that room like the Flash, the door slamming shut in her wake.

"I guess we're done here," Kelton said, standing.

Howard also rose. "Not so fast. Once I talk to the DA, Duke will be brought up on charges of conspiring with the Colombian cartel to sell illegal firearms. We're going to hold Duke until we can get a warrant for his arrest."

Kelton buttoned his suit jacket. "Are you telling me that you'll have the warrant within twenty-four hours? That's how long you can hold him, and I doubt you'll reach the DA and a judge by then since it's Christmas weekend. I would also like to remind you that Mr. Hart cooperated with the Boston PD during the incident at the junkyard. Not to mention, he saved your agent's life. Finally, Detective Hughes has one of his men on Duke."

"If that's true," Howard asked, "where is he?"

Kelton chuckled. "Outside by my car. Do you honestly think that Duke can do anything inside a federal building?"

Agent Howard collected his folder as a long beat of silence filled the room, his nostrils flaring. "Mr. Hart, you're lucky you have Detective Hughes on your side. We'll be in touch."

I had no doubt this wasn't the end of things. As Kelton and I were escorted out, I caught sight of Fallyn in another windowed room, her arms flailing around as she stood in front of her dad.

The look on his face was one of pure rage, but when he saw me, he stormed out of the room.

"You motherfucker." He marched in my direction. "I should call in my favors and put you away for the rest of your life."

I raised my good arm. "Slow your roll. I didn't kill your son."

"But you knew who did," he shouted.

Office workers and other agents watched in quiet fascination.

Fallyn rushed to his side. "Dad?"

I held up my chin, standing at his height. "If someone like Brian or me came to you with the news right after your son's death, would you have believed us? No. You would've brought us in, interrogated us, probably set us up to take the fall because the government can do that."

"McCauley is probably lying to protect himself," Fallyn's dad said.

"Then bring him in," I replied. "Question him."

"Mr. Maxwell," Fallyn said, "I suggest you take your client and leave."

Kelton touched my arm. "Come on. They know where to find you if they have any more questions."

I laughed at the sight of agents surrounding us with their hands on their sidearms. They were itching for me to give them a reason to shoot me dead.

Instead, I gave Fallyn a disgusted look before Kelton and I walked out. As much as she still affected me, she and I were a bad match for each other.

34

FALLYN

My fingers were aching from the force of my own nervous biting as I impatiently waited for Neal Fitzgerald to be brought into the ATF office. My head was spinning, like I'd spent days on a merry-go-round, from questioning Duke just six hours prior and from the tense encounter between him and my dad.

Every word Duke had said to Dad was spot-on. No matter if Brian or Duke had come clean back then about Neal, government officials wouldn't have listened.

Regardless, it was clear Duke didn't want anything to do with me. The hate on his face before he'd left the building confirmed that very thing. I shouldn't be surprised, and in part, I wasn't. Hurt was more like it. But I had to tell him how I felt, assuming he would even listen.

"Sweetheart, you need to sit down." My dad had almost passed out after I told him about Neal Fitzgerald. His anger toward Duke had raised his blood pressure to the point that we almost had to call the paramedics.

I laughed. "Says the man who was ready to throw Duke threw a window. I'm going to send Neal through it."

I'd been scouring Maggie Hart's old files and watching her news segments on her coverage of Jason's death, and I found something that had given me reason to pause and believe Duke.

While Maggie had been on camera outside Jason's apartment the day authorities found my brother's body, there was a person in the crowd, but his face had been obscured by a ball cap and sunglasses. I wouldn't have looked at him twice until the camera panned out to show more of what was going on in the area. That man had gotten into a government-issued vehicle. All I could think about was the picture Gwen had shown me of Neal with Brian, but I couldn't read the license plate number. I'd only been able to see the U.S. on the plate.

Even before Duke had come in for questioning, we were already investigating and combing through our database to find out which vehicles had been in the area that day, since all government vehicles had trackers on them. Our tech guys had yet to discover anything. None of us in the ATF office, and even my dad, wanted to believe one of our own would take out a colleague, especially the FBI director's son.

"I'm not sitting until I know for sure if Neal is guilty," I said.

"He's not going to admit to that," Dad said.

The lights of Boston's skyline began to twinkle as dusk set over the city. I wanted all this mess put behind me. I wanted to finally get the closure Dad and I were looking for. I wanted to curl up by a fireplace, preferably with Duke, but that wasn't about to happen.

My dad patted the table in front of the chair beside him. "Please sit for me."

I huffed and gave in, blowing out a heap of air as I sank into the leather seat. "Why are you so calm now? You were ready to knock out Duke earlier."

"Believe me, sweetheart, I'm still as furious as hell not only with Duke but about what could be true about Neal. But let's talk about Duke and you. I have been skirting the elephant in the room for the last several days, which was one reason I laid into Duke."

"I don't want to talk about him."

He regarded me with his fatherly expression that I'd seen many times when he was about to give me a speech or punish me. "We're going to. You've been on edge since Duke was shot. I know you have feelings for him. I'm not thrilled about that. He's not the right man for you."

I couldn't stop laughing even if I wanted to. "There's nothing to worry about, Dad. Duke hates me. You saw the way he looked at me."

Dad glanced past me and stiffened.

I turned to find Gwen and Bruce hauling Neal Fitzgerald into the conference room.

Finally.

Dad and I would have the opportunity to interrogate Neal while Bruce and Gwen stood by as witnesses.

"What's this about?" Neal asked with fear on his pockmarked face as Gwen shoved him into a chair across from Dad and me. "What is the former FBI director doing here?"

"Looking for my Christmas gift that Santa hasn't delivered to me in the last few years," Dad said with a bite to his tone as he flipped over the photos in front of him and slid one over to Neal. "What were you doing with McCauley in this photo that was taken in October?"

Neal studied the picture. "DEA business is none of yours."

"Are you undercover?" Dad asked.

"McCauley is an informant of mine," he said.

"Liar," I mumbled.

My dad showed another picture to Neal—a screenshot taken from the video footage when Maggie was covering my brother's story. The photo depicted a man in a ball cap among the crowd. "Who's this standing behind the two young ladies?"

Neal took one look at the image, and his head shot up. "I don't know."

I glared at Neal. "Careful."

"Where were you four years ago when my son was found over-dosed in his apartment?" Dad asked.

"You expect me to remember that far back," he said, his eyebrows lifting.

"The pic in front of you is time-stamped the day Jason's body was found in his apartment." I squared my shoulders. "In that photo is a government vehicle. Were you driving it that day?"

"You're trying to pin his murder on me?" His mouth dropped open.

"Who said he was murdered?" Dad asked.

Neal glanced at Gwen and Bruce, who were guarding the door, as if they could come to his rescue.

"We know you shot Jason with an overdose of drugs." I didn't know that, but I wanted to see his reaction.

Neal just sat there. "I want my lawyer."

My dad was on his feet and slapped his hands on the table as he leaned over in Neal's direction. "Did you kill my son?"

"I said I want my lawyer."

The veins on Dad's neck bulged. "You're going to need more than a lawyer by the time I get done with you."

Both Gwen and Bruce flinched.

"You know that government vehicles have tracking devices, right?" I asked.

That comment did faze Neal.

I was on the table and throwing myself at Neal. "You son of a bitch. Answer the questions." My hands were around his throat.

Gwen rushed over. "Fallyn, we need him if we want the truth."

I let go, and Neal choked out a laugh. "You have nothing on me."

I climbed off the table as Neal popped out of the chair.

"We have a witness." My stomach knotted as my hands shook.

Neal laughed. "Who? Brian McCauley? He won't testify. He would only be incriminating himself. His ego is too fucking big to do such a thing."

"Oh, you think Brian will go to jail for what?" I asked.

"Drug running," Neal said. "Not to mention, if he knows who killed Jason, then he's liable as well."

My dad's laugh sent shivers down my spine. "You know, I will roll out the red carpet for McCauley where he won't see the inside of prison."

"You can't do that." Neal's brown eyes were wide with fear.

"Oh, you don't know the influence I have," Dad said confidently. "To murder one of your own is a sacrilege."

"No jury will believe a thug like McCauley," Neal argued like he would win against my dad or even a jury.

"I'll make it so a jury convicts you," Dad said.

It was as if Duke had given him that idea earlier when Duke intimated in so many words that the government was corrupt.

Neal turned as white as a ghost. "You can't do that."

"Want to try me?" Dad fired at him.

"Why did you do it?" I asked, even though Neal had yet to admit his guilt.

Neal sighed loudly, defeat washing over him. "Jason was about to narc on me."

My dad dropped into his chair, holding his chest. "You motherfucker." His voice cracked.

"I tried to reason with him that night," Neal continued. "But he wouldn't listen."

Gwen stood, ready to intervene in case I lashed out at Neal again.

"So you pumped a ton of drugs into him?" I asked, my tears flowing freely.

Sweat beaded on Neal's forehead. "Not right then. I waited until later when he was passed out. Word was he was hooked on drugs, and he had a lot of them in his apartment."

"Take him," Dad ordered Gwen and Bruce. "Lock him up."

Gwen clutched Neal's arm and all but dragged him to the door.

"I'm not going to prison," Neal said.

Suddenly, déjà vu slapped me across the face as I remembered Mateo's words right before he pulled the trigger.

I couldn't have stopped time even if I tried when Neal grabbed Gwen's gun from her holster. The two fought as Bruce drew his weapon, but Neal already had Gwen's gun, aiming the weapon at Bruce then Gwen.

"You don't want to do this." Gwen backed away, raising her hands in the air.

"Man, drop it," Bruce ordered, ready to fire.

"He wants you to shoot him," I said to Bruce. "Neal, you're not about to get out of this that easily."

Neal smirked. "Watch me." In a flash, he pressed the gun to the underside of his chin and pulled the trigger.

For the longest moments, no one moved. Dad finally came over and wrapped his arms around me.

I couldn't say it felt good to witness Neal take his own life, but maybe now Dad and I could finally get the closure we'd been hoping for.

35

―――――

FALLYN

Christmas came and went. Dad and I had spent the holiday watching football and movies while his new four-legged companion, Rosie, snuggled up next to us. While I was content that the mystery of my brother's death had been resolved, I still felt on edge. If anything kept me awake at night, it was the unresolved issues I had with Duke—or rather, the lack of opportunity to say my piece to him.

And then—color me surprised—Duke had called and asked if we could talk. I'd jumped at the chance. Although we were waiting for a warrant to arrest Duke, he was still a free man because it seemed few judges worked between Christmas and New Year's.

I rode the elevator up to Denim's penthouse where we were meeting. I knew it was over between Duke and me. I knew we could never be a couple. Did I want that? I wasn't sure. For now, I did want to get some things off my chest.

The elevator came to a stop, but my pulse sped up as the doors opened into the penthouse.

A Christmas tree twinkled in the living room. The dining table

238

was no longer in the wide space between the kitchen and living room where it had been during Thanksgiving.

Duke stood in front of the wall of windows directly ahead of me, looking out at Boston's skyline. "I always loved living here."

I stayed close to the elevator, not sure what to do or even say. I had a speech planned. I'd even practiced it on the drive into the city.

But when he turned around, I forgot my words for the moment. He looked better than when I'd first met him at the cemetery. Gone was the coldness in his eyes. In its place was warmth and, dare I say, peace. His sandy-brown hair had grown, and it curled on the nape of his neck. His close-shaven beard was groomed nicely, and I was digging the jeans and button-down shirt he was wearing.

"You look happy," I said.

He strode half the distance toward me and stopped, his gaze sweeping over me. "You look tired."

I laughed. "I have a lot on my mind. Where's Jade and Denim?"

"They're at Dillon's house so we have privacy to talk."

Tension strung us together so tightly that I was having trouble breathing.

His unwavering gaze was nail-biting, and I had no nails left after the Neal incident.

"I'm listening," he said.

"You have nothing to say?"

He leaned his shoulder against a round beam. "I have a lot, but I understand you've been wanting to talk to me. So ladies first."

His nonchalant attitude was unnerving. "Did you hear about Neal Fitzgerald?" I asked.

"Kelton told me," he said. "I also heard Brian won't be touched by the Feds, and neither will Vince."

I shrugged. "The ATF doesn't have anything to charge Brian or Vince with. But both of them should find legal ways to make money. Rosario will be charged with murder and the selling of illegal firearms. I suspect she'll be behind bars for quite some time, unless she has a really good lawyer."

Silence dangled for a beat as I thought of what to say next. Again, I'd planned several things to say, but looking at him, I was losing all thought. I just wanted to feel his arms around me. I wanted him to tell me everything would be okay between us. But that was a pipe dream, especially if he was going to prison.

"Are you happy, Fallyn?" he asked.

My name on his lips was a chef's kiss. "If you think I'll apologize for doing my job, I won't."

"That's not what I asked," he bit out, seemingly angry all of a sudden. "Frankly, if you did, then you aren't the woman I thought you to be."

"What kind is that?"

"Gritty, tomboy, take no prisoners. The person I witnessed at the junkyard is not standing before me either. Nor was she in that conference when your boss thought he had my case sewn up."

I snorted. "Agent Howard is a good agent and a good man."

"I don't give a shit about your boss. I want to know if you're happy. You got everything you wanted."

My eyebrows drew down. "Did you call me here to act like an asshole?"

"I want to see the woman I fell in love with," he said. "I want to see Joy. The person I see right now is different."

"This is a test?" I asked. "I'm not any different. Joy was just a name. Maybe I was acting on some occasions, but I never acted when we made love. That was real for me. I didn't lie when we were in the gym that first morning. I did want to fuck you. I did want us to get past the sexual tension. The way we kissed wasn't fake either. I was falling each time you kissed me. We aren't any different, Duke."

His gaze roamed wild and free, and he didn't say anything for a few beats. "Yeah. How's that?"

"I had a job to do, and so did you. Nothing would've stopped you from saving your sister or finding those guns. You tucked your feelings away and did what you had to do. I did the same, although that night I was about to tell you how I felt. But you never gave me the chance."

"Here we are," he said, not showing any sign of emotion. "I'm all ears."

"You know what?" I ground my back teeth. "I'm out." I started for the elevator, holding in the scream that was stuck in my throat.

In three strides, he was grabbing me by the arm then spinning me around. "We're not done yet."

I let out a strangled laugh. "I think we are."

"We won't work," he said.

"Says who? You can't help who you love. I'm in love with you, Duke Hart."

He moved hair off my face. "You can't be."

"Stop fighting this." I wanted to stomp my foot. "What are you afraid of?"

"Never seeing you again," he said quickly and emotionally. "Never being able to touch you, like I'm doing now. Never breathing in your scent. Never seeing your smile. Never having another chance to make love to you."

I seated my hands on his waist. "You don't know that will happen."

"Regardless, if I go to prison or not, I need space. I need time to think, time to find who I really am."

"You still want me? I might be sending you to prison."

He swiped a finger over my lips. "No one is responsible for what I've done except me. And by no means should you take credit if I'm incarcerated. Let's be real." He sighed. "You didn't have any evidence on me. Sure, you overheard shit, but that wouldn't hold up in court. I made the decision and planned to save my sister. If the guns had been there, then I would've taken the heat. My actions leading up to this moment were all me."

"Who are you, Duke Hart?"

He smirked, sexy and dangerous. "I'm the man who's in love

with *you*." He pressed his forehead to mine. "I'm the man who would never ask you to compromise your morals for me. I'm the man who has never said 'I love you' to a woman in my life."

Between his confession and his scent, I was having a difficult time concentrating on my own feelings. But I didn't have to. The way my heart was ramming against my chest, the sweat on my palms, the dryness in my throat, the unshed tears, and everything else coursing through me at breakneck speed was evidence enough that I was so deeply in love with him that it hurt. The pain was greater because we might not be free to be together for five or even ten years, if my superiors got their way.

I was done thinking. I was done waging war on whether we would make a good match. Love wasn't perfect. Love was messy, and I wanted to be his mess.

I started to rise up on my toes but didn't have to as he lowered his head and cupped my face. "I'm so in love with you, Fallyn Williams. Whatever happens from here, know that you have my heart and soul."

I blinked away tears, melting in his arms as our lips locked— soft, gentle, slow, and sweet.

"I love you," I said between breaths. "I'm yours, Duke. I've never loved this hard before. I never felt elated and pained all at the same time. I need you."

I was crying as I thought about him going to prison. It gutted me to think it could be years before I would again get the chance to feel his arms around me, see the way he looked at me when I walked into a room, or experience all the other things he did that made me love him.

"My world makes sense with you in it," he whispered as he tugged on my bottom lip.

I wanted to stay in his arms forever, but sadly, destiny had other plans.

A phone rang somewhere in the room.

He froze as if he knew who was calling.

"What's wrong?" I asked.

"My lawyer is here," he said, sauntering over to the phone by the elevator doors. "He called this morning to tell me he was meeting with the DA and a judge." He lifted the receiver. "Yeah. Send him up."

I shook my head. "Do you know the verdict?"

He hung up. "I don't. Will you stay?"

"Of course." Talk about a panic attack. I started practicing my breathing as if I were going into labor.

Duke was rather pale as he waited for the elevator doors to open. Minutes later, when they did, I felt sick.

Kelton Maxwell stepped into the penthouse with one of those deadpan expressions, but when he regarded me, questions danced in his blue eyes.

"Just saying my peace," I said.

"What's the verdict?" Duke asked, shoving his hands into his jean pockets.

"Do you want her to hear this?" Kelton asked.

"She's cool," Duke said.

"Judge Dixon had a chance to weigh the facts in the case, including how you worked with BPD and saved Fallyn's life and that this is your first offense. The DA fought for ten years. I fought for time served. After all, the government has the source of the weapons, Rosario Mendoza. Plus, there were only three assault rifles on-site, which can't be proven to belong to you. But—"

Duke and I said "fuck" in unison.

"The judge feels you need to pay for your role in this mess. He slapped a one-year sentence on you, but you can be out in six months on good behavior."

Happy tears streamed down my face as I threw myself at Duke. "This is great news." At least I thought so, considering how adamant Agent Howard was to lock Duke up for at least ten years.

He held me tightly for a beat, shaking in my arms, before securing Kelton into a hug.

"Thank you, man," he said to Kelton, sounding choked up.

Kelton laughed as he eased away. "Dillon always said you were a cold bastard. Could've fooled me."

"He's right." Duke grinned. "I don't hug many people. I really appreciate you going to bat for me."

"Don't thank me just yet," Kelton said. "You'll need to pay a fine of two hundred fifty thousand, and the ATF is seizing the Monarch. I'm sorry, but I wasn't able to save your club. They're planning on auctioning it off."

I had rather liked working at the club. "That's all they're seizing?"

"Yes," Kelton said. "Duke doesn't have much more than that."

"No bank accounts?" I regarded Duke.

"Not important," he said. "When are the cops coming for me?"

I got the feeling he had more assets than the club, and I would bet they were hidden.

Kelton glanced at his Rolex. "They should be here within the hour. You might want to call your brothers. I'm also required to wait here with you, but I have calls to make. Do you mind if I use Jade's office?"

"Go ahead," Duke said. "You're her boss anyway."

I remembered Jade telling me at Thanksgiving that she worked for a lawyer, but that didn't matter.

"How do you feel?" I asked Duke when Kelton was out of the room.

Duke pulled me into his arms. "Free. Relieved. Happy. It could've been so much worse." He pecked me on the forehead. "I never thanked you for saving my sister."

"And I never thanked you for saving me. I'm sorry I shot you, though."

"Would you do me a favor?" he asked, rubbing the scar on my forehead.

"Anything."

"I can't ask you to wait, but could you watch over Grace?"

"Of course. Is there something going on?"

"She's raw, emotional, has PTSD from her ordeal in sex trafficking, and sometimes she likes to take matters into her own hands when she sees women on the street being abused. But she's supposedly starting at Boston University after the New Year. That should keep her busy. Just in case."

"You really would die for those you love," I said matter-of-factly.

His response was a fierce, desperate kiss, needy and emotional, that left me breathless and dizzy. "Especially you."

No matter what happened from here, Duke Hart would always have a place in my heart.

36

———

DUKE

ELEVEN MONTHS LATER

The sun on my face had never felt so good as I walked out of prison. I thought I would've been out in six rather than eleven months. I hadn't gotten into any brawls. I'd kept my head down, minded my own business, and done as I was told by the guards. But the government tape and paperwork had taken longer.

With the exception of my brothers, no one knew I was leaving prison today. We hadn't wanted to tell Grace and get her hopes up in case something with my parole fell through the cracks. Plus, my brothers wanted to surprise her at a birthday party Denim and Jade were throwing for her in a few days.

I hadn't seen Grace since Christmas last year. The day my lawyer came to Denim's penthouse to deliver the news about my sentence, I only had time to call her and my brothers before the cops showed up to take me in. Besides, I couldn't bear to see anybody in my family in tears, especially Grace.

During my incarceration, I'd decided that I didn't want any visitors either. However, I had spoken to my family maybe three times when I had phone privileges. I wanted to create as much space from the outside world as possible to give me time alone to think, decompress, and find myself. I'd never had a chance to understand who I really was.

As a kid, I'd been a father to my siblings. They'd come first. As an adult, I did whatever it took to survive, always running, protecting, and doing my best to stay alive.

I wouldn't say that prison had been cushy, but it gave me time alone when I didn't have to bark orders, run businesses, or worry that an enemy would try to kill me. Lying in my cot at night with deafening silence rather than the loud music of the nightclub, I'd thought about what my future would look like—the boxing gym I wanted to open, the self-defense classes I wanted to teach to the battered women from Dillon's shelter, the family I might want to start. The last one scared the fuck out of me, though.

I wanted only one woman to start that family with, but I didn't know if Fallyn was even available. In fact, if one of my siblings had brought her up when we talked by phone, I would have cut them off. I couldn't handle hearing about her or if she had a man in her life. That would've made me go ballistic, and I might've done something stupid to increase the length of my prison sentence.

The cold November wind blew over me as I strode toward Denim. It had been one year almost to the day that the shitstorm started that night of the ambush. One year since I'd met Joy—or rather, Fallyn. She'd been the star of my dreams and the keeper of my heart for the last three hundred days.

I'd wondered constantly what she was up to, if she thought of me, and if she missed me like I missed her. But again, I hadn't wanted to see her or hear about her.

Now that I could finally breathe in fresh air, she was definitely someone I wanted to track down, but I was scared out of my fucking mind that she had moved on, found a guy, gotten married, and become pregnant.

Denim and Vince stood by my SUV, grinning like kids in a candy store.

"Vince? Holy shit. How are you?" In one of my calls with

Denim, he'd told me that the Feds had questioned Vince, but since he hadn't been at the junkyard or involved in how things had gone down, the Feds had nothing to hold him on. Brian had also been questioned but not about guns. Rather, the Feds had wanted to know about Neal Fitzgerald.

Denim flicked his thumb at Vince. "I brought this guy along."

I gave them both the hugs of all hugs. "I've never been happier to see you."

Denim chuckled. "Prison sucks, doesn't it? At least you were only in for eleven months. I was in for six years."

"You're a stronger man than me." I would've dealt, though, if I'd gotten that ten years the ATF had recommended.

"You look relaxed, man," Vince said, his blue eyes glistening. "I don't think I've seen you in better shape either. Seems to me prison suited you."

"I wouldn't go that far. But there's not much to do other than eat, sleep, work, and exercise." Truth be told, I'd actually enjoyed the boxing matches I started during the free time prisoners had to exercise. I also had the opportunity to spend time learning about architecture. I drew the layout of that gym I wanted to open, and I'd found that I wasn't actually bad at design.

"What about you, Vince? You seem happy," I said.

"Life has been okay," he said. "Amber and I are probably leaving Boston soon. We're looking to settle near her family in Colorado."

I would hate to see him go. He and I had been together since our late teenage years. He was like a brother to me. I'd thought about leaving New England as well. Maybe I would one day.

"We should get together before you do," I said.

He gave me a nod as he got into the back seat. "We'll have plenty of time."

Denim circled the hood to the driver's side of the SUV. "Anyone try to shank or fuck with you?"

"Not really." I climbed into the passenger seat. "If so, we aired out our differences in the ring. Guards loved it because they could bet on us."

Laughing, Denim pulled out of the lot. "Sounds like you had a better experience than me."

"I wouldn't go that far," I said. "So, tell me, how's my niece? How's fatherhood?"

"Amazing. I wanted kids but never thought I would see the day I would become a father, especially when I was in prison. But Lily Rose Hart is the most precious thing ever. She has black hair like her mom—and wouldn't you know?—she has blue eyes like me."

I cleared the emotions from my throat. "I'm proud of you, bro."

"Jade wanted to name her Savannah, but I argued against it. The name is too raw for our family."

"For everyone," Vince chimed in, knowing what I'd gone through for years.

As much as I still thought about Savannah, I'd made peace with her death and with my guilt over what had happened to her. I'd even talked to the prison counselor about Savannah. She'd recommended that sometimes the best therapy was journaling, which I found cathartic.

I leaned an elbow on the console. "It would've been okay."

"Not for me," Denim said. "As much as I love my wife, I didn't want a constant reminder of my past, and Savannah was just that since I'd been her dealer. We need to move forward, Duke. We had a fucked-up childhood. Our teenage years in gangs weren't pretty, and most of all, you and I didn't take the right paths like Dillon did. I won't even start on Grace's life."

"Can we make a stop in Weston at the cemetery? All of us can pay our respects, which might help each of us. Plus, I need to see her grave before we head to your place. My counselor recommended not to forget those you loved."

"I wouldn't mind," Vince said. "I'm trying to clear up some of my own demons as well."

He'd had to deal with her drug addiction as much as I had.

Denim looked at me like I was a nutjob. "You really have changed. I didn't even have a counselor in prison. Or rather, I chose not to talk to one. I was too fucking angry with the world."

Denim's phone rang, and Dillon's name came across the SUV's monitor.

I hit the answer button. "Hey, man."

"It's so good to hear your voice," Dillon said excitedly. "I would've been there, but I'm in the midst of moving the shelter to its new home."

"You should see Duke," Denim said. "Our older brother is broader and leaner than ever and sounds like he found himself."

Dillon laughed. "I can't wait to see you, Duke. Also, I know you wanted us to keep your early release hush-hush, but I just learned that our eavesdropping sister overheard me talking to Denim on the phone this morning. She dropped by to pick up more of her clothes. I told her to keep her mouth shut for now."

"Does she know about her birthday party?" Denim asked.

"No," Dillon said on a sigh. "Duke, Grace is doing well at BU. You'll be proud of her. She's also living in the dorms and loving the whole college experience."

"That makes my heart so fucking happy," I mumbled.

"I need to run," Dillon said. "Denim, make sure you fill him in. I'll see you guys later."

Once Denim merged into highway traffic, he sighed. "Jade has a room ready for you."

I eyed my brother, waiting. "Fill me in on what?"

He regarded Vince briefly. "I'm trying to figure out how to tell you."

"Just say it, man," Vince encouraged Denim.

For the first time in a while, my stomach sank with that feeling of gloom and doom. Fuck. I hadn't felt that since the day I was carted off to prison.

"Who died? Please tell me it's not someone close to me."

Other than my siblings, the only important people in my life were Brian, Vince, and Fallyn, and Vince was in the car. I prayed nothing happened to Brian or Fallyn. But my mind went to Fallyn. Considering that she was a federal agent, her job was as dangerous as mine had been.

I gently backhanded my brother on the shoulder. "Speak already."

"You didn't want us telling you about Fallyn while you were inside," he started as he moved into the high-speed lane. "She's fine, by the way."

I sighed loudly. "But?"

"She quit the ATF," Denim said. "About a month after you were in, she decided to leave her job. She came to me to make sure Dillon and I would watch over Grace. Of course, we always do, but apparently, you asked her to keep an eye on our sister. But Fallyn needed to put distance between herself and the Hart family. Her words, not mine."

"Please tell me she's not married." My gut churned with anticipation.

I wouldn't fault her if she were. It would've been selfish of me to ask her to wait for me.

"No ring on her finger," Vince said, easing my misery.

I hung my head as relief coursed through me.

Denim sped past a slow-moving vehicle. "She's Grace's mathematics professor at BU."

My eyes widened. "From agent to professor. That's a swing. Boyfriend?"

"Not according to Grace," Denim said. "Our sister has been trying to befriend Fallyn, but Fallyn has kept her distance. Still, we're trying to surprise Fallyn as well as our sister at Grace's party. That's why Dillon told Grace to keep her mouth shut. We wanted to surprise you, but we know you don't like them, and we wanted to give you time to process in case you don't want to see Fallyn."

Vince's hand landed on my shoulder from behind. "She looks

good. Amber and I ran into her at a restaurant a month ago. She asked about you."

My heart was freaking out at the thought of seeing her. A mix of emotions—excitement, hope—rifled through me along with questions. Would she still feel the same about me as she had the day she told me she loved me? Could we have a relationship? I was new at the relationship thing, though.

Then again, none of that mattered as long as I could see her and know that she was happy.

Three hours later, after we stopped at the cemetery in Weston, grabbed a bite to eat, and dropped Vince off at his apartment, Denim pulled into the underground garage at his penthouse.

I'd barely climbed out of the car when Grace came running toward me with the biggest smile on her face.

Holy hell, tears shot free as she jumped into my arms.

"I missed you," she cried. "I'm mad at our brothers for keeping your release a secret."

I set her on two feet. "It's not their fault. I asked them to. The government kept changing the date."

"I'm glad you're home," she cooed, taking my hand.

"Does Fallyn know?" Denim asked.

"I didn't tell her," Grace said. "Otherwise, Dillon threatened to chop off my hair in my sleep."

Denim and I laughed. Grace's hair was down to her butt and beautiful.

"So when can I tell Fallyn?" she asked as we headed toward the elevator.

"You can't." Denim narrowed his gaze at her. "Duke will decide."

I appreciated that my brothers wanted to surprise me with Fallyn at Grace's birthday party, but I didn't want to see Fallyn for the first time at a party or with my family watching my every move and emotion.

"She might already know," I said as we entered the elevator. "Her ATF colleagues might've gotten word and told her."

"I don't have her class until tomorrow afternoon," Grace said. "So I can't say if she knows you're home or not, but she hardly talks to me outside of class."

Either way, I had my own plan on how I wanted to reconnect with her.

37

FALLYN

I was running late for class. I hadn't had a chance to go over my lesson plan. The morning had been filled with meetings between students and faculty. As the new adjunct professor on the block at BU, I was overwhelmed keeping up with my schedule. I'd accepted a part-time teaching assignment while I studied for my doctorate.

Nevertheless, I was enjoying the workload. It kept my mind preoccupied.

Since I'd said goodbye to Duke roughly ten months ago, I'd quit the ATF. It wasn't because I promised my dad either. I'd lost interest in the job after my undercover assignment—and not because of Duke. But after Neal Fitzgerald shot himself in the head, I was tired of seeing dead bodies.

Then, sadly, my dad had a heart attack not long after New Year's. That alone had hit me square in the face. As soon as he recovered, he and I left New England for a couple of months and ventured down to the Georgia coastline, where the weather was warm, the atmosphere was laid-back, and the area was quiet and serene.

The beach house we'd rented had been perfect for his recovery and for me to spend time with him while thinking of what I wanted to do next, as far as a career.

Dad encouraged me to do what I'd planned all along—teach college classes. He'd heard that BU had several adjunct openings for the upcoming fall semester. So I applied, and I couldn't have been happier. I loved the college vibe, the students, and even the long days.

I ran down the hall, my messenger bag strapped over my shoulder, my feet aching in my heels, but I came to a screeching stop about ten feet from the classroom.

A familiar brunette who'd been my rock since I'd gone under-cover was waiting impatiently outside my classroom as students walked by.

"Gwen, what are you doing here? Did something happen to Duke in prison?" I'd called her on occasion to check in with her and to see if she knew anything about Duke's well-being.

I'd tried to see him at the onset of his prison sentence, but he declined visitors. Grace had mentioned that her brother wanted time to himself, to wrap his head around his life and future. He was one of those individuals who operated with the out-of-sight, out-of-mind mentality.

I tried to adopt his motto but failed when I was lying in bed at night or any time I was alone with my thoughts. I'd prayed constantly that nothing bad happened to Duke in prison.

"Do you have a minute?" She sounded like she had bad news.

"Not really, but hold on." I poked my head into the classroom. "Today's topic is correlation coefficients. Study up. There'll be a quick quiz in ten minutes."

Students complained as I returned to Gwen. "What is it?" My tone was sharp and biting.

"Have you seen Duke?" she asked.

Just hearing his name made my damn heart hurt. "Is he out?"

Her blue eyes flashed with something I couldn't figure out. "I think he got early parole."

I dug my fingers into my chest. "But you don't know for sure?"

She shook her head. "Scuttlebutt in the office. Agent Howard is nervous. He's still angry that the judge didn't send Duke away for ten years."

I wasn't surprised. I'd seen Agent Howard a couple of times since I'd quit, and every time he'd asked me two questions. *Do you talk to Duke? Why do you like him?*

My responses were always the same. I replied no to the first question, and the second one was even easier to answer. I saw a side of Duke only a few people had seen. Take away the criminal component and there lay a man who wanted help, could love deeply, was compassionate, and cared.

"Duke won't return to his old ways," I told Gwen confidently.

Her eyebrows shot up. "Are you sure about that?"

I glanced around the now-empty hallway. "He wanted redemption. Of course, some people can regress. Prison isn't a surefire way to take the criminal out of the person. But I know in my heart, Duke will be a changed man, and if he's still in love with me and wants a life together, I will do whatever it takes to make sure he never reverts to his old ways."

"You really are that in love with him," she said.

"More so than ever. I've had enough time to think, and each day that passes, I fall more in love with him. The day he was officially arrested, I knew then I would wait for him."

"I'm happy for you, Fallyn," she said, sounding downtrodden. "Envious too."

I crossed my arms over my chest. "Why? I fell for the enemy. Surely, that isn't the reason."

She snorted. "Not because of Duke, but you stuck to your moral code during your assignment despite how you felt for Duke. I couldn't have done that."

I sighed. "Gwen, you're a badass agent. You're selling yourself short."

"Maybe," she said. "I should go. We need to meet for dinner. I miss you."

I wrapped my arms around her. "You're a good friend. Why don't we plan a day next week? I need to get into class. I'll text you if I see Duke or hear that he's out."

As she started to leave, she hesitated. "How's your dad?"

I grabbed the handle on the door. "He's doing great. He met someone."

"Really? Good for him," she said.

I was happy for my dad. Between his dog, Rosie, and Charmaine, a pretty brunette who adored Dad, I didn't have to worry too much anymore. He and I had long talks about love and the future. He was slowly coming around to the idea that I had feelings for Duke and the possibility that Duke and I could be together one day.

Gwen's phone rang, which was my cue to head into class.

The rest of the day was one big fog, while I wondered if Duke had been released from prison. In between my afternoon classes, I tried calling Denim, but he didn't answer. Grace wasn't even in class. That led me to believe that the rumor about Duke was true.

Goose bumps blanketed my body at the thought that I might see Duke after eleven long months. But as the day ended and night set in, I was a basket case. I didn't want to rush over to Denim's or Dillon's place, acting like a crazy lady. I stopped by Grace's dorm, but she wasn't there.

If Duke was, in fact, a free man, then I suspected he was catching up with his family, and I had to take it down a notch. Or maybe he didn't want to see me. That thought made me nauseated.

I had my messenger bag crossed over my body, my purse around my shoulder, and two eleven-by-seventeen envelopes of test papers in my hand as I walked to my car. I stopped halfway between the building and my car and fished the keys out of my purse, something I should've done before now but forgot as I left my office.

Once I had my keys in hand, I resumed my trek to the parking lot, looking around, a habit I had from my days with the ATF. To always know your surroundings wasn't just something that the ATF taught. My dad had ingrained that in my head as far back as I could remember.

When I reached the sidewalk along the building, I looked left first and froze. The envelopes dropped from my hands, my purse glided down my arm to fall beside the test papers, and my stomach pitched and rolled like a boat in high seas.

Standing against his SUV beneath the campus streetlight was Duke—the man I was so in love with that it pained me to think about him at times. Anything could've happened to him in prison, including death and a longer sentence that might have doomed him to life behind bars.

A twisted smile spread across his face, and instantly, my body went numb. My feet were rooted to the pavement, unable to move as I blinked several times to be sure I wasn't seeing things. After all, I'd been in a fog since Gwen had come to visit me.

He was even more handsome than I remembered. His sandy-brown hair was cropped close to his head, accentuating his chiseled features. He looked relaxed, happy, and ready to conquer the world.

He watched me watch him as my heart pounded against my breastbone like a caged animal desperate to be set free.

Then he pushed off his SUV and strode toward me with a predatory grace, hunger steeped in his eyes. But the closer he got, the more I could see it wasn't hunger but love and desperation.

"Hi," he said in that raspy voice that made my body hum and sing hallelujah.

"Hi." I blinked away happy tears.

We stared at one another, our breaths colliding, and I would bet our hearts were in sync, racing and fluttering.

"You're more beautiful than I remember. You've been in the

sun." He swiped his thumb over my cheek, my scar, my lips. "I want to hear all about your new job and learn everything about you, if you'll still have me."

I gulped down my emotions despite the tears flowing down my face. "I don't ever want to let you go." I threw myself at him.

He wrapped his arms around me and sighed, burying his nose in my hair. "I love you, Fallyn. I want to marry you. I want to make babies with you."

I giggled and cried. "Are you asking me to marry you?"

"If you'll have me," he said, seemingly holding his breath.

"Of course I'll be your wife. But I think we should practice making babies first."

He laughed, wild and free, picking me up and twirling me around.

I freaking loved his laughter, the happiness bleeding through it, and him. I had no idea where the road would take us, but I was willing to travel it with Duke Hart—the man who had my heart and soul, my soon-to-be husband, and, I hoped, one day, the father of our children.

EPILOGUE
DUKE

August on the North Carolina coast was hot and humid and the perfect climate to enjoy our honeymoon. Fallyn and I had gotten married several weeks ago, but we couldn't celebrate properly until I'd gotten permission from my parole officer to travel out of state.

Leaning on the railing, I twirled my wedding band, gazing out at the breaking dawn, where yellows and oranges streaked the horizon in the distance. In the nine months since I'd walked out of prison, life had been a whirlwind of chaos.

It had taken me time to adjust to a new normal. Checking in with my parole officer, living with Fallyn, and finding a job had been odd. Luckily, I had enough money that I'd stashed away for emergencies to keep me on my feet. In the meantime, I was helping Dillon at his shelter, training battered women in how to protect themselves from the assholes who'd beaten them.

My plans for a boxing gym were in the works, but I didn't want to rush into it, and I wanted to wait until my parole was up in another year before I opened a gym.

"Duke?" Fallyn asked in a sleepy, sultry tone.

I turned around, and my breath lodged in my throat, my heart sputtering the way it did every time I laid eyes on my beautiful goddess. The humid weather suited her. She had sun-kissed skin, hair up in a messy bun, hazel eyes that sparkled with happiness, and, the best thing of all, a growing stomach.

Yep, she was five months pregnant, and I was freaking out. One of the reasons I couldn't sleep. Would I be a good father? Was Boston the right place to raise kids? Would I get any blowback from my former life as a front man for the cartel?

With the Alvarez brothers six feet under, they weren't a threat anymore. As far as Rosario, she had nothing against me. When she and I had planned to rescue Grace and her daughter, Alexa, we both knew the potential consequences. Still, Rosario was serving ten years behind bars. The charge of murdering Mateo had increased the length of her sentence. But she could've gotten life if it hadn't been for the fact that she had a good lawyer. He'd argued that Rosario had only been protecting Fallyn and me.

But Brian and Vince weren't taking any chances. Brian had sold his dealerships and moved with his daughter to Tennessee, where he enrolled Fran in a private school while he opened a restaurant, of all places. Vince, on the other hand, had whisked Amber out of Boston and settled in Colorado. I suspected, though, with Rosario out of the picture, the Mexican cartel would be taking over the gun and drug trade in Boston.

"Did you hear me?" Fallyn's sweet voice penetrated through my haze. "You have that worried look. What's going on?"

I kissed her palm. "Just thinking about where's the best place to live for us. With our daughter growing inside you, her safety and yours is of the utmost importance to me."

She dragged a hand over my two-day beard. "Duke, breathe. No one is going to come after you or us. If they do, we're both pretty good with how to handle any situation."

I sighed as I admired her sapphire wedding band. Fallyn didn't want a rock, just a simple band with a few stones in it. "I still can't believe you're my wife," I said, switching the subject. "You've changed me in ways that I'd never thought were possible."

Now wasn't the time to worry but to enjoy my new life, free from the seedy criminal world, with a beautiful woman who was both my partner and the mother of our soon-to-be child. I couldn't ask for anything more.

"You should be proud of yourself. I would like to think that I had something to do with the new Duke, but it was all you. And redemption looks good on you."

"You look good on me," I retorted.

She gave me a blinding, flirty smile. "I would look better if you were inside me."

I chuckled, blood pooling in my dick as if he'd heard her.

She winced. "Oooh." She took my hand and placed it on her belly. "Emma is moving."

I lost my breath when I felt her kick. We'd decided on the name Emma Anne Hart, a tribute to Fallyn's mom. While I wasn't hung up on names, I loved that Fallyn lit up when she said "Emma Anne."

I grabbed her hand. "I have a surprise for you, Mrs. Hart."

"Please tell me it involves sex," she said as she followed on my heels through the beach house and into the kitchen.

"Patience," I teased as I lifted her onto the white marble island.

"Are you going to cook for me? Oooh, bacon? I have a craving for maple and jalapeño bacon."

I wished I could say I was a good cook, but I'd never made a dish of anything. I went over to the pantry, where I'd hurriedly stuffed the gift I'd purchased yesterday from a shop in town while Fallyn had stayed behind to take a nap.

I pulled out the pink bag and handed it to her.

She regarded me with hesitation. "What's this for?"

I settled between her legs. "For loving me. For marrying me. For everything. I love you, Fallyn. There shouldn't be a reason to give my beautiful bride a gift. I saw it and thought it was perfect."

She removed the velvet box, biting her bottom lip, easing the box open as if what was inside was about to jump out at her. When she laid eyes on the contents, she pressed her fingers to her mouth.

I took out the necklace, which had a charm with baby feet and two stones. "They're topaz, since that's the December birthstone and Emma is due on Christmas."

She threw her arms around me. "How did I get so lucky?"

"I'm the one who is lucky." I brushed my lips over hers. "You're the best thing that has happened to me."

She crashed her mouth to mine, and our tongues tangled in a passionate kiss.

I got lost in us, her beauty, and the way she made me feel both physically and emotionally. She tasted of heaven and home, of freedom and bliss. I knew with her at my side that I would realize everything I'd wanted for myself, for her, and for us. We were two halves of a whole, and in each other's arms, we were complete.

The end.

The next book in the Hart series is Hart of Hope. To learn more visit https://sbalexander.com/books/hart-of-hope/

Other books in this series:
Hart of Darkness
Hart of Vengeance
Lear more here >>> https://sbalexander.com/series/the-hart-series/

ABOUT THE AUTHOR

Award-winning author **S.B. Alexander** writes sports and paranormal romances and heart-pounding romantic suspense. Dive into her character-driven romances and meet the hot heroes and feisty heroines who steam up the pages of every book with all the feels, family drama, a sprinkle of action, and a dash of intrigue as they embark on their happily ever afters.

S.B., or Susan as she likes to be called, is a Navy veteran, former high school teacher, and corporate sales executive. She loves sports, especially baseball, although nowadays, you can find her on the golf course, swinging for that elusive hole-in-one.

Her motto: "Life is too short to waste. So live every moment like it's your last."

You can connect with S.B. Alexander in the following ways:

Facebook Reader Group: http://sbalexander.com/sbareaderroom
S.B. Alexander Book Store: https://sbalexanderbooks.com
Author Website: https://sbalexander.com
Newsletter: https://sbalexander.com/newsletter
Email: susan@sbalexander.com

facebook.com/sbalexander.authorpage

instagram.com/sbalexanderauthor

tiktok.com/@susanbalexander

ALSO BY S.B. ALEXANDER

MAXWELL SERIES

New Adult Contemporary Romance

Dare to Kiss

Dare to Dream

Dare to Love

Dare to Dance

Dare to Live

Dare to Breathe

Dare to Embrace

THE MAXWELL FAMILY SAGA SERIES

Young Adult Sweet Romance

My Heart to Touch

My Heart to Hold

My Heart to Give

My Heart to Keep

THE VAMPIRE NAVY SEAL SERIES

Paranormal Romance

On the Edge of Humanity

On the Edge of Eternity

On the Edge of Destiny

On the Edge of Misery

change based on reader demand and the author's schedule. Subscribing to the author's newsletter or following her on Facebook is the best way to stay updated with planned new releases.

Buy direct from S.B. Alexander - signed paperbacks, save on bundles, and more. https://sbalexanderbooks.com

Subscribing to the author's Newsletter at http://sbalexander.com/newsletter

Or following her on Facebook is the best way to stay updated with planned new releases. Join S.B. Alexander's Reader group on Facebook at http://sbalexander.com/sbareaderroom